The Second Marriage of Kunju Namboodiri
&
Other Classic ~Malayalam~ Stories

OTHER BOOKS IN THE SERIES

Maguni's Bullock Cart and Other Classic Odia Stories
A Teashop in Kamalapura and Other Classic Kannada Stories

The Second Marriage of Kunju Namboodiri

&

Other Classic Malayalam Stories

Series edited by Mini Krishnan
Translated by Venugopal Menon

HARPER**PERENNIAL**
An *Imprint* of HarperCollins *Publishers*

First published in India by Harper Perennial 2025
An imprint of HarperCollins *Publishers*
4th Floor, Tower A, Building No. 10, DLF Cyber City,
DLF Phase II, Gurugram, Haryana – 122002
www.harpercollins.co.in
2 4 6 8 10 9 7 5 3 1

English Translation © Venugopal Menon 2025
A Note on the Series © Mini Krishnan 2025
Copyright for individual stories vests in their respective writers

Though every effort has been made to trace the copyright holders of the stories published in this volume, it has not been possible to do so in all cases. Any omissions brought to our notice will be rectified in future editions.

P-ISBN: 978-93-6569-842-8
E-ISBN: 978-93-6569-752-0

This is a work of fiction and all characters and incidents described in this book are the product of the authors' imagination. Any resemblance to actual persons, living or dead, is entirely coincidental.

Each individual writer asserts the moral right
to be identified as the author of their work.

All rights reserved. No part of this publication may be reproduced, stored in a retrieval system, or transmitted, in any form or by any means, electronic, mechanical, photocopying, recording or otherwise, without the prior permission of the publishers.

Typeset in 11.5/16.2 Adobe Caslon Pro at
HarperCollins *Publishers*

Printed and bound at
Thomson Press (India) Ltd.

This book is produced from independently certified FSC® paper
to ensure responsible forest management.

Dedicated to my parents who showed me the Right Path.

A special dedication is due to the very few persons who supported and encouraged me to translate in my sunset years.
Of these is one who practically bore my flame in cupped hands against the strong winds of doubts and indecision. No coeval deserves this dedication more than this mentor.

CONTENTS

A Note on the Series	ix
Introduction	xv
Translator's Note	xxvii

1891 Anonymous: INSTINCTIVE MISCHIEF	1
1893 Vengayil Kunhiraman Nayanar: DWARAKA	7
1894 C.P. Achutha Menon: MY FIRST FEE	16
1900 K. Ramakrishna Pillai: OH NO! NOT THIS WAY!	36
1903 C.S. Gopala Panicker: A BRIEF MISSIVE	43
1905 Kalyanikutty: I FELT ASHAMED	56
1909 Moorkoth Kumaran: JUST A GLIMPSE	67
1911 M. Saraswatibhai: WITLESS WOMEN	78
1913 Lakshmikutty Varasyar: SO WHAT NEXT?	91
1913 Chembathil Chinnammu Ammal: A CASE OF HOMICIDE	96
1915 B. Kalyaniamma: NAMBIAR'S SECRET	110

CONTENTS

1916 Abhinava Chandu Menon (Thelapurath Narayanan Nambi): THE SECOND MARRIAGE OF KUNJU NAMBOODIRI — 127

1919 Thachatte Devaki Nethyaramma: AN IDEAL WIFE — 136

1920 Ambadi Karthyayani Amma: CONSCIENCE AND AVARICE — 143

1920 V.A. Amma: A SLEIGHT OF HAND — 152

1921 E.V. Krishna Pillai: THE SUPERINTENDENT'S BRIBE — 162

SOME PERIOD PRIOR TO THE 1930s Malabar K. Sukumaran: CUNI'S REMEDY — 168

1927 V.T. Bhattathirippad: ILLUSION OR DELUSION? — 184

1930 C. Kunhirama Menon (M.R.K.C.): THE DEPOSIT AT MANIMANJATHU — 201

1930 C. Kunhirama Menon (M.R.K.C.): THE LIFESPAN OF AISSAKUTTY UMMA — 214

Notes on the Authors — 226

A NOTE ON THE SERIES

A POEM ABOUT READING begins 'I opened a book and in I strode / Now nobody can find me' and ends by saying 'I finished my book and out I came ... But I have a book inside me.' Anyone who has read a work of fiction (is it ever wholly fiction?) knows what it is to return repeatedly to the memory of this or that character or event. Sometimes everything is forgotten except the impression and emotion those pages conjured up. This is particularly true of short stories: literary lightning that tears through you and exits leaving a wordy high.

I collect translated stories the way other people collect watches or potted plants, recipes or paintings, or something that gives them the pleasure of possession; my collection of stories belongs to their writers and translators. They possess me. That's just how literature is. Along the way, I have had a whole lot of unoriginal thoughts: Is our portmanteau of words enough to convey the complexity of our lives? Why do some languages appear to have more words than others? How might we convey what cannot be said? Coincidentally, all these questions about language and life apply to the art and effort of translation—some might say trans-adaptation—as well.

The idea for this series came from a collection of Malayalam stories I received from Dr M.M. Basheer, who edited and published *Aadhya Kaalathe Stree Katha* in 2010—stories by early women writers. Why only women, I thought to myself, but there were too many other things to do and deadlines to meet and the moment faded. But the seed was sown. For a while, I rattled along with the idea of a most neglected genre—the long story, which fell between the short story and the novella—until David Davidar published a collection I put together for Aleph Book Company: *Tell Me a Long Long Story* (2017). Five years before that, through Oxford University Press (India), I edited a series of novellas. After I retired, I tried to secure the interest of publishers in volumes of long stories from different Indian languages. Again—closed doors. Very slowly, and around the same time, it became clear that all the big prizes for translated fiction were reserved for novels by living writers. Naturally, publishers shifted focus to the map of that heaven. What, I thought to myself, will happen to those writers who were no longer with us but were the reason we are where we are in terms of tastes, styles, experiments and themes? The sun setting on our literary past, where pre-modern met modern, began to bother me. So, I came up with what I thought was my next big idea—anthologies of EISET: Early Indian Stories in English Translation. Fortunately, my editor, Rahul Soni, saw some potential in this apparently forgotten zone.

The evolution of fiction in Indian languages is linked with the development of prose—in some languages, a relatively recent medium for literary expression. To be sure, storytelling itself evolved from the earliest human societies and is the oldest form of enchantment through entertainment, closely linked with song and India's long culture of orality. India had sophisticated poetics and complex orature at a time when modern European languages were just emerging. Tamil, for instance, was a fully developed language thousands of years ago, well before Sanskrit became the power-and-prestige lingua franca. But printed fictional works came to be evaluated largely in terms of their closeness to Western models, and at least eighty years of Indian short fiction from the last quarter of the nineteenth to well into the sixth decade of the twentieth century were strongly influenced by Western norms riveted in place by British models or translations of European works into English. As schools, colleges and popular reading materials proliferated, maintaining the complex balance between the intimate and the universal fell into the hands of the writers and promoters of fiction, projecting as they did an illusion of life and truth, which is the function of literature. For a very long time in social and academic contexts that reverenced the classics as the only things worth studying, fiction was seen as second-class literature. With this stands the raging question of plural heritage, both local and imported. Was there a conflict? Or a smooth hybridization swallowed whole by a readership from which the writer himself or—on rare occasions—herself originated?

In an interview, Dorothy Figueira said that though early translations were inspired by pragmatic colonial needs to understand Indians better in order to rule and control, it was not entirely unidirectional; Indians responded to commentary from the West. It was a dialogue from the beginning. This was possible probably because the translingual sensibility lies deep in Indians educated in any language, though that immediately reminds me and everybody else that even illiterate populations in our country are effortlessly bilingual. E.V. Ramakrishnan does not agree. In paper after paper, he discusses the massive shifts in the cultural domain when English began to displace Sanskrit as the Indian subcontinent moved towards colonial modernity. He calls this time of cultural and linguistic violence a time of rupture.

It is routinely said and printed that there are more speakers and readers of English in India than there are in the Anglophone world, and the pressure this single language applies today upon our language empire is incalculable. There can be no argument about the fact that the biggest intervention in the social energy of our languages was the arrival of English. At some cost to our languages, while simultaneously enriching us with outside influences, it has nudged us into a sense of needing to keep up with world literature—a trend that has led to a sudden visibility for translations of Indian literary works.

Languages are like opposing reigning powers, and translators are the ambassadors who flit between two kingdoms. The encoding they pack at one end and unpack at the other for another language readership naturally calls for great skills. Translation is a deep reading of a text. Every story or poem has a voice. Inward, human. It asks you to believe the feeling locked into the printed word m and it reaches you through your reader-ear. We read as listeners because the origin of stories is orality. Imagine the translator's workshop, created in a phantom space between two languages, in some sense, a linguistic outer space where there do not appear to be any recognizable norms. Monolingual peoples have tried hard to arrive at rules, many of which suit them but most of which break

A NOTE ON THE SERIES

down when translators function in a multilingual context such as ours in India.

Let me say something else here. The multiple flavours and successes of a translation depend a lot on the personality of the translator—how ethical, how vain, how patient, how adventurous s/he is—to say nothing of that invisible meddler called the editor or facilitator. To plunge within, in order to extrapolate outwardly what another said, calls for utter honesty. No grandstanding or vanity must be allowed to intervene and contaminate the rendering. Is the translator competing with the original or seeking to supplant it? I can never decide, but I do think successful translations run just a little ahead of their originals as if clearing the way for the author, becoming in fact a third entity that is neither the source nor the target language. Gustave Flaubert said that a translation should free itself from the translator; is that—could it be—true? At a time when identities are not only plural but fluid, and we are continuously told what to think and how to think, our translated literature should be seen for what it is and can be: not just a part of history, but a bank, a treasure house of our own pasts because memory is the cement of our identity. The translations in this series offer a rich mix of the music and sounds of some of our languages.

As we age, as technology inexorably overtakes us, as we balance the intimate with the universal, with what might we fill our memory baskets given the extreme fragility of the past? What but stories about ourselves and others by writers who were both like us and unlike us?

—Mini Krishnan
Series Editor

INTRODUCTION

The evolution of Malayalam short stories can be traced back to the period between the concluding years of the nineteenth century and the early part of the twentieth century, arising from the initiative of contemporary publishers and those lovers of language who could relate to Western literature. Modern prose, especially literary prose, came into being only in the nineteenth century. The efforts of the Christian missionaries should be remembered with gratitude because they were the pioneers of liberal education and the translation of religious and moral texts into Malayalam, which had an impact on the popular imagination.

There are a few who believe that the first short stories in Malayalam were the stories published for children by Kerala Varma Valiyakoil Thamburan (1845–1914). Those stories were compiled and published under the title *Keralavarma Kathakal* (1983). The distinctive features of those stories were their small format and allegorical content.

INTRODUCTION

Such publications that emerged during that inceptual period did have a tale-to-tell in each, but lacked the form and character of the short story of modern literature.

The first true-to-character short story of Malayalam is 'Vasana Vikruti'—published as 'Instinctive Mischief' in this collection, originally published in 1891. It is believed that this story was written by Vengayil Kunhiraman Nayanar. However, researchers now say that the publisher of the story, the literary magazine *Vidyavinodini*, did not print his name as the author. The compilation of Nayanar's stories titled *Kesari*, published before his demise, does not include this story. The foreword to this compilation was written by C.P. Achutha Menon, the editor of *Vidyavinodini*. Were the story written by Vengayil Kunhiraman Nayanar, he might have indeed indicated it. 'Vasana Vikruti' exhibits all the distinctions now deemed mandatory for short stories. It is about the folly of a thief. The man, who fell into the trap of the police—thanks to his own folly—decides that he is not suited for his occupation and goes on a pilgrimage to Kashi. The story is written in first person as narrated by the thief who is discharged after serving a six-month sentence in jail.

'Dwaraka' (1993) by Vengayil Kunhiraman Nayanar (1860–1914) is considered to be the first ever 'fantasy tale' in Malayalam. The author, in his dream state, wears a watertight submersible suit and descends into the ocean where the ancient city of Dwaraka sank, along with a fellow officer of his ship. It is only when he is jolted awake by someone that the protagonist realizes that it was only a vivid dream. As reality and illusion intermingle in this story, it can be termed fantasy.

The story by C.P. Achutha Menon (1852–1937)—'Ente

INTRODUCTION

Aadyathe Fees', published without fixing his name—was first published by *Vidyavinodini* in 1894. According to S.N. Krishnapilla (as published in *Atmaposhini* in 1920), who wrote the first critique on Malayalam short fiction, the story was by C.P. Achutha Menon, which bears credibility. The gist of the story is that an advocate, Shankarankutty Menon, seeks the hand of Ammukutty, the beautiful daughter of his client, to settle a dispute in court. The author has engaged a style of storytelling that intermingles gravitas with frivolity.

'Alla! Ee vidhamo?' ('Oh No! Not Like This!') is a story by K. Ramakrishna Pillai (1878–1916)—published by *Vidyavinodini* in 1900—which does not assign his name to it. That this story is by the famous Swadeshabhimani (patriot) K. Ramakrishna Pillai has been confirmed by A.R. Rajarajavarma in his compilation of stories titled *Katha Ratnamala* (1910). A son informs his father that he is in love with a girl and wishes to marry her. In his reply, the father tells him that if he does not marry the girl chosen by his father—a relative of his friend, the Peshkar (Administrator)—he, the son, will forfeit his inheritance. The son, however, goes ahead and marries the girl he was in love with. He is under the impression that the girl's father's brother was the 'servant' (a menial employee) of another man. It is only when her uncle, the Peshkar, arrives to visit them that the man realizes the true stature of her family. He had married the very girl that his father had intended for him. Although we can see fantasy in this tale, the forthrightness of narration and the realistic tone of conversations are noteworthy.

The story by C.S. Gopala Panicker (1872–1930), 'Oru Neelam Kurannya Kathu' ('A Brief Missive') is the tale of a transaction. The vile Kunyunni Menon expunges a line from the letter sent

INTRODUCTION

by Krishna Menon, thus falsifying its content. He also goes ahead and files a case against Krishna Menon for not adhering to the commitment, now altered in the letter. A clever advocate establishes the guilt of Kunyunni Menon in court. Gopala Panicker assimilated the fact that a short story must relate an incident or reflect the empirical element in it.

Moorkoth Kumaran (1941–1974) relates in his story, 'Orotta Nokku' ('Just a Glimpse'), the conflict between Govindan and Krishnan over the custom of thaalikettu kalyanam (child marriage)—one for and the other against—which leads to the untimely demise of a young girl. For the trifling reason that she attended such a ceremony without his permission, Vasudevan, son of Krishnan, contemplates divorcing Madhavi, Govindan's daughter.

Thaalikettu is an ostentatious ritual conducted even before a girl child comes of age. A man ties the sacred knot in marriage and, within no time, annuls the bond. All the Hindu societies in Kerala adopted this practice during that period. Many leaders of several clans spoke against it. Later, it was accepted generally that tying of the sacred knot (thaalikettu) needed to be performed only at the time of the actual wedding. Moorkothu Kumaran was a staunch crusader against all unseemly rituals like thaalikettu and manifested his disapproval through stories and other forms of protest.

'Kooniyude Chikitsa'—'Cuni's Remedy'—was published by *Kathapallavangal* in 1924 by Malabar K. Sukumaran (1876–1956). The story is a satire on the popular Nature Therapy in vogue during that period. In order to diminish their household expenditure, a husband and wife embark on a regimen of starvation called Cuni's remedy. The abstinence from food minimizes expenses, but the couple cannot sustain the crash diet physically. They begin to steal from their own kitchen at night. The realism of the characters and the humour in their dialogues enhance the joy of reading.

Thelapurath Narayanan Nambi's (1876–1924) 'Kunju Namboodiriyude Randam Veli'—'The Second Marriage of Kunju Namboodiri'—brings into sharp focus a strong subject of the times. Kunju Namboodiri seeks a new alliance on the pretext that his current wife lacks both status and wealth. He loses consciousness in a boat accident, is taken to his wife's house by his friend on the pretence that it is the house of his fresh alliance. Namboodiri, who experiences the pristine qualities of the nursing woman, realizes that it is none other than his own first wife and repents; he commits himself to the oath of perennial monogamy. This story campaigns against the practices of the Namboodiri community, in which men married multiple times into their own community as well as into other castes—and the lack of grace they exhibited in their personal lives.

'Suprandinte Kaikooli' ('The Superintendent's Bribe')—first published in *Kalakaumudi* in 1921—by E.V. Krishna Pillai (1894–1938) is a story about the prevailing corruption in the police department. It portrays a police superintendent who is given to register cases on a whim and uses 'agents' to approach the victims with compromise talks, finally extorting money from them. This culminates in the man taking a bribe from his own father. Humour, sarcasm, strong criticism of the evils in society, a lucid narration are among the strong points of this story.

Writer and social worker V.T. Bhattathirippad (1896–1982) published the story 'Mayayo Manmatibhranthiyo' ('Illusion or

Delusion?') in 1927, attracting much communal antagonism. It speaks of the trauma in the life of a typical Namboodiri girl. She could not marry the man she loved and is instead obliged to marry an elderly Namboodiri. The young girl's husband dies four days after the wedding. She escapes from the husband's house and is found unconscious at a railway station. Her old student companion happens on the scene, whereupon she hands over some papers she had scribbled and succumbs thereafter. On these sheets she has described the anguish-ridden lives of the Namboodiri women. The narration is from the perspective of a visiting friend of the author who relates the tale. Powerful social criticism enraged reactionary members of the writer's own community.

By the beginning of the twentieth century, the women of Kerala began to make a mark in all walks of life. Their contributions began to appear in literature too. A literary magazine called *Sharada* (1905) was launched in Thrissur exclusively for women. The story, 'Nanichu Poi' ('I Felt Ashamed')—first published in *Sharada* in 1905—by Kalyanikutty is a love story. The story is about Kalyanikutty, who wanted to marry a man she had met on a train journey but could not because of societal restraints on inter-caste marriage. Kalyanikutty is a high-caste Nair, and Krishna Menon is a Chaarnna Nair deemed inferior in caste. Kalyanikutty dreams that she marries Krishna Menon and lives happily. She materializes through her dreams what she could not attain in real life. The name of the character in this story has been adopted as the name of the author. It could be the pseudonym of a writer (either gender) of the period. There are critics who claim that this is the first story by a woman in Malayalam.

In the story 'Thalachorillathasthreekal' ('Witless Women')—first

INTRODUCTION

published in *Bhashaposhini* in 1911—written by Saraswathibhai, the protagonist Govindan Nair, who is a literary figure, would repeatedly ridicule his wife, Kalyaniamma, saying that women were by nature brainless and could not understand literature. When Govindan Nair finds out that the name of a prominent writer is the pseudonym of his own wife, he is stunned. The story expounds the fact that women can engage in intellectual pursuits like writing stories and that their menfolk must not demean them in any way. The author echoes the dictum that men and women must share equal status in society. A stern finger is pointed at the misogynistic traits of some men.

The story by Lakshmikutty Varasyar titled, 'Ini Entha Cheyka' ('So What Next?')—published first in *Lakshmibhai* in 1913—is a satire on the predilection for the English language. Girls were smitten by the language and by those who spoke it. When a girl assumes that the person accompanying her uncle was a student at an English-medium university, she falls madly in love with him. The gist of the story is about the humiliation after the wedding, when she learns that the man is studying Sanskrit. The author brilliantly mocks women who thought it undignified to marry someone who lacked an education in English.

The highlight of B. Kalyaniyamma's (1884–1956) story, 'Nambiarude Rahasyam' ('Nambiar's Secret')—first published in *Atmaposhini* in 1913—is humour. In order to impress his wife, the husband plagiarizes stories and sends them to publishers under his own name. The concerned editor and reporter together catch the perpetrator red-handed. The culprit apologizes and introduces them to his wife. As this story has been narrated with due gravity, the reader takes a while to absorb the humour and ridicule in it.

INTRODUCTION

The story 'Oru Yadhartha Bharya' ('An Ideal Wife')—originally published in *Lakshmibhai* in 1919—by Thachatte Devaki Nethyaramma defines the role of a committed wife. Unable to bear the incessant torture of her husband, a woman plans to elope with a friend. But seeing her husband lying in a pool of blood by the roadside, she discards her lover and returns to nurse her husband. Even the jilted lover feels a surge of admiration for the lady. Husbands who beat their wives have always been prevalent in our society. But such a wife as this is indeed rare.

How a wife reforms a neurotic husband with the help of a vaid (apothecary) is narrated in the story, 'Oru Podikkai' ('A Sleight of Hand')—first published in *Lakshmibhai* in 1920—by V.A. Amma (?). The natural flow of dialogues and the simplicity of narration with a touch of humour make this story remarkable.

Notably distinct from the rest of the stories from *Aadyakaala Sthree Kathakal* (early tales by women writers) is the story 'Manassakshiyum Mohavum' ('Conscience and Avarice'), published originally in *Kairali* in 1920 by Ambadi Karthyayani Amma (1885–1990). The story depicts the internal conflict in the mind of a murderer, between his conscience and his greed. Having killed the shopkeeper and pilfering whatever he could from the shop, the man's desire appears before him as an apparition. A battle between Conscience and Avarice in conceptualized form was not known to the literature of the time. The depth of the concept and the probability of it makes this story perennially relevant.

Chembathil Chinnammu Ammal's 'Oru Kolakkessu' ('A Case of Homicide'), first published in *Lakshmibhai* in 1913, is an investigative short story. A nephew is about to hang for the crime of killing his uncle. A proficient lawyer proves instead that the uncle committed suicide. This story proved that women could write detective stories.

'Manimanjathile Nikshepam' ('The Deposit at Manimanjathu') by Chengalath Cheriya Kunhirama Menon (M.R.K.C) is a story about an aristocrat who chances upon a manuscript and the scabbard of a sword among the heaps of ancestral junk in his crumbling tharavad. He realizes that the clue to the hidden treasure is locked in a verse-riddle inscribed on the palm-leaf manuscript and sets out to locate the vanished Manimanjathu House. His persistence and determination lead him to the treasure hidden in the ruins of the vanished tharavad.

Another story is 'Aissakutty Ummayude Ayussu' ('The Lifespan of Aissakutty Umma'). Set amidst the gore and turmoil of the eighteenth-century attacks on Malabar by Tipu Sultan, the story is a gem of a historical recreation, rooted in fact. The reigning Premier's niece delivers a baby girl, the only heir to the kingdom, and dies alone, covered in gold ornaments. A Muslim finds the infant and raises her as his daughter, supporting himself with whatever he had found on the corpse, which he disposes with dignity. Aissakutty, as she is called, thinks she is a Muslim. Her identity becomes known when her aged and impoverished adopted father attempts to sell the last piece of jewellery—an amulet with the royal insignia. The founder of modern Malayalam, Thunchath Ezhuthachan, is also mentioned.

Before Kerala was segregated according to languages spoken, both Kochi and Malabar boasted distinctive identities politically and administratively. However, there was a similarity and equality in the transformation that took place in both those regions. The writers who worked in the genre of short stories of the early period have contributed greatly to the social and cultural changes they witnessed, through their short stories. The stories written by both men and women writers portrayed the palpable progression in the social order, the influence of the English language and the opportunities that emerged for the emancipation of women at large, which resulted in their occupying positions of power as also their strong presence in all fields of growth.

The transition from joint families to nuclear families, the karanavar (head of the family) who would stop at nothing to tame his recalcitrant nephews, husbands who fake illness to torment their wives, tender-hearted wives who reach out to needy husbands, the upliftment of the Dalit section of society, the curiosity evinced by them in political matters, the compulsion of women to assert their identity in the world around them, personal acquisition of wealth augmenting the status of the individual—many such factors have been the cause for the growth and transformation of the social milieu of Kerala.

We can see these variegated situations of life depicted in the early Malayalam short stories.

A glimpse of the past and the way things were then is an irresistible indulgence in nostalgia. To return to the late nineteenth and early twentieth centuries with the sole intention of reviving the literature of an era gone by is a task of earnest commitment to that very cause. Most of the stories were written during the timeline mentioned, but ruefully, leave alone the authors, even some of the publishers of the time no longer exist. The compilation of the short stories for this series was accomplished, therefore, by 'bivouacking', as it were, at the Kerala Sahitya Akademi intermittently, with only my spouse for company and sustained motivation. Often, I had to

INTRODUCTION

transcribe the scripts from the archives in the Akademi by hand as those were the days when photostat machines were not prevalent in Thrissur.

Incipient as it is, the commitment to write is a gateway to profound thought processes. Each story stands alone in character and in its telling. We tend to trip over 'blind spots', unless the incumbent writer visualizes a given scene in its most minute detail—we did encounter ambiguity in the detailing of certain episodes. These were the thoughts foremost in my mind as I set out to compile stories for the Early Fiction series.

Motivation is multilayered: I wanted to personally engage in the 'treasure hunt' for a style of writing lost forever, that they be read by latter generations who can gain insight into an atmosphere that prevailed in the Keralam of the time, pausing briefly in their rushed lives to relive the intrinsic values our forebears upheld.

Another encouragement for this project came from Mini Krishnan herself—who came up with the suggestion of a turnaround series—as one who has always been a prime mover in translated literature in India.

Never the least, but last to mention here, is my better half, Mrs Zuhara Basheer, who is forever the driving force in all my ventures.

I hope this series of early value-driven stories will be cherished and enjoyed by a wide section of readers committed to serious literature.

—**Dr M.M. Basheer**
Kozhikode, 2025

TRANSLATOR'S NOTE

Sourced largely but not exclusively from a Malayalam collection titled *Adya Kala Kathakal*, this is a volume of short stories meticulously selected by Dr M.M. Basheer, the renowned writer and literary critic on the suggestion of Mini Krishnan, a promoter and editor of translations from Indian languages. This book is part of a larger scheme that encompasses vintage writing from several Indian languages, rendered in English, reaching out to an Anglophone readership scattered in India and outside it. It was therefore a privilege to be invited to join the venture as a translator.

These stories in Malayalam were published between 1891 and 1928, a crucial time in the history of Kerala society, emerging as it was from its medieval state in its encounter with colonialism and its influences. They portray the values of a period and the collective social philosophy that prevailed in those decades, lost to us forever, and found only in books. A noteworthy aspect that struck me is the preponderance in more than one story, of the most coveted occupation of a time when the British ruled us—the legal profession and in consonance, law and order. The protagonists of several of the stories are either aspiring lawyers or practising advocates. The coveted social distinction then was the BA degree—evoking an inexplicable nostalgia of our ancestry in a certain section of senior citizens.

Translation of this collection often became challenging when a writer resorted to aristocracy's propensity for Sanskrit and Manipravalam,[1] interweaving stanzas and verses in those languages with the base narrative, creating thereby a tangible ambience in a given situation to coax the reader's focus. To overcome this hurdle, I sought the help of Dr A.J. Thomas, poet, translator, editor and a literary figure of international repute, who gracefully explicated these words and phrases to help me round off the assignment. My grateful thanks to Dr Thomas, who also shared a list of stories with me to choose from.

Prevalent in Kerala in those times was the Namboodiri clan's misogynistic oppression of women, which was fearlessly attacked by V.T. Bhattathirippad, who spearheaded a literary and social campaign in support of the community's crushed womenfolk. His intellectual integrity powered his social activism and unforgettable literary works. His tale in this series—and those of a couple of others too—use some of the expressions unique to the class of that hitherto 'revered' gentry to portray their presumptuous way of life manacled in, alas, a cloistered outlook.

---

1 A blend of Sanskrit and Malayalam defined metaphorically as the mixture of 'rubies and corals'.

TRANSLATOR'S NOTE

The story by V.T. Bhattathirippad in this collection ('Mayayo Manmatibhrantiyo') is one such poignant tale that leaves us distraught on reflection, being all the more powerful for its earthy narration, to render us so.

A short period preceding the nineteenth century also comes into focus in a couple of stories when the narrative by Chengalath Kunhirama Menon (M.R.K.C.) waxes quasi-historical, which makes for engrossing reading. Often the verbatim use of the speech of local communities, so delectable in the source language, has been both transliterated and sequentially translated herein, to retain the flavour of the times and to augment a feel of the locale. Images of nature, old folk customs, evocations of subtle caste differences and the rich play of jokes and dialects caused me to hover over a sentence or a page for hours. Even days. The joy of translation is fleeting but the overall experience becomes a part of one's personality. I experienced second hand the power of the writers as they poured life into their characters. I encountered another unfamiliar speed bump with the many poetic embellishments and quotations from classical literature, and ethical and religious texts. I consulted many knowledgeable people before translating them. Some of them are Shri V.T. Vasudevan, writer (s/o V.T. Bhattathirippad); Dr Suvarna Nalapat, author and researcher of repute; Dr K. Satchidanandan, renowned academic and poet; Dr A.J. Thomas; Dr J. Devika and Dr G.S. Jayasree. I extend my grateful thanks to all of them.

The hunt for the authors of the source texts brought me into contact with several personalities who were once associated directly with the writer or are related to them. Recovering the work of the writers, who lived between 1822 (earliest) and 1990, is an exercise in the revival of writing in a native tongue protracted over a period spanning nearly two centuries. Juxtaposed with the period of publication, naturally, most of the original publishers no longer existed.

The quest for information about authors not listed in the available search engines prompted me to visit the Kerala Sahitya Akademi in Thrissur, where all records of published literature in Malayalam are stored. Another venue of search had to be the Appan Thamburan Smarakam library, also in Thrissur, where all the periodicals over a century and more are stored. With the concerted efforts and help of the Librarian at the Akademi, Ms P.K. Shanta, to whom I am deeply indebted, I was able to access all records to find details of just one of the missing authors. Around seven authors still remained untraced, for whom I was advised to contact Dr J. Devika, renowned researcher and writer in Malayalam, and Dr G.S. Jayasree, editor and publisher of *Samyukta*, who also searched for those authors but to no avail.

A pamphlet compiled by Dr M.M. Basheer bore this passage dated 20 August 2004 about his own investigation into the early works, at Appan Thamburan Smarakam, the gist of which read:

> *All the records in ATS library are already in a state of decay and have begun to wither; it is of the utmost importance that all available data here must be converted to soft form and stored appropriately, for posterity. Several authors published in periodicals have used pseudonyms which make the referencing all the more challenging.*

TRANSLATOR'S NOTE

The Kerala Sahitya Akademi already had its archival data on a compact disk, which was checked thoroughly. I wish to record my heartfelt thanks to the Akademi through this note. Furthermore, may I add that I could not have brought this assignment to fruition were it not for the strong support all along of my wife, Rajani, who also accompanied me to Kerala Sahitya Akademi, prepared to spend long hours at the desk. The importance of preserving the records of our pioneering writers became more and more evident as the exploration progressed.

Besides translating the text of a story, up rose the challenge of a different kind: translating the title without the crutch of transliterating with a footnote. Ambiguity wrestled with accuracy. A few examples I would like to share:

In the story 'Vasana Vikruti', my first preference was to title it 'Instinct-Driven Misconduct'. This was because vasana is instinct and vikruti is erratic behaviour, so I thought of misconduct. The protagonist is driven by an innate and uncontrollable longing to steal and deceive, which he attributes to his faulty ancestry. On deeper reflection of the story itself and the title used by the author, the English title was changed to a compact 'Instinctive Mischief'.

Next came the story, 'Alla! Eee Vidhamo?', which I translated as 'Oh no! Not This Way?'. The literal meaning of the title in the source language is, 'Oh no! In This Manner?' During the proofing stage, 'Oh! Not Like This!' was suggested. Equally adaptable, this title could appropriately replace my own. Considering once more the Malayalam connotation of what the author called it, I wondered if there wasn't a difference between 'like this' and 'in this manner'. Often a meaningful yet harmless overlap is possible, which correlates with the context aptly. I'm still wondering!

TRANSLATOR'S NOTE

My grateful thanks must be recorded here to my daughter, Gayatri, who assisted me in deciphering and streamlining a unique portion of a story that needed expertise to tabulate and elucidate the primary description by the author.

From the moment the spark was lit—followed through by compilation, translation, the indispensable editing thereafter and frequent course correction by my Series Editor—this has been an unforgettable project taken to its thrilling culmination by Kartik Chauhan, my editor at HarperCollins.

The shadowy domain of translation can be illustrated in a quote from an article by Mini written in 2015 on the subject:

The struggle a translator faces when he/she has to translocate jasmine from Coimbatore to somewhere in Scotland ... would it retain its heady fragrance ... if it lost something, would it gain something else ... say size?

I close by saying that this note is intended to bring into focus the nuanced roles of those involved, for the benefit of readers who might have wondered what goes into producing a translation of heritage writing.

I pay homage to those authors who paved the path for us.

—**Venugopal Menon**

ANONYMOUS[1]

Instinctive Mischief

Among the people who have been punished by law, there is no one more unfortunate than I. This is not to say that there isn't anybody who hasn't suffered or isn't suffering more than me. But those who have deserved punishment for their own idiotic actions are rare. That is what makes me sad. There is no indignity in suffering the dangers brought upon us by God. To be outwitted by intelligent police officers is also bearable; falling into the trap set up by oneself is not insufferable. But there is no end to the regret born of knowing that even an intelligent child could tell that it was an inescapable trap. This is what they call insult.

My house is in the province of Kochi. All I want to say here is that it is in the vicinity of forest land. You must have seen for

---

1 The author is believed to be Vengayil Kunhiraman Nayanar, although his 'Complete Works' does not include this story. No publication has been able to confirm the rightful writer of this story.

Originally published in Malayalam as 'Vasana Vikruti' by *Vidyavinodini*, Number 1/March 1891.

yourself people of different complexions, fair or dark skinned, in the same family. The same goes for my own tharavad[2] too. The difference is not about complexion, but in behaviour. Some people are refined at all times, others are unfailingly crude. This difference didn't begin in recent times but was so even among my ancestors.

I was born into the unrefined part of the family. At least some among you must have heard of Ikkanda Kurupu and Raman Nair, two 'deities'. Among the two, the first mentioned is my fourth father[3] and an uncle of four generations ago. I have been named in memory of the man. Therefore, through two streams of lineage, both matrilineal and patrilineal, I have inherited an intrinsic flair for thievery and was fated to be a thief. In order to make sure that readers understand the greatness of my ancestry, I am compelled to add here that Ikkanda Kurupu's great-grandfather is Ittinarayanan Namboodiri. If there is some fool who hasn't heard the story of Ityaranan, well, I'm not writing this for him. Even during my childhood, some in the family attempted to wean me off the path of sin. If they haven't been successful, I am willing to vouch it isn't because they didn't try. Call it the strength of my instinct. It can never be said that I was a poor student. My own tutor bears testimony to the fact that all my classmates were less intelligent than I. There remain in many parts of the land of Malayalam, grand

---

2 An ancestral joint family.

3 *Naalamachan* or fourth father refers to the fourth consort of a lady according to the prevalent custom of the time where a Namboodiri established his right for connubial alliance merely by gifting the chosen woman—from other communities like the Nairs—a length of cloth to 'clothe herself'.

people who have learnt thirty anthologies in ten years and rejoice as experts in geometry, arts and science. I have studied five to eight anthologies, but I can't parade as an expert in them. However, if there was a reference text, I had the expertise to understand the meaning of the poems, without anyone's help. By the time I achieved this, because of traits inherited from both lineages, I lost interest in these matters.

Living on the edge of a forest and because I entered it and encountered wild animals every now and then, fear was never a part of my character. I used to get beaten badly during my student days, but by the time I turned twenty, my behaviour changed drastically. I gave up trivial stealth and aspired for the big stuff. I would glance at an object only if it was really precious. Wherever I stepped in, the result was the same. This way I amassed a lot of material assets. In my work, it wasn't my fourth father that I emulated. There are two ways of thieving. One is to go in a group with glowing torches at night; the other is to go alone. The difference between these two methods was like hunting in packs and hunting solo. If it is the former, you shoot down at least one prey; but you are not certain which you shot it—and the shared portions of the meat would be minimal. Tracking an animal alone takes a lot of time and once you find it, there is less thrill than anguish; but doesn't the thrill lie in the anguish? When it is over, there are no partners to partake of the kill. So, I thought it is better, any day, to hunt alone. My fourth father wasn't of this opinion—he was of the old school and here I am, a progressive man. Ittyaranan Esquire was the same ilk as I. To think that he had had such a modern outlook even so many years ago, it isn't difficult to understand why the people of Irinjalakuda called him a Superman.

After I left home, I went around and made some money. In the meantime, Kochi province got its new police force. During those days, I conducted a theft in a house near Thrissivaperoor.[4] It seems that the Englishman Gunther's people did not like it one bit. The theft was from an illam.[5] The householder's son proved to be a snitch. This fellow was a gambler and had incurred huge debts. That is how he came to me for support. I had given him a large quantity of opium to be mixed into his father's milk at night. I had warned him that only a quarter of the amount of the stuff I had given him was to be used. I went in and grabbed what I could. I wanted to carry off a jewellery box, which Namboodiri kept next to his pillow. I approached the box, still scared that I might wake him. That didn't happen. How could he wake? He had fallen into eternal sleep. That sinner of a son of his, who thought there should be no loopholes in his plans that night, had mixed the whole quantity of the opium into his father's milk. I gave all that I took from there, including the jewellery box, to my friend, Kalyanikutty. We were in love. One night, she picked out a stone-encrusted ring from the box and slipped it on the ring finger of my left hand, after which I became very attached to that ring. Though I could have slipped it off my finger, I never did.

Ever since the loot of the Namboodiri's illam became public, the policemen began to suspect me. During the same period, the Kodungalloor temple ornaments also went missing. Two more thefts were reported at the same time. The police intensified their investigation. All told, I realized that I couldn't stay there any

---

4 Thrissur, currently.
5 The house of a Namboodiri.

longer. Deciding to stay away for a while, I set out for Madras. I had no plans to work or anything of the sort. I took it as a vacation period of my 'court'. During the court vacation, the officers engage in searching for comfort and beauty, don't they? I decided to do just that. For a month, after reaching Madras, I went around sightseeing. One day when I went to Gujli Street, a very beautiful streetwalker had come to buy groceries. There was a small crowd in that shop. Among them was a dunce gazing at the girl, his mouth agape, showing his protruding, distorted teeth. When I saw this prince's stance, I couldn't resist the temptation to play a trick on him. I forgot my decision to desist from wrongdoing. I edged into the crowd. I dipped my left hand into the man's pocket. To be successful in such arts of theft, one must have practised the ambidexterity of Arjuna. If not, many errors could occur in the manoeuvre—that would foil the scheme. Drawing from the pocket just a notebook, I moved away and returned to my place of stay. When I fell asleep after supper, I dreamt of Kalyanikutty and woke up with a start. I was reminded of the bond between us through the gem-encrusted ring on my finger. When I felt for it, I couldn't find the ring. I was dismayed. I tried to figure out where I could have lost it but to no avail. The next day I went through all the streets and houses I had ambled through the previous day. I asked around everywhere and finally went to the police station and reported the loss. I committed that bit of folly thinking that they would most likely find it.

Later that day, after noon, a constable came to my lodge. As soon as I saw him, I thought my ring had been found. When I sensed a reluctance in him to return it, I flashed a five rupee note.

He asked me: 'Do you know how this ring reached me?'

I stood perplexed at his question.

When I came to, I had been hand-cuffed, searched and the notebook in my pocket was on the table. The sentence for this foolish act was twelve swipes of the cane and six months in jail.

Having completed my term in jail, here I am free once more. A man so incompetent if he continues in the profession, it would be a slur on his fourth father. People say that stealing is bad. Let me set aside my lineage and my profession. I must take a dip in the Ganges and pray at Kashi Vishwanath temple to rid myself of the sins I have committed and to never again think of performing such a deed.

My grandmother would recite every day at sunset:

> *Shruti smrutibhyam vihitha vrathadaya:*
> *Punanthi paapam na lunanthi vasanaam*
> *Ananta seva thu nikrunthati dwayee*
> *Mitha prabho thwalpurushaa babhashire*[6]

[Sacred rites and holy fasts mentioned in Vedas ... do not erase sins or purify

Nor do they erase the instincts in us.
Eternal service alone removes dualities.
So teaches Lord Vishnu.]
(Sd) Ikkanda Kurupu.

---

6 A stanza from Narayaneeyam, a treatise on Lord Vishnu, which describes the importance of Bhakti and service over learning and rituals.

VENGAYIL KUNHIRAMAN NAYANAR

Dwaraka

WHILE I WAS studying in Madras, Dr Duncan, who was the Director of Technical Education in the state, advised me to go abroad for further studies. Having passed my BCE exams, I was deputed as Second Mate on the famous steamship *Himavan*, under the captainship of Shri Martin James, a very affable person. Following the recommendation of William Hunter, the author of *A History of Bharat*, I was introduced to Lord Rippon, who was once our Viceroy—who in turn guided me to Martin James. This was the outcome of my great ambition to work under a reputed engineer as part of my course, before I returned to my homeland. This was a chartered ship taken on lease by a large foreign trading company from Aden, in keeping with the terms of the British Government, to research the viability of establishing a submarine telegraph cable in the city of Bombay.

Originally published in Malayalam as 'Dwaraka' by *Vidyavinodini*, Number 9/July 1893.

One end of the cable was to be fixed in the city of Aden and checked for its effectiveness by sending messages from the ship to Aden and back regularly. Some time during the summer months, our ship reached the proximity of the famous Hasthadweep,[1] not very far from the harbour of Bombay. We circled the island from the north and travelled east a while longer. One morning, just before we docked at Bombay harbour, it was noticed that the communication link with Aden was disrupted. It was evident that the cabling had been breached somewhere. We sailed along the route of the cabling to check the spot of trouble using electrical equipment. Almost a mile away from Hasthadweep, we detected that the fault lay somewhere near it. Knowing well that the only way to rectify the fault in the cable was to lift it above water level and set about repairing it, we began to make arrangements. Fortunately, at that point of time there was no turbulence in the waters or gusts of wind—the lack of which made repair work easy. During those months, the rising sun smeared the sky with hues of blue and gold—a sight very soothing to the eye. After sunrise, as the sun rose above the horizon, the sky turned the colour of pure gold in all its brilliance.

We raised the cable with great care, spooling it on the deck of the ship, and reached the spot where it had been damaged. When the cable laid on the seabed was brought out of the water, all kinds of seaweed and offal of small creatures and minuscule insects remained stuck to the cable. As we gradually rolled up the cable, we sensed that it was stuck between rocks and other stones under the water. We had to be more careful in stretching the already

---

1 Elephanta Island.

taut cable lest it snap, as James, a man of long experience, warned us. When he and I spooled the cable some more, just as he had feared, the cable snapped and the still uncoiled part of the cable sank into the ocean. The mishap seemed pre-ordained! We were aghast and frustrated to the core. All our efforts sank like a line scored in water! But that was no reason to sit back and do nothing. *Try, we must*—thought James, and he spoke to the navigators of the ship, and in order to make sure where exactly in the ocean the rest of the cable lay, he ordered the ship to cruise back the way we came. After sailing around a bit, a spot was finally identified as the exact spot where we could locate the sunken cable. Thankfully, it was not a very deep part of the sea. We dropped anchor there. Our next exercise was to raise the cable from under the water using the heavy-duty cranes on board. A few tugs by the crane netted no result. When the adventurous Martin opined that the only recourse we had was to don deep-sea diving suits and go in, I thought he was trying to be funny. But when he went on to explain that the spot located was not a deep part of the Arabian Sea and that water there could not be more than two hundred feet deep, I began to understand that Martin meant business. He began to tell us about the equipment used for deep sea diving and how pearl was mined from the seabed and other related matters. He went on to tell us about a famous American electrical engineer who had invented an apparatus for breathing underwater and its utility in deep-sea excavation. The equipment for underwater breathing currently in use could supply air to the diver, but the air ran out quickly. To make up for that, the people on shore had to pump in fresh air through a tube, to sustain the diver. Not just that, this equipment had other features too. Its natural weight was enough to send the wearer deeper into the water. Besides a cap made of light-weight material, integral to the breathing apparatus was a chamber to conserve the air we breathed, enabling the wearer to spend long periods under water without any difficulty. This diving suit was also a protection against predatory underwater fauna. I had read about this equipment in a magazine during my student days and seen a picture of it but had never actually seen it. I was thrilled to hear that Mr James had two such pieces in his possession. As our discussion progressed, we also talked about trying once more to extricate the trapped cable and raise it to the surface. This time round, we brought it to the surface of the water, as we did in our previous attempt; but this time too, it slipped out of hand and slithered back into the seawater. Many minds went to work and many suggestions surfaced, but not the cable. Finally, it was decided that we would give it another try, but only the next morning, and all of us dispersed.

Even before dusk set in, James and I had supper and went up on the deck, sat on the deckchairs and began to smoke cigars, enjoying the remarkably pleasant breeze. Talking about deep-sea diving kits, James said: 'Nair, I think that if we are unable to raise the cable with our crane, we will have to dive in ourselves to check. If we do that, God only knows what treasure we might find at the bottom of the sea. As described in detail in your Mahabharata and Shishupalavadha,[2] the lost city of Dwaraka must be around here somewhere—that's what experts report.' When he said that, my mind slipped into a kind of turmoil, and I do not recollect what my mental state was, just then. Our writers of epics tell us

---

2 A snippet from Mahabharata.

that after the advent of Lord Krishna, the city of Dwaraka was swallowed by the sea. Perhaps a tectonic shift caused the shifting of the city into the ocean. Even these days, it was not uncommon to hear of islands both surfacing and drowning in the sea due to undersea earthquakes. Therefore, it was perfectly logical that such a claim about Dwaraka might be true. But we did not know if the geographical location of the catastrophe was where we were anchored right now.

To the great poets of yore like Kalidasa, Dwaraka was a holy land of art and culture, as evidenced by the many creations originating there. I thought that to be able to actually see such an ancient city under the sea would be the most memorable spectacle of my life—with my head full of such thoughts, my desire to go deep-sea diving peaked. I said to James, 'Don't forget the deep-sea breathing equipment,' to which James answered, 'I remember; will call you when they are ready.'

With that, I retired to my cabin and lay down, all wrapped up, thinking of the next day's expedition till I fell asleep. Within a short span of time, I thought I heard someone walk past me. When I looked through the folds of my blanket, I saw Martin undoing the knots of a large bundle. Wondering what he was up to in the middle of the night, I watched him extricate two deep-sea diving costumes from the bundle and set them up for imminent use. Then he went over to another corner and came back with two underwater lamps that looked like the lanterns used by policemen. He came to me and said, 'Nair, Nair! Wake up. Don't you want to see Dwaraka?'

'It is not dawn yet...' I mumbled.

'So what? Diving deep into the sea wearing this underwater breathing apparatus is not acceptable to our old Captain. He keeps warning us that the sea is very deep around here. We must finish our task before he wakes. What difference does day or night make to us?' At that, I quickly got out of bed and both of us put on our deep-sea diving costumes along with the underwater breathing apparatus. We attached the underwater lantern firmly about our waists. We stealthily went to the rope ladder that dropped from the deck down to the waters. Martin James lowered the long rope—attached to the side of the hull—into the water. In no time, he vanished deep under. I had my fears, but summoning all my courage, I followed suit. Clinging to the rope, I climbed down the rope-ladder. Going down deeper, we touched firm ground. James sat on a smooth boulder comfortably, with no sign of fear. On the bed of the sea, we saw many kinds of pebbles, multi-coloured marine molluscs—cowries and conches. In the light of our lanterns, they seemed to glitter more than they normally did. All the stones were covered with algae and black mould. After a while, James left his perch on the boulder and began to walk, looking around. I too had become restless. As we walked through the seaweeds, we passed thousands of small, multi-hued fish flitting around us. Something that caught our attention was a granite rock, which was at least three feet in diameter. James used his penknife to scrape off the fungus that had formed on it (as we see on our compound walls during the rainy season) and decided that this was no natural formation. It was obviously the work of an artisan. When all the mould was removed from the rock, we saw some letters etched on it. It was evident to us that this was a stone carved a long time ago, in the now submerged city of Dwaraka. On seeing this rock, an ecstasy came over me, which was no less than the happiness of the Great One when He first beheld the nine celestial planets. We concluded that the Dwaraka of ancient lore must be right where we stood. Walking towards the east, we came across many more weeds and marine fauna. We progressed slowly, tripping and stumbling. When James grabbed me as I fell, together we began to fall into a depthless abyss. Finally, we touched ground once more. Being underwater, we felt no pain. As we got up and looked around, we saw a dome of intricate design that must have been around a hundred feet in diameter. My thought was how to get back to the surface of the water from the spot we were in. We continued to explore the seabed around us. As we fell a while ago, we heard a deep resonance that echoed even in the water. When the sound of the echo subsided, we began to dig into the sand below our feet. We found sculptures resplendent with carved petals, flowers and replicas of birds made of corals and similar gemstones. The walls around the spot where we fell were made of spectacular multi-hued stones. Anybody would be mystified at the artistic prowess of the sculptor who must have etched and carved it inch by inch. We stood petrified by the sight we saw. The view of the walls made of priceless crystals and the row of pillars, and the frescoes covering the walls—all made luminous by the light from the lanterns we had—reflected each other immaculately. We stood transfixed, alarmed and unable to distinguish one from the other.

Dwaraka—a place described in the epics of Mahabharata and Bhagavatham and great poems like 'Magham', which is also a sacred place. To think that I had the fortune to stand before one of the Royal Courts of such a palace, brought boundless joy mixed with a slight trepidation caused by the awe-inspiring vision.

The excitement and joy that Columbus experienced when he first set foot on American soil, or the euphoria of Vasco-da-Gama, who found a sea route to our own peninsula, and yet again, the thrill of the great Navigator[3] when he sighted the vast Pacific Ocean—all of them faded into insignificance in comparison to my own state of bliss right then.

To the right of where we stood on the western side of this altar, was a great door. When we passed the door and reached the opposite end of a passage, we came upon a staircase, still remarkably intact, with many beautiful carvings. When Martin James walked down the stairs, I followed him, meekly. At the bottom, what we saw was a smaller room—compared to what we had just left behind—but its walls were made of a smooth black stone that resembled polished granite. In the centre of that room, we saw a spectacular platform, fashioned like a lotus. In the middle of the lotus stood a gem-encrusted cauldron made of gold with a hundred lamps etched around it, which shone brilliantly even in that light. I tried to lift it, but even as I put my hand on it, it disintegrated and became a lump of dust right before our eyes. A brilliance that was equal to a million suns emanated from it. Our own lanterns became little wicks of flames in comparison. As soon as this happened, the jet-black walls seemed to sink lower and lower. As we stood there horrified, we saw a thin line of white smoke in the shape of a pillar rising from the spot where the walls once stood. We also saw a couple of grotesque, armoured demons following the smoke and approaching us. At the sight of these gruesome creatures, both of us fainted like people struck by

---

3 Ferdinand Magellan.

lightning. Just then, one of the demons brandished his mace and pounced on me to grab my neck with his free hand. That is when I screamed.

At the same time, I heard someone shout: 'Hey, Nair! *Nayare*! What kind of sleep is this? It is almost noon. Why did you yell? Did you have a nightmare? Get up! Don't you want tea?'

Startled, I looked around: What Dwaraka! What Himavan! Barrister Menon stood beside me, laughing!

Listening to his travelogue of several foreign countries, his experiences of the wonders of electricity, his sailing episodes, of the etiquette of the people of those countries, their penchant for innovation ... all garnished with a smatter of humour—my mind wandered and soon I fell fast asleep again: that is all.

C.P. ACHUTHA MENON

My First Fee

It has been seventeen years since I was first assigned to the Ramapuram District Court, waiting for a litigation to come my way. When I first sat among the other lawyers of the court, it was with the arrogance that I would turn the place upside down with my prowess. My mother and elder brother, too, shared my spirit: 'When the clients set their eyes on our Shankarankutty, would they ever give their case to any other?' Such was their confidence in me. But soon I began to realize that the clientele did not share this opinion. I had been squatting here for over six or seven months dressed in a jacket and a headdress but the parties did not even pretend to notice my presence. Apparently, I was to them just another piece of furniture. After some time, both my enthusiasm and strength began to dwindle. However, as there was ample wealth in my ancestral home and because I was the apple of the eye of my mother's eldest brother, who was the head of the family,

---

Originally published in Malayalam as 'Ente Aadyathe Fees' by *Vidyavinodini*, June 1894.

karanavar, I got by famously even without any income from the court.

Seven uneventful months sped by. One day, as I lay back in the easy chair at dusk, reading the newspaper, a servant walked in—

'Kalyaniamma of Poonkunnam requests you to call on her.'

'Kalyaniamma of Poonkunnam?'

'Yes.'

'Any idea why?'

'No. She said you must visit her right away, if not otherwise engaged.'

Poonkunnath Kalyaniamma was the wife of Ambalappat Gopala Menon, the Munsif. Soon after I began my practice as an advocate, I called on him twice, but the lady was not around then. When the court closed for vacation, the gent succumbed to paralysis.

When I heard that Kalyaniamma—who had never even met me—had sent for me, I became curious. If only I knew why. But it was the summons of a lady! Besides, I must bear in mind she was the wife of the late Gopala Menon. He had taken a strong liking to me. With all this on my mind, I set out to Kalyaniamma's house right away. The lady was waiting for me at the entrance of her house. She received me with joy and great respect and ushered me in.

This was our first meeting. As I said before, she had not been present when I had called on the Munsif. She was not more than forty; however, at first sight she did not appear any more than thirty. She was a beautiful lady of extraordinary intellect. Within minutes, I sensed that anybody who spoke to her even for a short while would become an admirer. I was desperate to know why she had summoned me. But she spoke of other matters to begin with.

'You have come here twice, haven't you? I wasn't here then, unfortunately.'

'My bad luck.'

'Not at all. My husband approved of you at his first meeting with you. Not a day passed when he did not talk of you. *You haven't met Shankarankutty Menon, have you, Kalyani? He is a boy with a future*—he would always say.'

I do not know if anyone exists who is averse to praise. Especially if that praise comes from the face of a pretty lady. If there are those who do not fall for it, I concede, that I am not one among them. When I heard Kalyaniamma's words, I was prepared to do anything for her.

'I am lucky that he thought so well of me, though I don't believe I am worthy of it. What a pity, that such a competent man as he is no more. A misfortune for the people at large.'

'The people? It is nothing but *my* own bad luck!'

Even as she spoke, she began to sniffle and weep. The matter was clearly serious—either because of my sensitive nature or because of my weakness; I can't bear to see tears, let alone tears from the eyes of a lady as graceful as Kalyaniamma. So, I felt distressed and grew restless. After a while, the lady regained her composure and spoke: 'My distress has disturbed you. When several matters came to mind, I couldn't contain myself. When you have heard me out fully, I'm sure you will be able to forgive me.'

Kalyaniamma told me all, in elaborate detail. Her narrative was often interrupted with sobs as she spoke intermittently—because

My First Fee

of which I am unable to relate her story here verbatim. Therefore, I shall confine my narrative to its gist:

Kalyaniamma, though born in an aristocratic tharavad, was sunk in poverty even as a child, thanks to the debts brought upon the family by its karanavar. Soon after the property was impounded and auctioned, the karanavar expired. Kalyaniamma had only her mother with her for solace. That is the period when Gopala Menon, the Munsif, began to court her. Needless to say, from then on, they were no longer troubled by poverty. The house she lived in now was the one that the Munsif had built for her. Besides the house, he had bought her property for ten thousand rupees. He had also given her four thousand rupees in cash along with ornaments and vessels. Although Kalyaniamma had five children, she had only two at the time of my visit. The older one was, a girl of sixteen called Ammukutty and the other a boy, Balakrishnan, aged about eight. The other three died in infancy.

Many days before he died, Gopala Menon had transferred a property worth eleven thousand rupees to Kalyaniamma's name. The Deed of Agreement had been signed by the Munsif's nephew, Krishna Menon, and attested by another nephew, Kandunni Menon. The property was leased out to three persons and the lease deeds were made out in Kalyaniamma's name.

When Kalyaniamma opened the box that contained the sale deed and the lease papers, she was startled to see them missing.

In order to find out what must be done under the circumstances, Kalyaniamma had sent for me to discuss the matter.

She said: 'If the money lost was only a small sum, I could have borne the loss. I am very reluctant to litigate with his nephews, particularly so soon after Gopala Menon's demise. But if I remain quiet, my children will starve.'

'How can you be sure that the nephews are the ones who cheated you?'

'I forgot to tell you that. It has been three months since the Munsif died, but I found out about the theft of the documents only yesterday. Of the three lessees, one goes by the name of Ikkoran, an Ezhavan. It was only when he came here yesterday and told me that Kunhikrishna Menon had asked him to rewrite the lease deed in *his* favour and when he, Ikkoran, objected to it, offered to pay him two hundred rupees to comply, that I became suspicious and checked the box to find the documents missing. In the uproar caused by Gopala Menon's impending death, the nephews snatched the documents; no doubt.'

'Doesn't anyone else know of the transfer and lease deeds?'

'No. Everything was done in confidence.'

'What about the witnesses?'

'Yes, they do know. Veerashuppupattar and Unnaman Nair are the witnesses, the latter for the lease deeds. When asked yesterday, they both said that they knew nothing about it! Veerashuppu's account was settled even while Gopala Menon was around.'

I said: 'The nephews have cheated you, no doubt. Such rogues, aren't they? Strange that a decent man as the Munsif had such nephews!'

'He never trusted them. But I, on the other hand, mingled very cordially with them. I have never said nor done anything unpleasant to them in all these years. Leave that be. Now, tell me what we should do.'

My First Fee

I thought for a while. 'As far as I understand hitherto, they have sealed all loopholes while committing the crime. We must consult a reputable advocate of great experience and wit, as a beginning.'

'I haven't thought of that. I want you, Sankarankutty Menon, to find a solution for this. Were he alive, the Munsif would have entrusted this work to no one else but you. That is my firm belief.'

'I have never conducted a litigation. This is not a trivial matter. So, engaging an experienced person would be the best for you. I say so because this would be my first case ever, should I take it up.'

Just then a sweet voice spoke up vehemently from behind Kalyaniamma: 'Did the "experienced" advocate take up all those cases before fighting his first case?'

In the sight that I beheld when I turned to look, I forgot that very instant Kalyaniamma's sorrows, the misdeeds of the Munsif's nephews and shed all my nervousness at the same time. Leaning against the door jamb with an arm around a boy of eight was a girl in the prime of her youth, smiling shyly but diffidently. I stared at her without blinking for a long while. I sat still. Watching both of us, Kalyaniamma spoke up: 'They are my children, Ammukutty and Balakrishnan', and called them to her and seated them beside her. Never one to be perturbed in the least in front of an audience, I now became very nervous in Ammukutty's presence.

When Kalyaniamma asked them, 'Do you know Sankarankuttymenn ...?' Balakrishnan said, 'Is this Achan's *Shankaramenn?*' and Ammukutty said without any doubt, 'I know him'—my nervousness doubled. I had assumed what Kalyaniamma had said about the Munsif having a soft corner for me was mere courtesy but what these children said convinced me it was not so.

As I had not seen Ammukutty before, I was surprised by what she said and so asked her: 'Oh, how is that? I have never seen you before.'

'Does that mean that I couldn't have seen you?'

Kalyaniamma intervened (fondly): 'Nothing but insolence bursts from her mouth! Her father doted on her and pampered her silly.'

I did not think Ammukutty was being impertinent. I thought there was a wisdom beyond her years in her words.

'I wasn't being disrespectful. People will recognize prominent persons while the latter rarely enquire about ordinary folk.'

'Me and prominent? Hearing that for the first time.'

'The truly dignified are not conceited. That is why *you* feel so,' said Ammukutty.

I smiled and said to Kalyaniamma: 'If your case goes to court, it is better to name Ammukutty as your advocate.'

She replied: 'Leave all that. No end to her airs! What must we do about our case?'

'I can't figure out a way just yet. Let me sleep over it and get back to you tomorrow. Will suggest something then.'

I lingered there for a long time chatting and finally bid goodbye.

My thoughts on the way back from Kalyaniamma's house were confounding and contradictory. At the outset, I was excited to have received my first case of litigation. That joy doubled when I realized that this was a prestigious case that would garner fame. At the same time, I was sad to think of Kalyaniamma's plight and worried that I might fail to bring matters to a satisfactory closure. In the midst of all these thoughts shone brightly a youthful, beautiful and brilliant face. Try as I might to concentrate on any fixed matter, that face intruded and would not let me complete my train of thought. I wondered at the inconsistency of my mind. It was much later that I understood the reason for this turbulence of thought. When I recognized it was the powerful, inevitable onslaught of first love, I wound up all my other thoughts and permitted my mind to dwell on Ammukutty alone and revelled in that exquisite pleasure.

My readers would want to know more about the figure of that woman who stole my heart at first sight. Feature to feature, she did not possess any great beauty. Her complexion was not startlingly attractive, except that it was more fair than dark. Her head was a mite larger than usual and her forehead slightly prominent. Though her eyes were deep-set, they had a distinctive sparkle to them. Her cheeks were plump and she had a small pointed chin. While she spoke or laughed, her gums showed but her teeth were unusually attractive. Her hair was long and luxuriant. But I thought these features were not what attracted me to her. Ammukutty lured me not with the beauty of her features but with the liveliness of her face. Her overall youth, sprightliness, the sparkle in her very glance, the lighting up of her face when she smiled, her cute dimples, her delightful speech and the sweetness of its tone—all these, put together, gave Ammukutty irresistible charm.

When I thought all this over with a single-minded focus, I decided that my life would be wasted if I could not make Ammukutty my life partner. Judging from Kalyaniamma's respectful attitude towards me, I guessed that she might not have any kind of objection in this matter. But there was one obstacle. If, God forbid, I was unable to accomplish the task assigned to me by the family, it would be most demeaning of me to ask the mother for her daughter's hand. On the other hand, if I did conclude the case favourably, it would give me a certain privilege to ask for the girl's hand in marriage. Makes it easier for them too to consent to the match. Therefore, I made up my mind that I would not rest till I made the nephews of the Munsif return her property rights to Kalyaniamma; I began to make my plans to execute this task.

Had I ten years of experience in fighting lawsuits, matters might have been much simpler. I could have put together the evidence required to substantiate Kalyaniamma's plea within the span of four hours. But as an honest lawyer born to an aristocratic household and being fresh at his job, that line of thought did not even occur to me. I could only plan ways to find admissible evidence that would expose the nephews for the culprits they were, in court, and thus win the case.

The state of the matter was dire. Many knew that the property had been in the name of the Munsif for several years. Only three lessees and Veerashuppupattar knew that it had been transferred in the name of Kalyaniamma. It was evident that two of the lessees and the pattar[1] would fight the case instead of helping her out. Overall, it appeared that only Ikkoran might appear as a witness in favour of Kalyaniamma. But that alone would not ensure winning this lawsuit. It must be remembered here that in those days there was no practice of registering sale deeds.

On the whole, there was no sign of winning the battle. Both Kunhikrishna Menn and Kandunni Menn had sealed all loopholes in casting the dice. Whichever way you looked at it, it appeared

---

1 Slang for Brahmin.

My First Fee

surrender was inevitable. Thinking over these things late into night, I finally fell asleep. Even as I rose the next morning, this is what first came to mind. In that state of mind, I surmised that as Veerashuppupattar was a money lender and a trader, I could expose his underhand deeds by examining his account books. If I could find evidence against him, I could threaten him and influence him. How might I check his account books …? I did have a few dealings with him. He was a person who would stoop to any level for money. Still, I was not sure that I could easily trap him, because I knew that the pattar was cunning enough to escape being caught in the worst of situations. All the same, it was an avenue that must not be left unexplored. Since the deed papers had been stolen in the month of December or January, and he claimed to have paid back the money in the month of November, either all his accounts must have been re-written or there must be a mistake in the journal of accounts. I decided to meet the man personally and set out to his house in the morning.

While making small talk with him, I suddenly dropped the subject of the missing documents of Kalyaniamma as something I had overheard somewhere. About which, he said: 'Oh, you too heard of that? I was under the impression that the lady is of a decent sort. I never thought that she was capable of enacting such a farce!'

'How are you so sure it is a lie?'

'How am I so sure? She has said that I have signed as a witness in the document, whereas I haven't even dreamt of it. She also says that the receipt that I gave her has gone missing. That transaction was concluded in the month of November itself.'

'You do have proof of that, don't you?'

'Our accounts book is itself the proof. What court will refuse that piece of evidence? If you wish to, you can yourself examine the books.'

Saying so, the man picked up the accounts journal, turned to the relevant page and showed it to me.

'I don't distrust you; why would I check your accounts?' Even while voicing all this, I still picked up the book to check. I found no misappropriation in it. There were no slashes or corrections. Like he said, any court of justice would accept this as evidence. I therefore decided that following this path would lead me nowhere.

Karunakara Menon, who had become the Kalaripuram Munsif a mere two months prior to this transaction—after serving as an advocate in the apellate court for years—was the younger brother of my mother's brother-in-law. All the transactions of the Munsif pertaining to property were conducted by him. When I sat disillusioned with no recourse to a solution for my problem, I remembered this connection. This gent might have heard of the transfer of property done by the Munsif in favour of Kalyaniamma. Even otherwise, only good could come out of discussing this case with Mr Menon, I thought. I was confident that he would do anything in his power to help me because I knew he looked upon me as a son.

Soon after I thought of this way of tackling the matter, I began to sleep well again. Sleep had eluded me for the past few days because of the unrest I suffered without a solution to my problem. But that night I slumbered peacefully. The next day, after an early breakfast, I set out for Kalaripuram; I did not inform Kalyaniamma

My First Fee

of this. I sent word to her that I had to go home for an emergency and might take about two days to return.

I started my journey and reached Kalaripuram the next day. Karunakara Menon received me most cordially, needless to say. After discussing matters of family and asking after me, when he asked me if there wasn't any specific reason for my visit, I told him all about the case. Although he kept silent all through my narration, I could read from his face that he was very angry and disgusted at the tale.

'Kandunni Menon and Krishna Menon are not known for their decency, but I didn't think they were such scoundrels. How unscrupulous must they be if they can persecute a helpless lady like this! All right, we won't spare them but teach them a lesson. Thank God, I have with me the munition to do that.'

Saying this, he went indoors. I couldn't understand the import of all that he said, but it was clear that a solution was in the offing. Karunakara Menon returned and handed me two letters. When I finished reading them, I rose trembling from head to toe. I was thrilled that I could now make Kalyaniamma's foes fall at her feet.

'I must go back right now.'

Karunakara Menon smiled and asked me: 'Hold on! Don't get excited; you can return after supper. There are a few things we must discuss. What are you planning to do with these letters?'

'As soon as I get back, I shall file a criminal suit against them for stealing those documents.'

'Do you think Kalyaniamma will consent? You haven't understood the lady properly. She is the kind who would prefer to lose everything she owns rather than let any harm come to her husband's nephews.'

'Yes. That is true. But isn't it wrong to let those fellows get away?'

'It would be unfortunate. Still, don't do anything without the lady's consent. Returning the property to the lady herself will be a good punishment for those greedy guys. What then about Veerashuppupattar? He indulges in all kinds of crime. He ought to be straightened out.'

'But to do that, these letters will not suffice.'

'No. If there is any other evidence, that might help this case as well. It is certain that the man has falsified his accounts. The amount was returned in the month of November, says the pattar. For a thousand rupees, he is not one to desist from altering the accounts of two whole months. Only after finding proof of this felony and seeking the opinion of Kalyaniamma must you do anything more.'

I agreed and returned that very evening. I met Kalyaniamma as soon as I returned. She was very happy to hear that there was a possibility of retrieving her property. I did not go into all the details of the developments. As for suing the nephews for criminal offence, her response was just as Karunakara Menon had predicted. To whatever I said, she had only this to say: 'I will be most happy to get back my property without any litigation. Even if I lose all my property, I shouldn't be the cause of any harm to befall his nephews.'

Ammukutty spoke up: 'Amma has no problem in poor us starving. All she wants is for those heartless creatures to live unharmed.'

'How can you even call them cruel people?'

'Oh! No, not cruel, but thieving gentlemen!'

'You insolent girl! You are inviting the curse of elders upon yourself!'

My First Fee

Ammukutty retorted: 'Even if they have a lot of curses with them, it can fall upon me only if I choose to accept them.'

Kalyaniamma smiled: 'I have nothing to say to you,' saying which, she began to ask me about various matters. After a long while, I bid them goodbye and came away. I needn't reiterate here that the more I saw of her, the more my desire grew to marry Ammukutty.

I thought the whole night of various methods by which I might corner Veerashuppupattar, but couldn't arrive at a satisfactory conclusion. It was obvious that the man had altered all the figures in his account books. It had been done in total secrecy. So, it wasn't easy to expose the fraud through evidence or proof. However, I decided to summon Ambalappattu Krishna Menon and Kandunni Menon along with the pattar to Kalyaniamma's house the next day. I only wanted to see if I could expose their deceit through threats.

The next day, after noon, I had Kalyaniamma send for the nephews of the Munsif. The message sent was that an urgent matter had to be discussed. I doubted very much whether they would come at all. At least in that matter, I was not disappointed. Kunhikrishna Menon arrived at around 4 p.m. As we saw him approaching, we sent a messenger to Veerashuppupattar too. The message was that Kunhikrishna Menon had sent word to him to come over to Punkunnam for a talk.

Kalyaniamma received Krishna Menon with great respect. As she made small talk with him without hinting at the real reason for the meeting, Kandunni Menon walked up, followed shortly by the pattar. The minute they saw each other, they grasped the situation. It was clear from the way they smiled that none of them had the slightest fear of being exposed.

Till that point, the three men did not have any inkling of my presence in that house. When the three settled down and finished with their formal courtesies, I entered the room. Despite the fact that they were all past masters of cunning manoeuvres, they winced almost imperceptibly on seeing me there. I only knew the pattar personally but had a casual acquaintance with the other two, enough for them to know that I was a lawyer. Their discomfort was evident because now they were not dealing with a simple and defenceless lady but with an advocate—and a man, to boot. Veerashuppupattar introduced me to them, and I sat down. In the normal course of things, the three of us conversed politely about this and that. Talking sweetly with those fellows was very difficult for me but I did so merely for Kalyaniamma's sake.

I opened with: 'The documents of the deeds of property the late Munsif transferred to Kalyaniamma's name have gone missing from the box in which they were stored. As we heard that you oversaw the lessee rewriting the lease deed, we are compelled to believe that only you could have removed the documents from the box and that is why you have been called here by Kalyaniamma.'

Kunhikrishna Menon spoke in a sombre tone: 'It is not clear what right you have to be talking about this. Whether you have the right or not, it is not becoming of a decent man to insult gentlemen of repute with such an accusation. So, I refuse to speak with you.'

'Kalyaniamma has given me the brief to represent her against you in a formal litigation in court.'

'In that case, there is no point in discussing the matter here. We shall meet in court.'

'That suits me too. However, Kalyaniamma is upset about your being arrested and therefore wishes to settle the matter amicably.'

My First Fee

Kunhikrishna Menon: 'An out-of-court settlement doesn't seem probable. If you don't want to go to court, *we* do, now. Do you think respectable men like us will lie low if you accuse us because some lowly thief pilfered your documents?'

When he spoke so with the conviction that he had manipulated the act with perfect immunity, I was furious; but as I was sure that I could make them fall at my feet in court, I suppressed my annoyance and said simply: 'If you think you can frighten me with your bravado, it is because you don't know whom you are talking to. I had realized soon enough that you were not people with whom a decent settlement of the issue was possible. Kalyaniamma hoped to do so only because of her innocence.'

'If I knew you had summoned me to insult and conduct a mock trial, I wouldn't have come at all. I won't make this mistake again.'

When Krishna Menon stood up to leave, Kalyaniamma spoke up: 'Oh no! Please don't take offence. You can leave after hearing out the whole matter at hand. Swami! Why aren't you saying anything?'

Veerashuppu: 'Menons! Don't rush things. Listen to the whole story. Shankarankutty Menon, these people say they know nothing about the deeds. Then why do you accuse them of the offence?'

'What are you trying to say? Weren't you a witness to the document the Munsif signed off to Kalyaniamma? When they stole the documents, didn't they pilfer that receipt of yours for a thousand rupees that you had given to the Munsif and passed it back to you? Don't pretend you know nothing!'

'You are trying to harass us without reason. Talking through your hat doesn't speak well of your status.'

'You are the one who is blabbering. Read this.' I gave him the first of the two letters Karunakara Menon had given me. Fearing that the pattar would destroy it, I was careful not to give him the original. As soon as I brought out the letter, there was a change in the countenance of all the three. The pattar read the letter aloud.

I give below only what is relevant to this episode.

Uncle has decided to sign off property worth eleven thousand rupees to his wife. He insists that I comply with the deed and give it in writing. This transaction is not acceptable to me or anyone else for that matter. As this deal was done after Uncle became bedridden, isn't there a law for quashing it after his death? If we argue that the deed was signed during his illness—when he was mentally unstable—due to the instigation of his wife, can we get a favourable verdict? Only after getting your opinion on this will I get entangled in the ploy.

Hearing these words—written deliberately and heartlessly—innocent Kalyaniamma began to whimper and sob. I said to the pattar: 'Swami! I haven't shown this wretched letter to anyone yet. I let you see it only because my hand was forced. Do you now think that I was blurting out what came to my mind irresponsibly?'

Pattar and Kunhikrishna Menon stood as if turned into stone. Kandunni Menon spoke: 'Uncle did tell us about the transfer of ownership. It is true that we weren't in favour of it. That is why my brother wrote this letter. But Uncle died before the deed agreement was drawn. That is all.'

At this, Krishna Menon's face lit up. But I felt like laughing. 'In that case, Swami, please read this letter too.' I handed over the second letter. That letter was written two days after the document of transfer of ownership was filed. It clearly said that the deed had been signed, that the Munsif was on his death bed and should he die, the property must be immediately handed over to Kalyaniamma. On hearing this letter read out, those men who had been waxing eloquent till then looked shaken. Such people who have no qualms about cheating and stealing from a simple lady are, despite their display of outrage, intrinsically cowards. At this point, they stood transfixed for a long time, unable to utter a word.

Veerashuppupattar asked: 'Dear Krishna Menon, were these letters written by you? If so, you have no choice but to apologize to Kalyaniamma.'

Pattar remained composed and indifferent—till now these two letters had no bearing on him and could do no harm to him. Realizing that I could not alarm him unless I assumed an impudent stance, I said to him: 'Don't be so complacent because these letters are no proof of all your fraudulent practices. There are other similar proofs with me to prove that you have tampered with your account books. I won't tell you now what they are. While these other two confess to their crime, I won't let you off unless you record in writing what your role was and what your nefarious actions were in this case.'

The man's composure snapped on hearing this. Seeing the dread and panic of the three, I continued: 'A "fool" like me is not inclined to let off you "upright" gentlemen. But Kalyaniamma doesn't have the heart to see you taken to jail in chains. I don't think you have the wisdom or goodness to perceive her nobility of thought. We can resolve this problem if you return the deed papers intact or, if destroyed already, prepare a new valid legal document of ownership in her name. Whichever way, the matter must be concluded before sunset tomorrow.'

What more need be said? Before noon the next day, the nephews brought the deed papers and Veerashuppupattar, the money. Kalyaniamma was beside herself with joy and gratitude towards me. My self-satisfaction too knew no bounds. But she did something that was very awkward (to me). She placed before me three hundred rupees as a fee. How can I describe the embarrassment I felt at that moment? *Could I ever accept money from Ammukutty's mother?*

Kalyaniamma said: 'Isn't it proper for you to accept compensation for all the trouble you took?'

'Trouble? Never in my whole life have I enjoyed anything as much as I did while dealing with this case.'

'Still, how could I not do something to show my gratitude?'

'I won't say that you mustn't do anything at all. But I have a wish. All you have to do is to grant me that.'

'If it is something within my means, consider it done.'

'I do agree that I don't have the stature to ask this. But I am expressing my misplaced desire to you because I am certain that my life will go waste if I can't get Ammukutty as my life partner.'

Kalyaniamma: 'Oh! This is like icing on the cake. Having already done us a big favour, do you want to still better that with this? Misplaced desire! My God! Even when my husband spoke of you the first time, I began to hope for this match. He too hoped that such a thing would come about.'

It has been seventeen years since this episode. Not a day has passed without our talking with delight of the Munsif's nephews' misdeeds. Somehow the news of my outwitting them spread around town. From that day onwards, clients began to pour into

My First Fee

my office. Till now, our life together has been quite happy but when I think of Ammukutty's good fortune, it is negligible compared to my own. Ammukutty, who has been standing behind my chair, reading over my shoulder, held my hand at this point and refused to let me write more. She doesn't want me to make public the joys we shared with each other till now. It is also impossible to describe it in words.

K. RAMAKRISHNA PILLAI

Oh No! Not Like This!

I am in receipt of your letter. Couldn't reply due to the pressure of work here. I am stunned to hear that you are in love with a girl called, 'Bhavani'; that you desire to seek an alliance with her. You haven't mentioned anything about her lineage. I advise you not to have any relations with her. I fixed someone for you long ago. You may not have heard of the District Administrator from the Palace. You will do well to obey what I tell you to do. If you do, all my savings will be bequeathed to you. Otherwise, if you don't, you will receive only a sum of thirty rupees every month as allowance—bear that in mind.

I am going on a tour. I don't know where I shall be while in transit in the two or three months to come. So, don't send any letters now. I believe that you will rely on your sense of judgement, and with a mind seasoned with the study of English, respect my words—and do as you are told.

Your affectionate father,
Ramankutty Menon

Originally published in Malayalam as 'Alla! Ee Vidhamo?' by *Vidyavinodini*, Number 10/August 1900.

Oh No! Not Like This!

I SAT STILL, HOLDING the letter. I don't remember now what transpired in my mind then. But the lady of the house where I boarded told me that my face had contorted with changing expressions. It is a month since I wrote to my father. Proposing to Bhavani and her instant acceptance of it had come together. I was in no mood to give her up.

Unfortunately, my father did not support the match. Bhavani had already promised that she would never backtrack on me. We had agreed that as soon as we learnt that I had passed the BA examination—the results of which were due in a month—we would marry. Now, what could we do? She insisted that I show her my father's reply the moment it reached me.

After dinner that night, when I went over to Bhavani's house, the servants had not yet retired to their respective quarters. Bhavanikutty was seated, reading. I went inside to meet her mother and others to greet them before going to where Bhavani sat. We talked a lot about some poems and similar creative works; then I handed my father's reply to her. When she had finished reading, what she did was to look at me and burst out laughing. Oh! Her laughter is so unique! I tried to maintain my gravitas but couldn't. I too began to laugh. After a long while, Bhavani said to me:

'Forgive me. Oh no! This is certainly a joke. Funny that your father found a bride for you and didn't even ask your opinion about it ... What do you think?'

I fumbled for words. 'No, he ...'

'Anyway, it is her good fortune.'

'Whose?'

'Oh that—that—other girl's.'

'What! Bhavanikutty! Have you forgotten that we have plighted our troth? Will you alter that?'

Bhavani picked up the letter to read it once more. She went through it again and again. She laughed till tears filled her eyes. Then she said: 'Then what about the property? Your father will disinherit you!'

'Property, indeed! I don't give a damn about property. If thirty rupees a month doesn't suffice, I will find a job.'

'You are young. You are competent to pick a bride of your choice. Would you deny it?'

'Of course not! What do I lack? Bhavanikutty, listen! I have already decided to forego my inheritance. And why? Because I don't want the woman that my father has selected for me.'

'Would you actually do that?'

'Certainly. Either I live with you or I shall remain like this till the end of my days.'

'In that case, I have also decided: either you or a spinster for life. By the way, won't the results of the examination be announced by the end of next month?'

We continued to talk about other matters and also spoke about some of our relatives.

Bhavani said: 'You seem to have a lot of relatives!'

'What about you?'

'Just one. My father's younger brother. I don't think you will approve of him. But I am very fond of him.'

(She gave me a sidelong glance.)

'I will like him. Why do you doubt that?'

'Hmm ... Do you know what his status is? How else can you like him?'

'Tell me.'

'What must I tell you? He—he is … Maybe you know him already—is a dasan[1]—not heard of him?'

Facing Bhavani's mischievous glance bravely, I said: 'If I marry you, do you think I will speak ill of your relatives? Especially someone who has been good to you—would I ever deride him?'

Although I said so much with great style, what Bhavani said about her uncle did send an arrow through my heart. Pity! What is the stature of a dasan! What if it turns out that her uncle is a lowdown bloke who worked as somebody's servant—What would I do? I knew that she had lost her parents early. But only now did I know that such a person as a dasan looked after her affairs. My God! What a mess we would be in, if my father found out! My mind filled with such thoughts, as I stood there. Bhavani (looking sharply at me) said: 'I am the apple of my uncle's eye. How many things he sends for me from time to time! I see him as my own father. Whenever he comes to my house, he has complete freedom here. I love and respect him so much.'

'Yes, yes! You ought to worship him forever in your house. Okay, tell me where he lives.'

'He is mostly in the capital of our state; you have no objection to his coming over, do you?'

'Oh no! I am all for it.'

Bhavani heaved a sigh of relief as if a load had been taken off her head. She came closer to me and said softly: 'My heart has fused with yours.'

---

[1] 'Dasan' means servant. 'A servant in residence' is the narrator's assumption.

A month went by. In the meantime, we were already in a relationship with each other. I settled down in Mangalathu's house. Kochi was not very far from there. I joined a firm in Kochi and began working. My remuneration was twenty rupees per month. Suffice it to say that I lived quite well on a total monthly income of fifty rupees. If ever I felt unwell, it was only because of what Bhavani had said about the inheritance denied to me. I continued to assuage her fears.

Her pleasing face, bright joyful eyes, her small talk and her glances, all made me euphoric. When I was dull in spirits after a day's humdrum work, Bhavani's words gave me limitless joy.

One day, as we sat talking, the postman arrived with a letter for Bhavani.

'Oh! It's from my uncle,' Bhavani said in gleeful anticipation.

'Good handwriting. But one thing—isn't it unbecoming of him to be using his master's letterhead? Can servants do that?'

Bhavani, who was reading the letter with great concentration, did not hear what I said.

'Hear this! It says that by noon my uncle will reach here!'

'Oho! Will he reach before I return from my meeting with Secretary saheb? In that case, you must prepare a grand meal for dinner.'

'Dinner?'

'Why not? Isn't an early dinner better than a late lunch?'

'Uncle isn't very fussy about these things.'

'You know better; do as you please.'

I was later than usual returning from work. The time was about six o'clock in the evening. The evening tea after lunch at noon was exceptional. Even when I heard some strange voices in the corridor, I surmised that the uncle had arrived. I walked to my room thinking that I would meet him after placing my papers and books on a table and a quick change of clothes. Just then, the servant came running to me, looking at me meaningfully. When I showed my surprise about some new articles in the room, he said in a subdued tone: 'Bhavanikutty Amma's uncle brought them.'

'Oh is that so?'

The servant continued: 'My, my! Look at all the things …'

I could only wonder how this uncle of Bhavani's could cheat his master and bring such valuable things.

'He is an important man, no doubt,' said the servant.

I wasn't happy about all this. I thought I was witnessing all those stories about servants who cheat their masters.

When I went to the corridor for lunch, all the plates for the meal had been laid out. I saw a tall and sturdy man talking to Bhavanikutty. He was dressed in a mundu,[2] the way the lords and royal officials wore them, wore diamond earrings and three or four rings on his fingers; over his shoulder was a folded cloth—these were his adornments.

'Oh, there he is! Why so late? This is my uncle.'

I asked Bhavani: 'What is his name?'

Bhavani: 'Oh no! That is funny! Haven't you heard of the Palace Chief Administrator?'

I was taken aback.

'I am an old friend of your father's.' When I heard him speak these words, it struck me like fuel poured over fire. Seeing my

---

[2] Mundu is a length of unstitched cloth fastened at the waist falling to the ankle, a dress worn by both genders in Kerala.

discomfort, Bhavani stood laughing. The uncle spoke, watching her laugh: 'Bhavani is playing the fool with you. She hasn't changed a bit since her childhood.'

'It isn't that. She had told me that you are a dasan.'

Bhavani: 'Yes, dasan—Rajarajadasan [special envoy of the Royal Highness]. The Kovilakam Peshkar [Minister of the Palace].'

Mumbling, Rajarajadasan … Kovilakam … Peshkar—I began to think: friend of my father—yes—why—what—now why should I think of all that? The girl father had chosen for me was none other than Bhavani herself!

Bhavani: 'Yes, yes! If I weren't the person your father referred to in that letter, do you think I would have accepted you?'

'Oh no! Not this way!'

C.S. GOPALA PANICKER

A Brief Missive

'The matter is a complete mess. That obstinate fellow has gone and filed a lawsuit. Now there is no way but to give it some serious thought.' Saying so, Krishna Menon walked into the office room. I had had my breakfast and reached there by about eight or nine in the morning, checked four or five suits to be taken up that day and dispensed with the clients—that is all. That is when Menon blew in.

'Kunyunni Menon has filed a suit, hasn't he?'

I said, 'I heard about it three or four days ago in court but could not grasp the essence of the matter. I knew that you would come here when the summons reached you and thought I would get all the details of the case. That fellow is a crass, convoluted guy as you well know from past events. I myself have told you this often. That being so, it was a mistake on your part to even think of a deal with him.'

Originally published in Malayalam as 'Oru Neelam Kuranya Kathu' by *Rasikaranjini*, November-December 1903.

'No point saying all this. Please check all the records ...' saying which, Krishna Menon untied the bundle of papers.

'When I decided to sell my property—Poovalliparambu, the pathayapura[1] and a piece of land contiguous to it, it was decided in January when he came to my house that I would give it to him for one thousand nine hundred rupees. Around four or five days later, he sent me a letter:

> *I request you to send a reply with the bearer of this letter regarding the matter we discussed. Folks around here tell me that the amount you ask is way too much. I could strike a fair deal only if you reduce the amount significantly. I await your reply.*
>
> *To Ra-Ra Attuparambathu Krishna Menon from Adalodakathu Kunyunni Menon (Sd)*

'Following is the copy of my reply to that letter. Please apply your mind to it.

11 Vrishchikam 1078[2]

> *I am in receipt of your letter asking for confirmation on the matter we decided upon, in person. Reducing the cost of the property from what was agreed upon earlier would be a great loss to me. We had decided that Poovalliparambu, the pathayapura and the piece of land attached to it would be sold for a sum of one thousand nine*

---

1 Outhouse.
2 Malayalam year – circa Jan 1899.

hundred rupees only. I am agreeable to the deal as fixed before. The amount cannot be lowered.
—Krishna Menon (Sd)
//Copy//

'In reply to this, see what Kunyunni Menon wrote to me. Here:

I have received the letter you sent me yesterday. As discussed during our meeting, I shall procure Poovalliparambu and the pathayapura for the agreed sum of nine hundred rupees. Since you say that you cannot reduce the cost, there is no point in arguing about it. The money is ready with me. I am sending someone over for the documents. Let us conclude the deal today itself.

—Kunyunni Menon (Sd)'

'What? Nine hundred rupees? Your letter clearly states that the amount is one thousand nine hundred rupees!' exclaimed Krishna Menon.

'Yes, that is what my copy shows. But there was a flaw in the writing of the original letter. That is what caused all this confusion. We took two sheets of paper and first wrote the copy in one. The original was then copied from the former and this was put into an envelope and dispatched through the courier who had come from Kunyunni Menon. It was only when I obtained the copy of that letter from the court now that I understood what had happened. What is written in that copy is that I had agreed to sell Poovalliparambu and the pathayapura for nine hundred rupees only.'

'This is the meaning of the saying, *Property you cannot protect will be snatched away by unscrupulous persons*. Now that man will cling to it … It is wiser to grab what you get now and dispose of the property at the earliest.'

'Don't you say that, yet. I agree I made a foolish mistake. There is no course but to think of an escape route from this mess. To Kunyunni Menon's letter, I sent back a note. Look!

I do not understand the meaning of your letter wherein you have written the sum of sale as nine hundred rupees. Nothing has been mentioned about the piece of land adjacent to the pathayapura. You know very well that I have not agreed to sell Poovalliparambu and the pathayapura for nine hundred rupees. If the parambu and pathayapura are to be sold, the contiguous piece of land will not be useful to any buyer—that is why I said one thousand eight hundred rupees would be for Poovalliparambu and the pathayapura and a hundred rupees would be for the adjacent piece of land, thus making a total of one thousand nine hundred rupees only … you had agreed to buy the property accordingly, and we parted then (after that first meeting). Subsequently you sent that letter asking for confirmation of the deal and I wrote in reply. If you are not prepared to stick to what was agreed upon, I withdraw from the transaction. If 'nine hundred rupees only' has been written in my letter, it is obvious that it is a typographical error as you can well understand. I shall be obliged if you could send me that letter for me to check.

—Krishna Menon (Sd)

'In reply to this letter what Kunyunni Menon sent me is a registered letter:

A Brief Missive

14 Vrishchikam 1078

I received your letter sent the day before yesterday. I understand from that letter that you are now not prepared to execute the sale as originally agreed upon when we discussed it in person and according to your letter of 11 Vrishchikam. This will cause me to incur great loss. I do not remember agreeing to buy Poovalliparambu, the pathayapura and the piece of land, all together. Moreover, I had made clear to you even then that I do not require that extra piece of land. In good faith of your commitment, both verbal and written, I have promised to lend the premises to Mr Ittikkoran, criminal advocate, from the 20th instant. Therefore, if you do not execute the deed of transfer of ownership and hand over the property to me in five days, I shall be compelled to file a litigation against you and claim damages from you for the losses I would incur for which you are wholly responsible.

—Kunyunni Menon (Sd)'

Krishna Menon went on: 'This is the nature of the records of the case. His suit is to take possession of the property by implicating me through the letters I have written to him. Think of a solution along those lines.'

'According to me, the records of the case are against you. Isn't that Ittikkoran Menon a witness from his side?'

'Yes. Isn't he the only advocate practising in both Civil and Criminal courts?'

'If you wish to avoid paying for the losses claimed by the party, do as he wants, soon. The man has got you by the tuft on your head.

He is not likely to let go of it very soon. And Mr Ittikkoran too will not let him release it.'

'I am not too concerned about the loss part. Even if something worse were to come about, you know I have the means to bear it. However, my sense of guilt would arise from the fact that I knowingly or otherwise backed out from a word once given—though people in the know may not accuse me of it—and the loss of self-esteem I would suffer if it is known that I succumbed out of fear to the scheme of these two rascals ... these are the two factors of this case that perturb me now.'

'In this case, there is no cause for any pricking of conscience. You made a mistake due to oversight, that is all. If there is a way to thwart the scheme of the people who are deliberately trying to take advantage of your mistake, that is what we must think about and strive for. By the way, is there a witness to your first conversation with the prospective buyer when the deal was finalized?'

'No. But that the parambu and pathayapura together are worth much more than nine hundred rupees and that Kalakathu Raman Nair has offered one thousand eight hundred for that property can be proved.'

'Such a proof is required here. But how effective will that be to dislodge your handwritten consent, which would be held in evidence against you? Oh, no matter that!'

'Doesn't matter whichever way it turns out. We cannot desist from arguing the case. Let this Ittikkoran or Muttikkoran go to the high court and win a verdict and let them take away the property. I will not surrender the land voluntarily; that's for sure. I don't plan to give in to threats in violation of jurisprudence. Tell your peon to prepare a lawsuit and bring it here.'

'Wait a minute! My lawyer colleagues and I have decided that we will not take up any case involving Ittikkoran Menon, be it as lawyer or as witness, in order to demonstrate our disapproval of the man. Give this brief to our Raghava Menon. He is a smart young lawyer—intelligent and thoughtful. He is very polite with decent people but can be extremely aggressive with errant people like our adversaries. Even if he meets this litigant, he will snub or insult him wherever he is, rest assured. Therefore, when Raghava Menon is present, that fellow will not remain seated peacefully, even for one minute. Even when Kunyunni Menon learns that the defence lawyer is Raghava Menon, he will shake in his shoes. Explain the whole case to Raghava Menon and give him the case today itself. Together, Mr Menon and I shall examine the plaintiff's brief at the court in the original; tomorrow we will prepare the defendant's response and submit it to the court.'

He dispatched Krishna Menon to Raghava Menon's office along with a letter of introduction.

On the day the case was called, about ten to fifteen minutes before the judge arrived, all of us advocates and a few respectable clients had assembled in the solicitors' chambers. Our topic of discussion was Kunyunni Menon's case scheduled for the day and about the stories in circulation about Mr Ittikkoran Menon. There was not a single lawyer in the room who did not have a tale to tell, about 'Mister'. When one talked about his perjury in one case, another would tell us about how he fabricated a false document for a client of his. Then would come yet another story about how he dragged someone into a litigation and made a pauper of him. That is when Mister stuck his head into the room and promptly Raghava Menon greeted him with: 'Karanore! [Senior!] Do come in. We have cracked the case and once you are on the witness stand, all the shenanigans can be brought out!' and roused loud laughter in the room. In a flash, Mister withdrew his head and vanished from the scene. The general opinion of the lawyers was that Krishna Menon would fall victim to the foul play, finally. On the other hand, it could be surmised from his speech that Raghava Menon had found a loophole in the case and was confident that by submitting it during cross-examination of the witnesses, he could win the case. Even his client Krishna Menon had no inkling of what that point of debate would be. Krishna Menon merely hoped that he would benefit if it was proved in court that the statement in the letter—Poovalliparambu and the pathayapura for nine hundred rupees—had been written by mistake. Raghava Menon, on the other hand, had argued that the letter was genuine but the litigation was false. All of us assembled were curious to know how he would link the two lines of legal argument to Krishna Menon's advantage. Naturally, when Judge Janardhan Acharya sat on the bench, the bar overflowed with lawyers and the public at large.

Witness No. 1 for the prosecution, Mr Ittikkoran Menon, was sworn in on the witness stand. As his primary statement, he submitted what he knew before the court, which was as below:

The Defendant, Attuparambathu Krishna Menon, had announced that he planned to sell off his property, being Poovalliparambu and the pathayapura in it, hearing of which, the Petitioner, Kunyunni Menon and I visited Krishna Menon to strike a deal for the purchase of the property. That day after Krishna Menon quoted nine hundred rupees for both the items of property and Kunyunni Menon agreed to buy them for the price agreed on, we parted

A Brief Missive

company. This happened on the first day of Vrishchikam. Later when Krishna Menon sent a reply to Kunyunni Menon's letter to him, the letter was received in my presence. In that reply letter too, he has described the aforementioned matter, re-confirming the deal as agreed upon earlier.

(That letter was submitted to the court and marked as Exhibit A.)

Krishna Menon stood behind Raghava Menon fidgeting with his nose, glaring at Ittikkoran derisively.

The judge looked at Raghava Menon.

'Do you accept the submission of Exhibit A?'

'Yes.'

'What then, is the evidence that you propose to submit in this case?'

'We only want to examine the Petitioner, that is all.'

'In that case, begin the cross-examination of this witness.'

'Howsoever I cross-examine this witness and waste the court's valuable time, it will not benefit my case.'

Mr Ittikkoran, who feared Raghava Menon's strategic cross-examination for its sharpness and intensity, was greatly relieved to hear that Raghava Menon was not planning to ask him anything; he felt that he had had a providential escape from a fatal fall into disaster. He stepped off the witness stand and sat in the seat allotted to him. Krishna Menon was upset that Mister had been let off so easily. Most of the people in the bar felt so too.

Next, the Petitioner was put on the stand. Raghava Menon held aloft the letter marked A and asked: 'Is this Krishna Menon's letter?'

Kunyunni Menon: 'Yes, the one that he sent me.'

'Can you recognize Krishna Menon's handwriting?'

'Yes.'

Raghava Menon showed him the copy of Exhibit A, which Krishna Menon had submitted, and asked: 'Is this not Krishna Menon's handwriting?'

(That copy was marked Exhibit 1.)

Kunyunni Menon said: 'I couldn't say for sure.'

'You said you can recognize Menon's handwriting. Compare the two and tell me.'

'It looks like Krishna Menon's handwriting.'

'Is that all? Look again and tell me.'

'Yes. It is Krishna Menon's writing.'

Raghava Menon: 'The letter your side has marked Exhibit A and your contester marked Exhibit 1—between the two, do you see any significant difference ... if so, what is it?'

'In the document marked Exhibit 1, something has been added.'

'What had been added in Exhibit 1 does not appear in Exhibit A. Isn't that what you are saying?'

'No. What I am saying is that matter that is not in Exhibit A had been added in Exhibit 1.'

Raghava Menon: 'When you study document marked Exhibit A and document marked Exhibit 1 together, is there any difference between the two sheets?'

While Kunyunni Menon cringed on the stand, Raghava Menon abruptly changed his tone and, scowling harshly, added: 'If there are differences, speak up and tell the court what they are. Quick!'

Fearing that admitting to the obvious change between the documents would expose his deceit, Kunyunni Menon thought it prudent not to mention it just then. So, he said: 'There is no difference between the two. Both the sheets are alike.'

'Read the last line of the first portion in document Exhibit A.'

Kunyunni Menon: 'Poovalliparambu and the pathayapura.'

Raghava Menon: 'What is the last line in document Exhibit 1?'

'… along with the attached piece of land … one thousand and …'

'Now read together the last line of Exhibit A and the last line in Exhibit 1.'

'Poovalliparambu and the pathayapura along with the attached piece of land would be one thousand and …' read Kunyunni Menon.

'Bravo! If you still doubt that I have not understood the perfidy you have committed, discard it. Now read those two lines in proper order.'

'Except to read as I did, I know no other way to read those lines.'

'I know. Now put the second line in continuation of the other and read together.'

'Why can't you read it yourself? Why should I read it myself?'

'Remember you are under oath in court. Answer the question,' said the judge.

Kunyunni Menon perspiring profusely and trembling with fear: 'Poovalliparambu and the pathayapura along with the attached piece of land would be one thousand and …'

'Isn't that what we get when we read the last two lines of the first part of the document marked Exhibit 1?'

'Yes.'

'When you read the second part in both documents placed alongside each other, do you see any addition or subtraction in either?'

'No.'

'So, when we read the second part together with the first, we get: *Poovalliparambu and the pathayapura along with the attached piece of land would be one thousand and nine hundred rupees*—don't we?'

'Yes.' Kunyunni Menon stared at the judge and then Ittikkoran Menon with terror in his eyes.

Raghava Menon: 'You said before the court that there is no difference in the matter in both the documents. But I shall convince you that there is a glaring difference between the two documents. Hold the document Exhibit A over document Exhibit 1 aligning the top of the pages.'

Kunyunni Menon does so.

'Don't you see that the line, "… with the attached piece of land would be one thousand and …" in document Exhibit 1 sticks out below the lower margin of document Exhibit A?'

Kunyunni Menon cowered on the witness stand. He began to quake and perspire.

Mr Ittikkoran's face paled as the blood drained from his face.

'It does stick out, doesn't it? Say it. Don't bother that the scissors slipped at the middle part when that one line was clipped off document Exhibit A. Answer me, quick!'

What followed seemed to happen all at once. Those assembled instantly understood the offence committed by Kunyunni Menon. The judge Janardan Acharya blurted 'Rascal!' and glared down at Kunyunni Menon and Ittikkoran Menon—and Kunyunni Menon collapsed on the witness stand. Two or three bailiffs helped Menon out of the witness box as ordered by the judge and escorted him

A Brief Missive

outside the courtroom and laid him down on a bench. In all the commotion, our Mister leapt out of the court unnoticed.

A schematic representation is given below to apprise the reader more easily of the scissor work performed by Kunyunni Menon—

Exhibit A	11 January 1899 *Received letter written by you asking for a reply on the matter of the sale discussed in person. Reducing the amount from what was discussed would accrue great loss to me. Poovalliparambu and the pathayapura*	*Nine hundred rupees is what we agreed upon. I shall give the property to you at that rate. Anything less is not acceptable.* *To: Adalodakathu Kunyunni Menon* *From: Atuparambathu Krishna Menon (Sd).*
Last line of Exhibit 1	*along with the attached piece of land would be one thousand and*	
	First part of the letter	Second part of the letter

Kunyunni Menon's plaint was dismissed summarily, all costs to be borne by him. But the episode did not end there. Our Krishna Menon closed his record books only after dispatching two persons in different directions—Adalodathu Kunyunni Menon to jail in manacles and Mister Mukkidikkatte Ittikoran Menon back home bereft of his licence to practise law.

KALYANIKUTTY

I Felt Ashamed

It was already late when I set out from home after lunch. I had imagined that I could catch the train from Sultanpetta. But afraid that I might not make it, I went instead to Olavakkote. I reached the station, with only two minutes to spare. Achan bought the tickets quickly and guided the servants into a third-class compartment, along with all the luggage. By then, Amma and I had reached the platform. Achan began to scout for a vacant spot on the second-class compartments. All the compartments were filled with foreigners. The guard blew his whistle. The passengers in the train began to stare at us. It is difficult to explain my embarrassment. Achan led us to the eastern end. The door of one of the compartments was closing, and I think the train had begun to move. Seeing our despair, someone in the compartment opened the door for us. Somehow we jumped in. Oh! Only then did we begin to breathe normally.

Originally published in Malayalam as 'Nanichupoi' by *Sharada Pusthakam 1*, issue 6/May 1905.

The person who helped us was a Malayali. When we boarded, he made space for us and shrank into a corner himself. As he was busy counting all the bags, Achan seemed to have nothing to say. That gentleman opened his book and began to read. Merely by chance, he and I were seated face to face. When I peeked at the cover of his book, I saw the name *Henrietta Temple* printed on it: a novel I had read. He smiled when he noticed my interest. I couldn't guess the reason for it.

Let me tell the reader what my opinion was of his figure, when I first saw him. He must have been around twenty-two. Very fair skinned; not more than five feet tall. He was of proportionate build. He had a pleasant expression. Overall, a gentleman.

Once Achan had settled down, he began to talk to the gent. It appeared that his father and my father were the best of friends. The name of his family was Kaipalli. Place, Thiruvilwamala. He said his sister was in Kozhikode and that she had a daughter. We learnt that he was planning to stay in a house right next to ours in Madras. He said he wasn't married and was practising as an advocate in the high court.

Achan and this man continued to chat. After some time, I felt a little queasy. A pain began to bother me on the left side of my stomach. Initially, I ignored it. Not only did the pain increase, but I began to have trouble breathing. When I told Achan about it, he advised me to lie down. As there was a stranger among us, I tried to suppress my pain and appear normal. Achan and Amma began to worry. The gentleman across from me kept looking at me silently. Finally, I let out a cry of pain. Amma cried too, alarmed. This man stood up and told me to sit up straight. He looked at the left side of my stomach for a while. He asked me to remove my clothes around my stomach. By then Amma had undressed me partially. He then placed both his hands over the spot where I had the pain and pressed lightly. That very instant, I began to breathe easily and the pain dwindled. Never before or after that incident have I felt so much shame and nervousness. Thinking of that day, I still get goosebumps. In a while, the train reached Podanur Station. We had to go across the platform to catch the train to Madras. When we boarded the next train, the gentleman was nowhere to be seen. Achan said that he must have boarded another compartment thinking he was a bother to us. I felt cross. At whom? His leather satchel was on his vacant seat. So, I said that he would come back. At that very moment, he appeared with a steel tray on which were four cups of coffee. He served the coffee himself. When he handed me my cup, something happened. Either because I was careless or he did it on purpose, I don't know, but some coffee spilt on my mundu and his too. Amma said my hand had trembled. Then onwards, most of the talking was between that gent and myself, till we reached Madras. We mostly discussed books.

The next morning, at a quarter past seven, the train touched Madras. We first went to his place and had our breakfast there and then to the house reserved for us. The day after, he accompanied Achan to the doctor for his checkup. We stayed on in Madras for two months for the treatment, as instructed by the doctor. While there, the four of us would go to the beach every evening. Later, after dinner, he would come over to our house. On the west side of the room where my parents slept was a moonlit patio. The two of us would sit there and talk on and on. A distinct feature of his behaviour was that he didn't have the usual brashness of youth but rather great respect for women. He wouldn't say anything unwise; nor would he get upset at thoughtless statements others made. The mutual respect and affection we had for each other rose by the day. I began to feel that a life without him by my side would be futile. Two months flashed past like two days. Achan recovered and we scheduled our return trip home. When I thought I had to leave that man, I was cross at the doctor who had cured Achan *too* soon. When I say that, my reader will surely think how awful I must be. But the fact of the matter is that I was really sad to leave.

The night before the date of travel, as we sat on the patio talking, he said, choking on his words: 'You are leaving tomorrow. When will we meet again? The rest of my stay in Madras will be so dull. If I hadn't met you, I wouldn't have been unhappy now.' He sat silently staring westward. I knew that anything I might say to comfort him would be similar to the pot calling the kettle black but still, I said: 'Why don't you come back home during the January vacation?' I myself didn't know what I meant by what I said.

'Why wait for January vacations? I will be happy to go with you tomorrow itself. But ...' He stared at me for a long time and then: 'That would be improper. Not just that, it would bring us both unhappiness.'

That is when the gravity of the matter sank in. I trembled. My hands and feet turned chill. Perspiration covered my forehead. A lump formed in my throat, and I couldn't say a word. What a pity! When I thought that I was the reason for a young man's distress, tears welled up in my eyes.

'If only our Malayali world didn't have so many divisive caste systems ... how many more couples would be living in bliss!

What makes me sad is that because of my lack of thought, an innocent person—such as you are—is subjected to heartache. The seniors in your family believe that no alliance is permissible in the family except among persons of one's own community. But I am a Chaarna[1] Nair, don't you see? Only yesterday Shankara Menon told me this. I don't remember how I reacted to it then.'

We sat in silence looking at each other.

Then he said: 'The next time I see you, you will be the wife of some fortunate man. As soon as you marry, you must forget me. Otherwise, you will suffer because of your husband's lack of interest in you. All our dreams were in vain. Anyway, I shall never have a wife. You must give me a copy of the photograph you took last week.'

I went inside and fetched my photo.

'I too can't go on without you.' When I said that, he replied, 'You must forget me. Still, I shall give you a photograph of mine. It would be very sad if this makes you unhappy.'

As it was very late, he told me to go to bed and returned to his house next door.

I don't know how I spent that night. I considered telling Achan that I wasn't going back home with him. Then I reminded myself that my lover couldn't support me financially. I spent that night dreaming and crying my eyes out. The next day we departed to our home town. At the railway station, as the train began to move out, Achan's eyes filled at the sight of our friend's anguished face. Achan spoke of the man's virtues till he fell asleep. When Amma said: 'He is a good boy. If only he had money—' Achan quipped:

---

1 An accountant by profession, as ordained by the caste system.

'Kuttyparu can think of nothing but money; takes after her uncle.' Mother's face swelled with anger. Both of them slept after that. I sat looking out of the window, thinking of all the instances of the recent past, alternating between happiness and sadness.

Two weeks after we reached home, my uncle began to persuade my Achan to arrange my wedding. Achan told him about the man we had met on the train on the way to Madras, which my uncle did not concur with—that's what I guessed. Uncle began to pressurize Achan. What to do! In a matrilineal family, all matters are decided by the karanavar, the eldest maternal uncle. If the children turn out to be bad, the fault lay with the father; if they were good, the credit went to the ammavan (uncle)! In the end, what transpired was that ammavan's sixtieth birthday celebrations and the feast for my auspicious day of consummation were held on the same day.

My groom is my ammavan's second son, Vasu Menon—a very rich and good-looking landlord. Soft-spoken and very fond of me. He never does anything against my wishes. While I enjoy Vasu Menon's attachment to me, I often remember what *he* had told me—that I must forget him. It is like a Vaidyan's prescription that when you apply his oil for baldness, you mustn't think of egg or pumpkin. The minute you pick up the oil, you are reminded of them. Similarly, whatever I see or hear; whenever I see Vasu Menon or don't see him—I think of the man in Madras. Vasu Menon was aware of my love for the man I lost. But he never once mentioned anything about it. I behaved with Vasu Menon exactly as a dutiful wife would with her husband.

*

During this period, several calamities struck. I lost my father, mother and uncle. My brother Gopalan, who passed the BA examination, went to study engineering in Madras. All the affairs of the household were managed by Vasu Menon. One day, after dinner, I was seated alone. I had preserved *his* photograph in a certain small box, which Vasu Menon had never seen. When I took out that picture and looked at it, I was overcome with sadness, as thoughts of days gone by came rushing back to me. I couldn't check my sobs. The door was open. Someone standing behind me heaved a sigh when I wept. When I turned, I saw Vasu Menon's anguished face. He took the photograph from me and looked at it intently …

'Isn't this Krishna Menon's picture? You kept it locked all these days, didn't you? What if I saw it? You don't have to hide it now. Let it remain on this wall here.' Saying so, Vasu Menon hung the photograph over the table. I felt like a wanton cheat. From then on, Vasu Menon's love and respect for me increased.

*

The reader must have heard of the Park Fair held in Madras in the year 1903. Thousands of people had assembled there then. There were two more reasons for people to gather there. One was the Exhibition and the other the Bharata Mahajana Sabha conclave. To contextualize for the reader the events that followed, I shall give below Gopal's letter to me:

—*I had written before that I would be going to see the Fair. The roads were slushy because of incessant rains. Two or three of us*

I Felt Ashamed

stood at one spot as a group. Just then, there was a commotion near us. A horse had panicked and run away with the cart. Before we could shift from where we stood, the horse came upon us. The cart somehow hit me and I fell. Many prominent people were watching this. I remember one of them distinctly. He is a Malayali. I have seen him many times on the beach. All those times, he would stare at my face with interest. When I fell, he rushed to me and I think carried me into a carriage drawn by two horses. I don't remember what took place thereafter.

It is now six days since that day. I still can't sit up and write. The doctor's order is not to move me from my supine position on the bed, till he permits it. My fever has left me. The pain in my back remains. There is a slight damage to my spine. I must've fallen on a stone or something hard. Anyway, the doctor said this morning that in two weeks' time, I should be quite all right and can begin to attend college.

Above all this is another strange matter. I don't know where I have been brought. I can see a young lady by my side always. Cannot be more than sixteen years old. She looks well-off. Speaks good English. She is not at all nervous while speaking to the doctor. Furthermore, she is a Malayali. When I asked where I was, she said: 'Enjoy the hospitality; don't investigate.' This place is no hospital; it is obviously the house of a very rich man. All the servants are Malayalis. Looks like all of them are dumb. No one replies to any query. This girl alone is always by my bed. She doesn't reply either when I ask about her. I have no means of finding out whom we are obliged to. Please come here if you can. When I asked my 'foster mother', I was told that a vehicle would pick you up at the station *if you inform us about your travel plans. You can write to my old address. Nothing here to be alarmed about.*

Yours,

Gopalan

This letter was received at noon one day. It was too late to catch that day's train. I sent a telegram instead, to inform him that I would start the next day and reach Madras the day after. I was in a great quandary. Vasu Menon had passed away. All I have now is Gopalan to call my own. When I saw a different handwriting, I was worried. Even though he had written that he was well now, I couldn't contain my anxiety.

Right off, I called Gopalan's teacher over and prepared to travel the next day. And together, we left for Madras.

As the train approached Madras Station, I began to feel weak. The present crisis and the episode of eight years ago occupied my thoughts. When we alighted from the train, a Malayali received us and said, 'A carriage is waiting to take you to the house. I shall take care of the luggage.' He led us to a carriage drawn by two horses. The person who spoke to me seemed vaguely familiar. The horse carriage driver cracked his whip. That is when a weird suspicion rose in me. I asked Gopalan's master: 'Could this be a ruse?' The teacher replied: 'Oh no! Not at all.' I don't know where the coach took us. After about half an hour's run, the horses came to a halt in the portico of a stately mansion. The door opened. As we stepped down, the man who met us at the station was taking down our luggage.

'Is this where Gopalan is convalescing?' I asked anxiously.

A maid servant replied, 'Yes.'

I Felt Ashamed

'Where is he?'

'Mistress said that he is fast asleep now. You can see him after your bath and breakfast. Your bath is ready.' The maid took me to the bathroom. When I asked her whose house it was, she said nothing, merely smiled. When I finished bathing, she fetched clothes for me to change into. Even then I suspected something. The key of my suitcase was still with me. So, I guessed there were other ladies in the house. What surprised me even more was that I was given a newly crafted mundu—like the one I had worn on my first visit to Madras. Whatever the mystery, I thought, so be it.

When I finished my coffee, the maid came to me and said, 'Mistress would like to see you.' I asked her, 'Who is your Mistress?'

'She is the niece of the Master of the house.'

As I passed a room on my way to see Gopalan, I saw a lady of about fifty reclining on an easy chair. She turned her face away when she saw me.

When I entered Gopalan's room, the 'Mistress', who was a young girl, stood up. Gopalan said, 'I have mostly recovered.' Just then the lady I had seen in another room walked in.

'Though we didn't know Gopala Menon, Kuttan had his own doubts. That is why he brought him here.' I looked keenly at her face. On the wall opposite me was a photo of *him* and my own next to it. I concluded from Gopalan's letter to me and from what I had observed that day, that the old lady was his mother, the young girl his niece, and that the house belonged to him, which meant that he had reached a high stature in life and was now living well. My God! Had my daydreams come true? I felt dizzy. Someone supported me and took me to another room to rest. Someone sat on my bed and was fanning me, sighing from time to time. I recognized him as the man I had met so many years ago on the train to Madras. Would you understand the bliss I was experiencing? He wiped the sweat off my face and said, 'Kalyanikutty …'

When I opened my eyes, Achan said with a smile, 'What kind of sleep is this? Master has been waiting for a long time.'

I squirmed with shame.

I jumped off the bed and ran out!

MOORKOTH KUMARAN

Just a Glimpse

'How could you send her without my permission? Am I not her husband?'

'I didn't think you would object.'

'How would you know if I would object or not?'

'Even before this Madhavi has attended similar rituals. You did not protest on all those occasions. You would say—*Let her go wherever her father pleases to send her.* Likewise, this time too, I guessed you would take no offence to her going.' Kalyaniamma, Madhavi's mother, said defensively.

'The times have changed. My own father is against all your modernism. You know that well. We prefer to stick to traditions.'

'What do you call traditions? Do you call what goes on these days traditions?'

Originally published in Malayalam as 'Orotta Nokku', by *Vivekodayam*; December 1909.

'These are the gradual changes that have caught up with us. Isn't the discontinuance of the practice of tying the thaali[1] unacceptable to most people? What if people like you follow the trend?'

'Vasudevan, why do you speak like an illiterate? The practice of tying the thaali that is prevalent among us—what sanctity does it have? People like you have passed exams like BA, read a lot, travelled afar, met all kinds of people and liberated your intellect with worldly experiences. We women! What do we know? According to what my limited intelligence tells me, all this tying-of-the-thaali in weddings and other paraphernalia are nothing but wasteful expenditure—nothing else. What a fuss they make of a young innocent bride! They pretend that thaalikettu[2] is a sanctimonious act. Who is the priest who presides over it? The barber? You want all that is modern. But in all matters that concern women, they are content with obsolete tradition. You want to dress like the Europeans, cut your hair; and whatever else. Yes, even the women have brought about some changes in their attire; and why? All because when they travel with you on the train, their conventional clothes with eardrops dangling from sagging holes in the earlobes and garish bangles will invite sneers from people of other castes and traditions. So, you make your women wear sarees. Stitch up sagging ear lobes. Describe our ritual of thaalikettu to your European friends and see how they respond. Among the Brahmins, girls have to go through this ritual even before they come of age. The meaning of thaalikettu is to indicate

---

1 A symbolic chain of betrothal tied around the necks of very young girls.
2 The ritual of tying the thaali.

the status of a married woman. It is one of the preliminary rituals of a wedding—to them. Just as Pudamuri[3] means marriage for the Brahmins, it is thaalikettu for others. In imitating the Brahmins and adopting this ritual, what we are doing is grabbing the shadow and discarding the form. Imagine that we emulate the Nair community similarly. Among them, let's say there is a tradition that the pudamuri must be performed before the coming-of-age bath. Imagine we orchestrate a grand wedding before the girl comes of age, conduct a pudamuri overseen by the barber and hold a great feast at huge expense! How ridiculous would it all look? On the other hand, as all this has been simply following of age-old traditions, we are unable to see the absurdity of it.'

'You don't have to give me a long lecture like this. My father doesn't insist on the discontinuation of the thaalikettu ritual; but we still believe that marrying through thaalikettu is a big mistake.'

'That's your simian obstinacy! Since Madhavi's father is involved in this, your father merely wants to contradict him. Beyond that, all this has no meaning.'

'Oh yes? Only what you say and do is meaningful. We are fools!'

'I haven't said so.'

Vasudevan did not linger to hear Kalyaniamma's last words. He walked out in a huff. Kalyaniamma was upset that her son-in-law was offended. She feared that she might have said something unfair to him. Madhavi was Kalyaniamma's only child. Vasudevan had married her recently. Her father, Govindan, and Vasudevan's father, Krishnan, could not see eye to eye for whatever reason. Govindan

---

3 The symbolic ritual of gifting a piece of cloth as attire to the bride-to-be.

was a man of high self-esteem, proud of his caste and amiable by nature. He was an advocate with a large clientele and also very rich. He was a respected gent who spent time and money selflessly for the welfare of his community and people at large.

Krishnan was also a very rich man. Having entered government service of our European masters—though not through merit, but by sycophancy—he rose gradually and attained the post of a Munsif[4] and now received a pension. During his career as Munsif, he had accumulated wealth through corrupt practices. He and his family were enjoying the fruits of that wealth. Seeing Govindan's popularity among the townspeople, the seed of jealousy had subconsciously begun to sprout in Krishnan's mind. Now it had become a full-fledged tree, blooming with its roots spreading far and wide. That is when Govindan played a major role in the social emancipation venture launched by a few smart fellows. The fact that Govindan was an advocate of the league was reason enough for Krishnan to become antagonistic to the scheme. A whole lot of deeds take place in this world, reasons for which are unclear to most people. One such event was the alliance between Krishnan's son and Govindan's daughter. Vasudevan was a gentleman who had passed the BA examination and, furthermore, was now a government officer. He was not known to have any vices to speak of. Madhavi was an extraordinarily beautiful and well-mannered girl. As her father had educated her well, she was both mature and sensitive. Not many are as thoughtful and submissive at such a young age.

---

4 A subordinate judge.

The young couple lived in total harmony and in love. Their virtues seemed to proclaim the truth of the aphorism: a match of like-minded bride and groom brings perennial adulation to their parents.[5]

Vasudevan was particular to obey his father's every wish. All one can say is that what could be considered a great virtue was a mishap entrenched deep in him.

He did not believe in the verse that goes: *The one who disobeys must be abandoned, be he even a preceptor of repute.*[6]

Needless to say, it is common for those who obey orders unquestioningly to eventually fall into despair because of the vicious qualities of the ones who issue those orders.

There came a time when Madhavi was visiting her father. One day there was a wedding in the neighbourhood where the thaalikettu ritual was to be performed—a new practice those days. Krishnan and his cronies were against this, but he had not spoken about it openly. When Govindan attended that wedding, he took his daughter along.

That day, at noon, a young man called Padmanabhan, went to Krishnan's house. My readers must carefully take note of this man. Such people are rare in our country. He was short, always wore glasses over two globes for eyes, which looked as if cruelty and jealousy had been rolled into balls. Those eyes shifted as if they were trying to pop out of those glasses and decimate the whole world. He was very dark skinned; his nature was darker. When he walked, he stomped the ground with his right foot and gave

---

5 Malayalam verse translated.
6 Another Malayalam verse translated.

the impression of a tilt towards that side. Padmanabhan was a dependent of Govindan; which meant that he and his family lived off Govindan. Padmanabhan expressed his gratitude by using every opportunity he got to do something against Govindan. When he visited Krishnan and while talking of local matters, he went on to ask:

'Aren't you going to the wedding today?'

'No! Tying a thaali again and again on a girl who has already been through a thaalikettu ceremony. What nonsense! These fellows are insane.'

'Vasudevan must be going.'

'Would he go to a place that I wouldn't?'

'Oh, yes? In that case—'

'In that case—what? Tell me!'

'Oh, nothing much. Obviously, where the husband declines to go, the wife mustn't either, isn't that so?'

'Of course. My wife won't go either.'

'Not your wife. I ... oh, forget it. I have talked too much. As it is, most people don't like me.'

'Tell me, don't I have a right to know?'

'Nothing very important, except that your son's wife has gone for the celebration.'

At this, Krishnan jumped and asked: 'You mean Madhavi? Did you see her go?'

When Padmanabhan saw that his ploy was working, he spoke very slowly: 'I am coming from Mister Govindan's house. I left only after he and his daughter set off for the wedding.'

'How did that man take Madhavi to the wedding without asking our permission? Could Vasudevan have agreed to it?'

The last line was not spoken to Padmanabhan. Krishnan was asking himself. However, Padmanabhan provided the reply:

'Oh, no! Vasudevan hasn't allowed her to go. I heard Govindan tell his wife—"I will take Madhavi along with me for the celebration; let me see what they can do … I will settle his arrogance."'

Now all of this was false. Nothing of the sort was said by either Govindan or his wife. At this, Krishnan's anger knew no bounds. He gritted his teeth and went into Vasudevan's room. It was consequent to what transpired in that room then, that Vasudevan went over to his wife's house and the altercation followed, which has been described at the beginning of this tale.

That evening, when Govindan returned home with his daughter, he found a letter waiting for him. It was from Krishnan, furiously accusing Govindan of taking his daughter without her husband's or his father's permission to a celebration which was against his beliefs and rebuking the girl's mother for speaking haughtily to his son. The last paragraph of the letter read:

If you took your daughter to a celebration which is unacceptable to us to wreak vengeance on our alleged arrogance, and under the silly notion that my son will not get another bride, I inform you hereby that I am prepared to prove to you that your presumption is completely misplaced.

When he read this letter, Govindan who, by nature, was peace loving, became very angry. The audacity in Krishnan's letter was intolerable. As soon as he read the letter, he wrote a reply without consulting either his wife or daughter.

I am in receipt of your most obnoxious letter. I am aghast. I did not take my daughter to the celebration to quash your audacity. But it merely turned out to be a provocation for you to demonstrate it, I regret to submit. If you think that my daughter has committed an offence that is serious enough to annul her marriage, I shall consider it her fate.

—Govindan

Only after he dispatched the letter did Govindan reflect on the consequences that would accrue to his daughter and begin repenting having sent that letter. That night, he told his wife about the whole matter. Kalyaniamma was an intelligent woman who had studied Malayalam and Sanskrit in depth. Her opinion carried a lot of weight in that household. She listened to the whole story and said:

'I am convinced that Vasudevan loves Madhavi. If that kind of love can be forgotten in the matter of a day, it is better to be without it.'

That poor Kalyaniamma said this without foreseeing the great calamity that would befall her daughter is obvious.

Both father and mother managed to hide the matter from their daughter. Except sensing that there was a difference of opinion between her parents and her parents-in-law, Madhavi had no inkling of the gravity of the problem. Of late, her husband wasn't visiting her; nor did he take her along to his house. Her parents too did not talk about sending her over to her husband's house. All in all, the girl began to suspect something. If such issues are discussed among those who have the right to do so, there are plenty of people in the world who will volunteer information to the ones who wish to know.

One day, when Madhavi sat reading on the verandah, Padmanabhan walked up. Even when she saw his eyes through his glasses, Madhavi must have thought that they had been caged for them to one day leap out and turn the world to dust. He looked at Madhavi and said in a comforting tone soaked in subtle sarcasm: 'How can we escape experiencing what has been destined for us? Exactly like you, we too feel sorry.'

Madhavi blanched without understanding the meaning of it.

'Whatever are you talking about?'

'I was talking about Vasudevan's wedding plans. I heard that he has decided to marry Advocate Gopalan's daughter, Rugmini.'

When Madhavi heard this, all her fears fused and took a distinct form. She felt she had been pierced by a blazing arrow. But not speaking a word, she raised the book to cover her face. She neither looked at it nor read it. She could see nothing in it. She could only hear her pounding heart. When Padmanabhan saw that she was not responding to his report, he hastened inside to inform her mother about the good news. It must be pointed out here that all this information was false and fabricated. Vasudevan had not even given a thought to re-marriage. Although his father talked about it now and then, nothing had been settled. When Kalyaniamma was informed about it, she too kept silent. All told, Madhavi was in a terrible state. It hurt deeply that her fond husband had resorted to this heartless act. When she learnt of the reason, she was even more shocked. Every evening, Govindan would take his daughter in his car to the beach and other spots of interest. He cracked jokes and tried to raise her spirits in whatever way he could—but to no avail. Her mind and body began to wilt.

Vasudevan began to feel sad about having to separate from his wife in this manner. He was very fond of her. He sighed night and day, devastated at the thought of discarding his wife who was truly his better half in every way.

Two years went by. The skirmish over the thaalikettu wedding subsided. Krishnan and his troupe were the vanquished. The people in the vicinity understood the truth about the quarrel but the animosity between Krishnan's and Govindan's families continued. Madhavi's condition worsened by the day. Some local doctors said that she had contracted tuberculosis. Both her lungs were affected. All the doctors concurred that it was impossible to cure her. Kalyaniamma and Govindan could not bear their sorrow. Madhavi told her mother that she wanted to see Vasudevan just once before her end, in whichever way possible. Her mother passed this on to Govindan. He, in a desperate act to meet his daughter's last desire, wrote to Vasudevan.

Dear Vasudevan,

Madhavi is critically ill. It is clear that she will not survive for long. She wishes to have just a glimpse of you before she dies. If you can forget all that has passed between us, I request you to please come over and meet her—one last time.

—Govindan

How could one describe Vasudevan's anguish and sorrow upon reading this letter? He had learnt of his own father's atrocious behaviour and unjust deeds. He also understood Govindan's innocence. *All for the sake of a trivial matter, I was forced to forsake my beautiful soulmate, who was the reason for all my success in life; moreover, I am now the cause of her imminent end.* After reading

Govindan's letter, Vasudevan went into his room and collapsed on the bed, face down, and wept long and hard. He finally got up and set out for Govindan's house.

It was evening. The sun had begun to set. Crowds of men were trudging back to their houses, relieved after a long day's toil. The birds and the livestock revelled in the comfort of the soothing twilight in the wake of a blazing sun. Vasudevan walked up to the outhouse gate in Govindan's house and stood leaning against a tree in the courtyard. Two little birds chirped as if to welcome him. He slowly stepped on to the verandah. In one corner, he could see a completely emaciated form wrapped in flannels and blankets reclining in an easy chair. He could not recognize the person. It was Madhavi. As soon as she saw the lord of her soul, her heart began to pound uncontrollably. She placed her right hand over her heart. Vasudevan had not recognized her; he walked into the house where he met Govindan, who rose as soon as he saw Vasudevan and grasped both his hands. Tears streamed down his cheeks. For a long time, the two stood speechless, after which Govindan spoke: 'She is seated outside … didn't you see her?'

Both of them came on to the verandah and approached Madhavi. She raised her eyes and gazed at Vasudevan. Then she drew a sharp breath and closed her eyes … forever. She had begun her journey to the place that no man can ever know, where everybody will finally reach, if not today, another day … released from all the pangs and sorrows of her lifetime.

Vasudevan covered his face with his handkerchief and without speaking a word, walked out of the house. As he walked down the steps of the outhouse gate, another man was walking up the steps: Padmanabhan.

M. SARASWATIBHAI

Witless Women

GOVINDAN NAIR WAS not one bit convinced. For the wife of someone of his stature—a man of high birth and unmatched competence, the editor of a paper and a contributor to several journals—to consider accepting the job of a tutor! It was a matter of disgrace for him.

'A woman who works for a salary is an insult to womanhood and a slur on her husband's status. I do know of men who are happy to consider the wealth of their wives as their own, but I am not one of them. I am not prepared to live off my wife's earnings. The minute a lady begins to work for money, she loses her dignity and her femininity. Such a lady needn't remain my spouse ... What difficulty do you have now? For all your needs and help, you still have me.' Govindan Nair put his arm around his wife's waist and continued: 'Besides, what do you know about teaching children? Cicero, Aristotle, Plato, Spencer—have you read any of their works? You are mad. You will get strange ideas. How much

---

Originally published in Malayalam as 'Thalachorillatha Sthreekal' by *Bhashaposhini Pusthakam 15*, issue 8-9/ April-May 1911.

money do you want, don't you have me to provide it?' With this, Govindan Nair gave his wife a peck on her cheek and sent her in.

What could Kalyaniamma say! They still behaved like newlyweds. She loved him a lot but she had a secret grouse that he didn't treat her as an equal or acknowledge her intelligence. She said nothing because of her love for him.

Although she did not say anything when he asked her why she needed money now, that did not meet her immediate need for cash. The provision shop had to be paid, the milkman hadn't been paid for three months … The butcher and the baker had threatened to sue if they were not settled immediately. The supplier of ghee pressurized her every day. So too, the washerman.

Earlier in this story, I said that Govindan Nair was a great writer. If he had a ream of paper, he could fill it with articles in the course of a single week. Every time he said, 'This article will fetch us at least fifty rupees,' and sent it to publishers, all of them bounced back without fail. But Govindan Nair was never discouraged. He was, by nature, an optimist. On top of that, he was proud *and* conceited. If an editor rejected his article, it was only because the editor lacked the brains to appreciate the subtle humour in his writing. This is what the great writers of the world had had to endure too. Their genius was simply beyond commoners. He spent his days assuring his wife that he would be paid the following week.

Govindan Nair belonged to opulent aristocracy. But the only drawback was that he had no property. He was very well known in town as an excellent orator and an editor too. All the fame he had garnered was not entirely due to his own merit or verve. His opinions were far removed from those of the others. There was a theory that being different from others drew the attention of people. Govindan Nair's normal style of dressing was a display of status by itself. As far as possible, he preferred to conduct his lifestyle in the European fashion.

His alliance was from the decadent branch of a Nair family, which only had enough wealth to meet its day-to-day expenses. He boasted often that at the time of his wedding, his was the wealthier family than his bride's, and though he had offers from much more affluent families, his intention was not to live off of his wife's resources, but to elevate the status of a girl and her family … and that is how he wed Kalyaniamma. Kalyani and her mother lived alone. Seeing the prestige and fame of her son-in-law, that mother was prepared to undergo any hardship for the sake of the groom. All the help Kalyaniamma received from Govindan Nair could be summed up in a single lot: clothes, Benaras sarees, bottles of perfume, soaps … But that was a pittance compared to Govindan Nair's own expenses. In order to make Nair's life stress-free, the mother took care of the daily needs of the household. If she were residing with an ordinary man, she could have taken upon herself all the expenses of running the house too. But Govindan Nair's European lifestyle quickly eroded their inherited wealth. Nair said he would receive some money from his home at the beginning of every month—but there were the dues pending to the publishing houses for the books he had got printed. In this manner, a meaningless phase of their life sped by. What Kalyaniamma received by way of bequest, halved. Very soon, for whatever reason—either because of the anguish of having to watch her daughter's miserable life helplessly, or because she blamed herself for causing her daughter to have to run a house like this—or simply because her term on earth had come to an end—Kalyaniamma's mother expired. In the meantime, Kalyani began to have children one after another. That is when, realizing it was impossible to make ends meet without an extra source of income, she had asked Govindan Nair if she could tutor a couple of neighbourhood children. Little surprise that this had offended the great Nair no end.

Govindan Nair's style of writing did not appeal to most people. Kalyaniamma told him that she would like to listen to the stories and speeches he wrote before he darted them off to the publishers. Initially, Kalyani would comment on them analytically—not only did Govindan Nair not relish it, but he also insulted her by asking what she knew of literature, having lived in a kitchen her whole life. Once Govindan Nair realized that he was not receiving the praise he expected from his wife, he stopped showing her his manuscripts. Actually, his speeches were Latin and Greek to Kalyaniamma. The articles that he sent to publishers, which came back with rejection notes, Govindan Nair would crumple wrathfully and throw into a corner of his room. These would be picked up by Kalyaniamma and read over. She would then ask him: 'Readers may not be as erudite and intelligent as you are. The publishers will print the articles only if they are entertaining to the common reader. So, if *I* can't relish and enjoy your writing, you can safely presume that it is so with your readers too.' Govindan Nair merely laughed it off but never considered if there was any substance in what she said. Nair was very fond of his wife. But on the whole, he was contemptuous of women. He was ready to vouch in any court of law that a woman had not the brain to analyse literature. He was also prepared to prove that all the works published under the names of women had either been written by their husbands or a male acquaintance.

One day, Govindan Nair looked at all the rejected articles and said vengefully: 'All these numbskull publishers have united to conspire against me. I have no doubt about it. I had once submitted an article to *Swatantraghoshini* to expose many of them. They haven't overcome their ire yet. Otherwise what merit do Balakrishnan Nair's articles and speeches have over mine? Take any magazine and you see a story by Balakrishnan in it. Granted that his stories are passable. But he certainly doesn't have the vocabulary or articulation and gravitas that my writing has. He hasn't even a notion of Sanskrit. Such writers … not to deride them, Kalyani … although they don't possess the cadence of language … I must confess that I found delectable Balakrishnan Nair's "Self-inflicted Calamity" in this week's *Ghoshini*. However, if I were to write that story, I might have treated the subject differently.'

Govindan Nair babbled on. As Kalyaniamma was engrossed in stitching a blouse and had bent over to mend a stitch, Govindan Nair couldn't see the expression on her face.

Days passed this way. All the magazines carried Balakrishnan Nair's stories, whereas all the stuff that Govindan Nair sent for publishing came right back to him. Merely because Govindan Nair's name was recognizable in society, some of his articles on contemporary matters were accepted. But the remuneration he received from them was not adequate to sustain the man's lifestyle and daily needs.

Many days later, Govindan Nair rushed to his wife with a piece of paper in his hand and said: 'Look, Kalyani! What we sought has come seeking us. I have waited for long for a chance like this.

Now Sahityaparipalini Mahasabha [Academy of Literature] has asked for stories and the prizes have already been announced. The prize for an exceptional social novel is five hundred rupees! The second prize is three hundred. Third, two hundred rupees. I am sure that the first prize will be mine. Fortunately, as soon as I heard this announcement, a story has taken form in my mind. Be that as it may, even the third prize of two hundred rupees is no mean sum.

'The Academy people won't be prejudiced like the publishers. The winner is decided in the Academy by a group of esteemed people. Therefore, there is no scope for bias or vengeance playing a role here. Aren't your ornaments still with the pawn broker? Don't worry. The prize money will be settled in the coming month of October. You can go for the November fair in the temple, wearing all your ornaments. I shall also get you premium quality bracelets and buy you a Benaras silk saree, too. Our bad days are over. The prize money itself is five hundred rupees. Anybody will pay me one thousand rupees as a copyright fee for the primary print. That makes a total of one thousand five hundred rupees. Later, we can get it included in the syllabus of schools without much difficulty. Iyer will pay heed to my proposal. If that happens, they will need at least six prints of the book. At the rate of a thousand rupees per print, that would make a total of six thousand rupees. All in all, we stand to gain at least seven thousand to eight thousand rupees for the books. All you have to do is this: keep the children from crying. When I sit down to write, I want total silence. I will have to stay up late; therefore, you must tell the milkman to deliver another half litre of milk every evening, over and above the morning supply. We will pay him all together in one go. Poor fellow! He seems to be in difficulty. Let the money come. We could, maybe, pay him a hundred rupees upfront. With that money, he can buy some more milch cows, right? He can pay us back in instalments. Doesn't matter if he can't pay. Let him adjust it against the milk he supplies. Money saved is money gained ...'

Kalyaniamma, who was used to Govindan Nair's fantasies—which led to depression when none came true—told Govindan Nair that he could plan all this after they actually received the money from the Academy—which the latter did not like one bit. But because he knew very well that Kalyani did not have the education and brilliance of mind to recognize his calibre, Govindan Nair never got angry at anything she said.

Kalyaniamma took the paper from her husband and read the advertisement carefully and grew very thoughtful thereafter. Finally, she asked him: 'How many days will you take to write the stories?'

'Today is the 16th of Mithunam (June-July). The novel must reach the Secretary of the Academy before the 10th of Chingam (August-September). We have almost seven weeks on hand. I will need at least six weeks to complete the volume.'

'That means you won't get time to contribute articles and stories to other publications during that time.'

'From now on, we won't be able to write for magazines and newspapers. We can do without that income. We can manage without them.'

It was not clear if Kalyaniamma was taken in by this. Anyway, she said nothing in reply.

From that day onwards, Govindan Nair shut himself in one of the rooms in the bungalow and began to write. Kalyaniamma sat in the kitchen, making sure the children did not disturb him. By the end of the first month, the novel was half complete. Nair was totally immersed in the joy of writing.

Once he told Kalyani: 'Never before has anyone written a novel like this in Malayalam. I have brought into the story the gamut of human emotions. Our poverty will end soon. How did you buy the fronds to thatch our roof? When I met the milkman, I felt ashamed. But he did not ask me anything. These days, the shopkeeper has stopped pestering me for money. He merely asks if you and the children are fine. I do not know if he is planning to file a suit against us; but if that be so, why would he make small talk with me? All of them know that we will not hesitate to repay them when we get the money. That's it. By the way, the editor of *Anandadayini* of Kozhikode, Gopala Menon, and two of his friends are coming over to meet me today. We have to serve them coffee. I have called another four people from around here to receive them. You have to prepare coffee and snacks for eight. Mutton cutlets, poli, roti, plantains and coffee—this much will do. Everything must be ready by 4 p.m. These people think very highly of us. When we went to Kozhikode to attend the Nair Samaj meeting, you should have seen how well they received me. Therefore, we must do at least this much for them. Gopala Menon probably thinks I will invite him to stay the night. In our present state, we will avoid it. Be sure to be ready by four o'clock in the evening! Dress the children well with ironed clothes. Otherwise, don't bother! Just send them across to our neighbour's house. They can return after our guests leave.'

On another day, when the unabated stream of rejected articles annoyed him inordinately, Govindan Nair turned to Kalyaniamma and said: 'These dunces—editors—will never understand my prowess. They only relish the nonsense that Balakrishnan Nair produces. This fellow has become an enemy now. All the magazines and newspapers print his articles or stories. I can foresee it: this Balakrishnan Nair may turn out to be an esteemed writer one day. I don't concede that he has mettle. People want the kind of trash that he dishes out. If only that man hadn't appeared on the scene, all my articles and stories would have been printed. His appearance is proving to be my undoing.'

Engrossed as she was in some work, Kalyani said nothing till at the end, she spoke up: 'Didn't you say the other day that "Self-inflicted Calamity", published by *Ghoshini*, was quite entertaining?'

'Yes. When I said it was good, I only meant that it was better than his usual bland tales. Not that I enjoyed it. Anyway, he has become my nemesis. I despise the man.'

Kalyani hastened to stop him. 'Please don't say that. He must also be someone like us, trying to make both ends meet with his articles because he has no other option. Besides, merely because his style of writing and yours are poles apart, you mustn't see him as your enemy.'

'If someone like him sets out to reel off the kind of absurdities that people prefer to read, there will be no one left to read serious work like mine, which demands intelligence and deep thought. I will never again send articles to magazines.'

Govindan Nair finally completed his novel and sent it to the Academy before the due date. The novel was an exemplary one. The theme of the story was about a poverty-stricken man who, solely through hard work and perseverance, earns money and leads an ideal life thereafter.

A novel is much more than a story. It must also be a beacon of wisdom that leads its reader to the right path in life—this was Govindan Nair's philosophy. Most novel writers follow this precept in literary writing, but Govindan Nair's own method was something else altogether.

Having dispatched the novel to the Academy, Govindan Nair said that he now needed rest and lolled around at home doing nothing. The man knew very well that his wife loved him intensely. While he was writing, she never once distracted him. When the debtors came, she would handle them in her own way to leave Nair in peace. She would sit in the kitchen babysitting the children to make sure that they did not trouble her husband. She did not even step out of the house. The main door of the house was always kept shut, probably to seal off the sound of the children from reaching the outhouse where Nair worked. Her very behaviour changed to one of nervousness and secrecy as if the fear of people watching every move of hers had gripped her.

Morning dawned on the 25th of Kanni (August-September), the day the winners of the contest were to be declared. Nair had made arrangements for him to be informed as soon as the results were announced. By the next day's mail, a parcel and a letter arrived. Govindan Nair opened the packet with anxiety and curiosity. His face lost colour when he saw the contents. He yelled, 'My script has been returned. How sad, indeed! No reasons for its rejection either. I am sure they haven't even bothered to read the novel. Where do they have the time to read everything they receive! The prize must have gone to someone in their circle of friends. Let me see!' The accompanying paper was a report from the Academy. He checked the winners listed.

Kalyaniamma, who was usually calm by nature, anxiously held on to the edge of the table and asked: 'Who has been awarded the prize?'

'Need we ask? Naturally, it went to that rogue, Balakrishnan Nair. Didn't I tell you that his rise is the death of me?'

Kalyaniamma quickly took the paper and looked. *First prize— Rs 500—Balakrishnan Nair* was printed on it.

Govindan Nair let out a sigh. 'This man is destroying us.'

Kalyaniamma blurted out self-consciously: 'Please don't curse Balakrishnan Nair—*for I am he.*'

Govindan Nair was thunderstruck. 'What? *What!*'

Kalyani said calmly: 'I am the one who has been writing all those articles under the pseudonym Balakrishnan Nair. I did so because we had no other means to support our children and the whole family. After mother passed on, we have been struggling to run the family. Before that, every time I suggested something, you rejected all of them as trifles. Initially, I wrote a couple of stories to see if the readers would take to them. I sent them to some papers. They accepted my stories and went on to ask me to write similar articles and stories and, as advance payment for them, sent me some money too. It was at the time Amma had expired and you were running around for money to conduct the cremation rituals in a decent manner. Later, some journalists from publishing houses I hadn't heard of also approached me for stories. They also sent payments in advance. Due to our dearth of cash, I didn't return the money but began to write stories and articles for them. The more I sent them, the more they asked me to keep on writing. I have never received any big sum of money from my writing. Still, I did not yield to disappointment. It was never my intention to compete with you. So, please don't think of me as evil.'

Govindan Nair said in a tone of surrender: 'This means that all this time I have been living off the money earned by my wife. I never suspected this. Now I understand why our creditors stopped harassing me. All I have to say is this: I don't want to live on the money earned by a woman. Now it is clear that you are capable of taking care of the children and yourself independently. If I continue to live here, I will only be a burden to you. What has happened is in direct contrast to my desire to be of help to you at all times. I spent my days never realizing that the money I earned from the publishers was inadequate even to cover my lifestyle, never once pausing to think differently. From now on, I won't live here. I will leave today itself. I relinquish my relationship with literature along with my separation from you. I'm unfit to cater to the taste of the current crop of people. All my years of effort lie wasted. I will spend the rest of my life in my ancestral home, helping my brothers in farming or while away my time reading. Never again will I attempt to indulge in literary pursuits. I will never be jealous of Balakrishnan ... née ... Kalyani. If I was earlier, it was only because I thought some Balakrishnan Nair was usurping the welfare and esteem I wanted to pamper you with. I have been writing all these lacklustre novels and poems and continued to do so despite all the depression they brought me, only because I wanted to make your life a joyous one. At least now I am a contented man.'

Govindan Nair prepared to leave the house for good. When Kalyani told him that if he left her in her present state of pregnancy, she would become totally helpless, he consented to stay on till the delivery—but only as a guest.

The next morning, Kalyani gave birth. She asked for her husband at noon. Nair came to the door of her room and hesitated. She spoke in a weak voice: 'Please come in. I can't speak any louder.' When Nair went to her bedside, Kalyani said: 'You must take care of our children. They have no one else. I think I am going to die.'

Stunned, Govindan Nair held her hand and wept: 'Aiyyo, Kalyani, whom are you leaving me with? What will I do without you?'

Kalyani explained: 'This is better than having to live alone with the children. I must have wilted so much because of the long hours spent on writing that novel. Anyway, all is well. Please save that prize money and the money you get on the copyright too, for the protection of our children … Do you promise?'

Nair moaned: 'If you die, I will never touch that money!'

'And what if I don't?'

'If you don't … I will live according to your wishes. I shall, henceforth, do all that I can to support you in your efforts in literature and shall show my own writing to you and abide by your suggestions to make changes, if need be, as you deem fit. Tell me you won't leave me. There is no one else in this whole world I look up to and love as much as I love you!'

'You won't leave me, then?'

'Oh, no, Kalyani! Where could I go with my heart bound to you?'

'In that case, I shan't die. We will spend the rest of our lives together, contributing to the world of literature.'

Govindan Nair: 'Oh, dear Kalyani! Never again will I say that women have no brains. Promise!'

LAKSHMIKUTTY VARASYAR

So What Next?

At the age of thirteen, I was sent to the Girls' School in our village. I do not intend to say anything now about my lack of worldly experience at that point of time. When I think back on the story of how our lady tutor tormented us, my hands still tremble nervously. We had to solve many problems in Geometry in several ways.

As was my habit, I was looking through some of my lessons. Reading aloud was considered gross by some of my seniors who studied in higher classes, and I followed their advice.

One-two-three … I finished reading ten pages. I reflected on the matter I had read for a while as taught by our tutor. Ha! That is when I realized that I hadn't grasped anything at all. I thought that what someone said about our minds having a jumble of thoughts was more or less true. I was still reading the book silently. My mind—the fickle mind—followed the stranger I had seen that

---

Originally published as 'Ini Entha Cheyka?' in Malayalam by *Lakshmibhai Pusthakam 8*, Number 12/April 1913.

morning. Something I realized only now. I placed the book on the table and rested my chin in my cupped palm. For a little while—no for a long time—I sat lost in thought. It is better that you yourself train the course of your mind. It is not a good thing for women to allow men to ride on the wave of their thought process. I spent the whole day doing nothing else. The next day was no different. But why? The tutor's scolding increased steadily. At times even my mother began to berate me.

My rank in class dropped. I was not aware of all this. Something had blocked out these thoughts, restraining my mind. What was it? Infatuation or love? You can define it as you wish. I had developed a special liking for my youngest uncle's friend. How beneficial is the strength to control your thoughts! But I didn't have even a semblance of it. People who advise others tell me that one must use the mind as a bridle to rein in straying thoughts. To counsel is easy, to practise is the challenge.

My uncle and others began to ask about my indifferent moods; or so I thought. One morning, I was seated in my room after a bath, pretending to be preparing for school. But what went on in my mind must be plain to the reader. Amma (who seldom came to my room) entered. 'Kutty! What are you gazing at? Don't you have anything to read?' she asked. I replied that I was reading but silently, as is the norm of refined study.

Amma said: 'Kutty! I am told that Cheruve Chakrapani and you are to be betrothed.'

'Is it my uncle's decision?'

'It was a joint decision.'

'Have you chosen that never-do-well as my future husband?'

'What flaw do you see in him? Is he not stylish? Isn't he rich?'

So What Next?

'Are these the criteria that make a man eligible?'

'What else, pray?'

'How educated is he?'

'You and your education. If you shoo off the people who come forward to take your hand, you can sit there forever with your chin cupped in your palm. That is all.'

'A pity that you yourself set out to ask these questions. Have you nothing else to do?'

'His mother and others have come to know of your stand. That is why I'm here to ask you myself.'

'Tell them not to prepare for this match. Tell them so, bluntly.'

'Don't try to wash your hands off the matter with that conceit of yours. You have been pampered and spoiled. What can I do?' She stormed out of the room.

As usual I had my lunch, dressed for school and left.

'Dressed' does not mean that I put on the costume for a dance or a drama that I had enrolled in. In our village, girls went to school not in some casual dress as was common then. We decked ourselves out with trinkets and made up our faces, spending nearly an hour over it and went to school in a certain style. It is common for the mothers to dress their girls for school, thus making it a lifelong habit in them. They must have had a secret reason for doing this. Although I had no understanding of all this, telling myself *move with the times*,[1] I followed the custom.

Many days passed. I began to receive more and more information about the man I loved. I heard that he was brilliant

---

1 An adage meaning what the author says in Malayalam: *Kaalathinokkumoru Kolamedukkanam*.

and was currently studying at the University in Trivandrum. My love for him increased. It is always when you hear more of the virtues of your lover that love blossoms. I have never gone to my eldest aunt's house. Now I wanted to go just once; whom could I say this to ... If I did, they would imagine things. Keeping all this to myself, I spent my time turning these thoughts over in my mind.

One day, as if in keeping with my mother's curse, some people she had intended to visit our house came to discuss my marriage. They spoke to my eldest uncle. When our servant Ammu told me that my uncle had finalized the marriage, I was plunged into a peculiar kind of sorrow. My dreams of spending all my time sharing happiness with my lover withered. An inexplicable fear gripped me. Whom can I confide in, my dear readers! I went into my room and shut the door behind me. The waves of grief in my heart spilt over as streams of tears; because of its unusual flames, the grief turned to steam which led to deep sighs. It is impossible to describe the sorrow I felt overall. As if all this was not enough, my heart sank; I began to cry. My youngest uncle somehow came to know of this and came to my door and called out my name. He made me open the door and tried his best to console me. He said he would arrange my marriage to the one I loved. Though this gave me a lot of comfort, Amma and some others tormented me by talking about the match with that other moron. Much time sped by. In the end, the marriage I desired was fixed. My mother spoke of my lover boy's penury, his inexperience in contrast to the attractive qualities of the other man, and tried to make me change my mind. My mind—like a rock on the seashore that stands unaffected by the onslaught of lashing waves—remained firm. Probably because of my lover's 'poverty', the preparations for the wedding were lacklustre. Some relatives from my uncle's wife's side (all strangers to me) and some prominent people of the locality attended. And I was wed.

I had the feeling that I had attained the pinnacle of extreme happiness. Soon his college also closed for the holidays. I went to my husband's home and began to live there.

One day, we were talking casually to each other, seated in the corridor.

I asked: 'Will all this end when institutions reopen and you go back to Trivandrum?'

He replied: 'No; not if I pass.'

'Are you planning to quit studying?'

'There will be no classes thereafter. I am now in the Sixth Form (Pre-University Class). If I pass, I will get the status of a Tutor. I can then put an end to my studies.'

All this while, I had thought that he was studying English. I felt ashamed and deeply regretful. I sat there wordless.

What could I possibly do next?

CHEMBATHIL CHINNAMMU AMMAL

A Case of Homicide

Mullatharakkal Karunakara Menon sat on a chair in a spacious room in Chembakamittathu Tharavad, with a solemn expression, listening to the narration of a moustachioed man sitting across from him. On one side of the table sat Pichangottu Shekhara Kaimal listening to their conversation, his elbows resting on the table.

Karunakara Menon, who had earned a name for himself in the Malayalam domain,[1] had resigned from government employment and was doing some private business. His uncanny acumen for

---

1 The region where Malayalam was spoken was a part of Madras Presidency in those days.

Originally published in Malayalam as 'Oru Kolakkesu', by *Lakshmibhai Pusthakam 8*, Number 10/February 1913.

business was the talk of the town and people praised him for it. Although he appeared to be a heartless man, in practise, the man was not ruthless. It is doubtful whether anybody could see the man's dark curls and blazing eyes without flinching.

Karunakara Menon had arrived in response to a telegram from Chembakamittathu Padmanabha Kurup. It was his practise to take Shekhara Kaimal wherever he went, as he was a very close friend. Within ten minutes, Padmanabha Kurup walked into the room where they sat; the man with a luxuriant moustache was Kurup.

Kurup began to speak: 'I respect and trust you deeply because I have heard a lot about your intelligence and tact. That is why I troubled you to come all the way here—to solve a murder case that occurred in these parts recently. You must have heard of it as it is already a topic of much gossip.'

Menon said: 'I heard that Unikandan Nair of Anandavadi died on his plantation from a bullet to the forehead and also that just before the shot was fired, his nephew, Kumaran Nair and he had had an argument; aside from that I have not understood the intricacies of the case.'

Kurup began to explain: 'Unikandan Nair lives almost a mile and a half from here. Despite the fact that he was a cultured man and well-known, he was not popular. He condescended to acknowledge only Dr Rama Panickar and me. As Nair was a confirmed bachelor, the sole heir to all his property was his nephew, Kumaran Nair. The man nurtured this boy with great care and affection and educated him in the most reputed institutions of Madras. The boy passed the BA exam and returned from Madras to live in his own house. One day, on his daily walk, Kumaran Nair happened to see a lovely maiden with whom he fell in love at first sight. On making enquiries about her confidentially, he came to know that she belonged to a very poor family. Notwithstanding her status, he decided to marry her. His uncle was against it. Kumara Menon, however, married her—paying no heed to the elder's wishes. When his uncle came to know of this, an argument ensued between them. At the end of it all, Kumaran Nair warned his uncle that he would pay for all his actions and, with the money left for him by his mother, bought a house about a mile and a half away and began life there with his bride.

'Unikandan Nair was a chronic heart patient. Two weeks before his death, he had suffered a heart attack and had gone to Dr Kunhirama Panickar, who opined after a complete examination that Nair might not live for another month and that the end would be sudden. Not convinced, Unikandan Nair went to Madras to consult a reputed doctor; when that doctor gave him the same report, Nair returned disappointed to his house in Anandavadi. The day before his death, Unikandan Nair went over to his nephew's house. Kumaran Nair and his wife had gone on a visit when he reached there. Again, in the evening, the uncle went to his nephew's house. What we heard is that when they met, Unikandan Nair told Kumaran Nair that all his faults were forgiven and that future plans could be sorted the next day. Accordingly, Kumaran Nair went to the Anandavadi house at two in the afternoon. The two of them went out of the house, sat under a tree and spoke amiably to each other. Then they took a walk to Unikandan Nair's plantation where they paced around for a while. That is when a young girl who passed that way saw Kumaran Nair punch Unikandan Nair in the face and a while later she saw them patch up and make peace. Three hours later, a farm hand saw a corpse under a tree on Unikandan's estate—and began to scream. It was Unikandan Nair. A bullet had struck the centre of his forehead. It is evident from this that he was shot at point-blank range. Nair had a small hunter's knife with a blade as sharp as a razor. A few feet away, the revolver used to dispatch Unikandan Nair to his Maker was found half-buried in slush. Kumaran Nair's name was etched on the handle of the six-shooter. This is the evidence used to hold Kumaran Nair as the suspect. However, Kumaran Nair's version is that he was innocent of the crime—he said that his uncle had insulted his wife for no reason at all, even while the two of them spoke peacefully, which provoked him to punch Unikandan Nair in the face; the uncle was not seriously hurt. They spoke for some more time with no rancour at all but the uncle again began to criticize the new bride. Seeing that to remain there would only worsen the situation, Kumaran Nair had returned to his house—this was his defence.

'It was four-thirty when Kumaran Nair reached home. A labourer was still at the site. Though the facts of the case are as detailed, the general talk was that Kumaran Nair would be picked up—'

When Kurup finished telling the tale, Menon spoke:

'Having heard the whole story in detail, I think there are two factors which go in favour of Kumaran Nair: One, as people do not go around carrying a lethal weapon, the man who shot Unikandan Nair must have had prior intentions of murdering him; two, as his name is etched on the revolver, Kumaran Nair, if guilty, would not have discarded the weapon at the site of murder. Anyway, what did Kumaran Nair have to say about the revolver?'

Kurup: 'He said that there were many articles stored in his library, and the revolver was just one among all those, and he couldn't tell when and how someone took possession of it.'

'And the hunter's knife?'

'That knife has been long with Unikandan Nair. It is not known why he took that knife along on that occasion. All told, this has become a complicated case. Now that you have understood all the circumstances, what is your opinion?'

'The case is very interesting, to be sure. It is too early to comment on it. To begin with, can you send someone along with me to the spot—who has been there before the body was shifted?'

Kurup said: 'Since I was there, I could accompany you. The coach is ready; the coach driver is the fellow who first spotted the revolver.'

He summoned the coach.

Menon: 'Before he brings the coach, I have one more question. In the wake of Unikandan Nair's death, does Kumaran Nair stand to benefit in any way?'

'No, not a paisa. Because when the friction between them grew, Unikandan Nair made out his will in favour of a distant relative. Furthermore, on the eve of his death, he handsomely paid off a few labourers who did odd jobs in his house. Besides, he also wrote out some promissory notes in favour of some of his servants who attended to him. One of the beneficiaries is Govindan, a veteran.'

'Hold on! Does this Govindan know anything about these promissory notes and the condition that Nair was in?'

'Even if he may not know anything about Unikandan Nair's deteriorating health, he must know something about the promissory notes. I say this because Nair wrote out a promissory note for five hundred rupees in favour of Govindan for "all services rendered" in the presence of two witnesses. At that point, Govindan—summoning up all his courage—asked Nair: "Hope you haven't forgotten our young Master Kumaran Nair?" To which, Unikandan Nair merely said that they had worked out their differences and that he had planned a gift for him that would forever remind Kumaran of his uncle.'

Having heard this much, Menon said he wanted to meet Govindan right away.

He asked: 'Can you send word to Govindan to meet us at the site of the murder?'

Kurup agreed to do so. 'But if you have any suspicions about him, it may not be fruitful to try to obtain the facts from him ... However much you threaten him, he will not tell the truth. Such is his loyalty to the Nair family.'

'At the moment, I suspect no one.'

The coach arrived. Menon, Kurup and Kaimal got in and proceeded to the spot. Because of the trundling noise of the carriage, conversation was not possible. In their hurry to get to the place, the horse was driven hard, making it very tired. At one point, they had to get off the coach and walk the last stretch to the spot. The coachman tethered the horse to a tree and joined them. Hardly a quarter of a mile from there, they reached the venue. They walked around the place and checked it out. After inspecting the spot where the corpse once lay, Karunakara Menon asked Kurup: 'Where was the revolver found?' The latter led them to the slushy area where the six-shooter had lain half-immersed. They saw a heap of twigs that looked like a tent in the slush. When Menon looked through the twigs, he saw an impression in the shape of a revolver. He looked all around and snapped: 'Coach driver! Aren't you the one who first spotted the handgun?'

'Yes, sir! When I passed that place after the corpse was found, I saw a glimmer in the bog. When I went over to check what it was, I saw the gun. What glittered was a silver plaque on the handle of the gun.'

'Are you sure that this is the very spot where you found the revolver?'

'Yes. Thinking that I ought to leave the revolver where it was till the policemen came, I arranged the twigs around it, to mark the spot.'

'Twenty feet away, we saw another similar impression in the peaty soil!'

'I saw it too. Maybe the murderer had two handguns with him and in his desperation to escape the crime scene, flung them both aimlessly.'

Menon, who was totally engrossed in inspecting the crime scene, heard nothing of what the coachman said.

Kaimal spoke up: 'Mister Kurup! Even if you do not suspect Govindan, could he still not be the murderer?'

Kurup: 'Till now, nobody thinks so.'

Kaimal said: 'It may be so, the locals are wont to pass judgement even before the police investigate the case. Those fellows will not consider all angles. What was Govindan doing that day, after noon? Can we not assume that it was Govindan who went to Kumaran Nair's house and fetched the handgun?'

Padmanabha Kurup agreed. 'Yes, it could be so. Anyway, Govindan will come as soon as he receives my note. When he does, he will be forced to answer all the questions Menon has for him.'

Menon was deaf to all this talk. He went on with his exploration.

He said: 'Since we have nothing more to learn from the coachman, let him leave.'

Accordingly, Kurup sent the coach driver back to where the horse was tethered.

Menon said he wanted to inspect the spot where the dead body was found.

Kurup: 'Do you expect to see anything specific there?'

'Yes. I think something has gone missing.'

As they reached the spot, they saw someone approaching them.

Kurup said: 'There comes Govindan. You can question him all you want. But I doubt his answers will satisfy you.'

By then, Govindan caught up with them. The minute he saw Karunakara Menon, he withdrew the foot he had put forward. He lost his breath and seemed very agitated. But Menon seemed not to notice anything.

Kurup introduced Govindan to Menon. 'This man is Unikandan Nair's most faithful servant. Govindan, how many years have you served Mr Nair?'

Govindan: 'Master! I lived in his house for seven years. I became a resident there only after Kumaran Nair returned from his studies in Madras.'

Kurup: 'All right! This gentleman is a friend of mine. He is an expert at solving mysteries. He wants to ask you some questions—that is why we summoned you here.'

'I shall reply to all your questions with utmost honesty.'

Menon began. 'Is it true that your Junior Master kept guns at home?'

'Yes. A handgun made in Britain, and two other guns imported from America; so, he has three guns in all.'

'Go and fetch that British handgun and six bullets too, if you can find them.'

Govindan left to collect the things that Menon asked for.

Kurup spoke up: 'Mr Karunakara Menon! Looks like you have a firm grip of the situation.'

Menon merely nodded.

'When Govindan reacted the way he did upon seeing you, I got the impression that you knew each other from another time. It is difficult to describe how startled he was when he saw you.'

Menon recounted: 'Ten years ago, the man was arrested for burglary, and I had sentenced him and even tried to finish him off. He is guilty of many more crimes. Now he looks quite different, but I recognized him the moment I saw him.'

Kurup asked in despair: 'Knowing he is an incorrigible criminal, why did you ask the same man to collect the gun? Wonder if he will ever come back!'

'How long do you think it will take him to reach the house?'

'Maybe ten minutes.'

'Allowing for five minutes to search for the handgun and the bullets, he should be back here in twenty-five minutes—or say, half an hour. In the meantime, there is one more thing I want to be sure about. Let me focus on that.'

Although Kurup and Kaimal offered to go along with Menon, he preferred to go alone. The two of them sat below a tree to watch Menon in action.

A Case of Homicide

Menon traced and retraced his path, carefully examining both sides of it and reached the area where the soil was damp and soggy. He lingered there for a while and backtracked to his starting point, still lost in deep thought.

Kurup commented: 'What is this man searching for so keenly? Has he found something?'

Kaimal said: 'I have known Menon for a long time. I have never met another who has his power of concentration and agility of mind. Look! He is picking up something from the ground.'

Menon stooped to pick up an object lying a few feet away from the path and put it in his sling bag; he walked back to where his friends awaited him.

Kurup asked: 'Did you find something?'

'Yes.'

'Is that what you were looking for?'

'Remember I told you something had not yet been recovered? I have now found it.'

'Do you mind if we see it?'

'Not at all.'

Menon dipped into his sling bag and took out something and gave it to Kurup. It was a braided string of about eighteen inches in length, hardly half the thickness of his little finger.

Kurup gazed at it: 'I do not understand the link of this string to our case!'

'If you wait till Govindan returns, I shall explain.'

'Do you mean that you have figured out who the culprit is?'

'No doubt about that.'

'It isn't Kumaran Nair, is it?'

'Kumaran Nair has nothing to do with this case.'

'Let him not be the guilty party, by God's grace. I love him like my own son. Mr Menon, do you think Govindan must be arrested?'

'I do not have the right to punish Govindan. I am not here as an officer of the government.'

'You chose to send Govindan himself to collect the gun. Will he ever come back? Granted he does, he will be armed with a loaded handgun. Can't tell what he will do with it. Only God knows!'

Menon looked at his watch and said: 'It is only two more minutes to half an hour since he left. Still no sign of Govindan.'

Five more minutes passed after the half-hour mark Menon had estimated for Govindan's return. Just then, Govindan appeared holding two pistols.

Menon asked him: 'Didn't I tell you to bring only the British handgun? Why have you brought two guns?'

Govindan said: 'I thought it was better to bring two guns along. Master, have you explained everything to these people?'

'Kurup and I were just talking about you. I told him about your old case of breaking into a house. But I must say, you appear to have reformed now.'

'What you said, Master, is right. If you think I am involved in any way in this case, it is a mistake. If I wanted to kill the senior Nair, I could have easily done it long ago. But I am not one to do it. After I was acquitted, I have been living the life of a gentleman.'

Govindan placed both the guns at Menon's feet impassively. Menon picked them up and handed them to Kaimal.

'Govindan! I'm not punishing you. Firstly, I don't have the authority. Secondly, this case does not concern you in any way. I did mention your case of burglary here. But we are now convinced that you are a decent man.'

A Case of Homicide

Kurup: 'Govindan! You must swear that you have nothing to do with this case.'

Govindan did as asked.

Kurup turned to Menon. 'Mr Menon! We do not think that you suspect anyone else that we know of. You have already told us that you know who the murderer is. It is not fair to keep it from us any longer.'

Menon said: 'In a short while, I shall prove it all to you. Where is the braided string that I gave you?'

Kurup gave him the entwined yarn. Menon unentangled it and spun them loosely together again. He took the handgun from Kaimal, checked to make sure it was not loaded and told them to follow him.

When they reached the tree where Unikandan Nair's body was found, they stopped. There was a branch spreading out of the trunk five feet above the ground. Ten feet away from that tree was a sapling. Menon checked to see if a side shoot of the smaller tree would touch the branch of the former tree when bent far enough. He fastened the bent shoot to the branch of the first tree with the braided string, the branches barely touching each other, leaving a length of taut yarn in between. He then placed the handgun with its hair trigger on the side-shoot under tension, like a slingshot, with its barrel pointing to the part of the slushy area where it was initially found. When he plucked the taut bow-string, there was a twang-like sound of the strumming of a wire. Kaimal looked at Kurup in confusion.

Menon said: 'My dear friends, it will now be evident who or what caused the death of Unikandan Nair.'

Menon took the penknife from his sling bag and tested its blade. Though not as sharp as a hunter's knife, he decided it was sharp enough for the task at hand. He told Govindan to cut the string in a single stroke at the very moment that Menon gave him the nod. When Govindan did as told, the gun fired and the handgun itself catapulted and bounded off the soggy earth not too far away, skimmed to the soft mud farther down and came to rest there. The bent limb of the sapling having snapped back to its original position flung the string away to the slushy pool. On checking the marks made by the gun as it skimmed off and landed, it was seen that there were two of them—as was seen when the handgun was first found.

'I have now understood the intricacies of the case,' said Kurup. 'If someone has planned this sinful act, how much he must have hated Unikandan Nair! On the other hand, as the doctor had not given him much more time to live, if Unikandan Nair had planned to commit suicide—which is no more a matter for much sorrow—if he has done it to pin the blame on Kumaran Nair, even in death, how horribly mean is it of him! If it were not for Mr Menon's help, we may have never been able to prove the complexity of this crime.'

'The case is a rare one. But finding the proof was not as difficult as you had imagined. When I first saw the spot where Unikandan Nair's body lay, I deduced the case. When I saw that the impression of the handgun in the mud was at two places, my doubts were confirmed. That is when I told you there is still one more article of evidence missing. The penknife Nair had with him was used to cut the strings. Do I make myself clear?'

A Case of Homicide

'Oh, yes, Mr Menon, absolutely. My, my! Unikandan Nair was quite a mischievous character! This is a premeditated act to trap Kumaran Nair. But how did he get Kumaran Nair's handgun?'

Menon: 'Do you remember hearing that Unikandan Nair had gone to Kumaran Nair's house the day before this incident and that the latter and his wife were not home and Unikandan Nair lingered for some time in that house? Couldn't he have pinched the gun then? He told Govindan that night that he would give Kumaran Nair a "gift", which would remind him of his uncle all his life. Isn't that circumstantial evidence enough?'

'Anyway, we will always be indebted to you for clarifying the modus operandi of the case. Let us go now to tell Kumaran Nair the whole story.'

When Kumaran Nair was told the tale, his joy knew no bounds. All of them spent the night at Chembakamittathu and the next morning, informed the police. When the complexity of the case was explained to them, the police personnel felt ashamed of their own incompetence and declared that Kumaran Nair was not guilty. Kurup, Kaimal and Menon returned to their respective houses.

B. KALYANIAMMA

Nambiar's Secret

It was an evening at the peak of summer. The sun was about to set. A pleasant breeze blew across the land. Despite that, the heat in the publisher's office had not abated even slightly. The morning's post had been checked and those among them that deserved a reply had been dispensed with. The proof of the newspaper had been read. The reporters who had come with bits of news not worth a paisa—and preached about them as if they were of great importance—had been pacified and sent away. The editor's table was cluttered with heaps of paper—innumerable folded letters. Some well composed and in good handwriting, folded neatly and stamped; others scribbled, lay crumpled; yet others were folded and tucked into envelopes ... This way, the letters occupied space on that table, each a tell-tale token of the traits of its writer.

The editor had unfolded a letter of poetry and was reading through its first part. His publication *Sahityaratnakaram* was known for the liberal compensation it paid for first-class poetry.

Originally published in Malayalam as 'Nambiarude Rahasyam' by *Atmaposhini Pusthakam 5*, issue 8-9/January 1915.

When he saw the inordinately extended poem, the editor felt it must be relegated to the 'rejects'. He had begun to read it thinking it unfair to reject it without first checking its eligibility. The first part was not too bad; the second was better. As he read on, the editor began to enjoy the poem. Not unlike the way we turn to look again when we spot a face that looks familiar, the editor read all three sections once more. When he reached the fourth poem, a doubt arose in his mind; by the sixth, the doubt escalated. When he reached the end of Part I, he grasped the matter in full. After the last verse, he looked at the name and signature attested below it. He picked up the first poem and read its title. He then folded the papers and set them aside. He checked to see if a covering note had come along with the anthology.

The title of the collection of poems was *Parishkarabhramam*—a passion for modernity. The name at the bottom was Raman Nambiar. The letterhead of the pages the poems were written on had the name 'Manjeri Madhom' printed on them. There was no covering note. The editor found no other marks on the envelope that held the sheets. The address was written in the same hand as the author's—the stamp on the envelope showed the place of origin as Chandrapuram Post Office. Nothing was mentioned about the payment that could be sent to this address, if the poems were accepted. The editor had no idea where Chandrapuram was—whether it was in a town or in the suburbs.

The editor came out of his room and addressed the manager and the reporters seated there: 'Just for fun's sake—we have received a contribution titled *Parishkarabhramam*; it is a poem actually by Padmanabha Panickar, which appeared in the *Kavyavilasam* magazine years ago. When I was in the FA class, a few of my friends had heated debates about that poem. Now someone has sent the same poem without a single change of word or verse to us for publication! What should I make of it—is it someone trying to fool us or is it plagiarism in order to make some money on the sly?'

Needless to say, Nambiar's collection of poems was not published. Neither was it returned to Nambiar. The editor guessed that Nambiar would not lie low. Nambiar's verses were awaited as one would the work of great writers. Nambiar was not discouraged. He kept sending more and more poems and prose to the editor. They were all high-calibre poems previously published in some papers in other provinces. But just as Nambiar escaped the scrutiny of his editors, so too did his plagiarism the notice of his readers.

The editor and his team made every effort to locate Nambiar. They conducted investigations based on the signs and marks they found on the stationery and the envelopes he used. Some scoffed at them for trying to track down a trivial plagiarist with such verve. But there was a justifiable reason for such efforts. Anybody who steals the literary wealth of someone else and claims it as his own is a publisher's enemy. Besides, the editor of *Sahityaratnakaram* had another reason for his animosity. He thought these poems were a ploy to unseat *him*. If by chance he should publish any of them and be caught off guard, he would be exposed as an incompetent editor who had no grasp of literature or language and was therefore unfit to continue in that post—this is what he thought Nambiar's scheme was. He also felt that it was his duty to eliminate a fraudulent writer trying to make a quick buck.

Nambiar proved to be a smart man; the tricks he used to stay away from the editor's traps were admirable. On the letterhead of his second article was printed:

Unnai Warrier Memorial Library
Editor: M. Raman Nambiar

Nambiar must have used this stratagem either because he thought that not to reveal his address would lead to suspicion, or because he wanted the editor of *Sahityaratnakaram* to think that he was a reputed writer in the literary world. However, nobody had heard of such a library in the suburb of Chandrapuram. In his third article, Nambiar had given the name and number of a house in the central street of Chandrapuram; but on enquiry, it turned out to be an abandoned building.

Overall, Nambiar had made the editor of *Sahityaratnakaram* restless. The editor and his colleagues debated about Nambiar's motive. They formed two groups. One side said that Nambiar had filched only premier quality poems or articles, but not indicated details of his address. It meant that he merely wanted to be known in the field of literature and had no intention of making money from it.

The other side stated that Nambiar was suppressing his true address because he was afraid of being caught. If his matter were published, he would demand compensation right away, they argued. But the editor thought: *Would he have the guts after revealing his identity?* Raman Nambiar was unknown among the poets of Chandrapuram. Not a single poem of his had appeared in print in *Kavanakoumudi*. Even in the comprehensive article on modern poets published by *Bhashavilasam*, he had not received a mention. Besides all this, was it possible that the original author of that article had not located Nambiar?

Our editor made a plan. He placed an advertisement in the paper that read: *We wish to return the articles sent by one Mr Raman Nambiar. He must, therefore, furnish his latest address forthwith.*

That worked.

Within two weeks, Nambiar sent one more article of quality, along with which he had given his detailed address. As soon as the editor received this, he put together all of Nambiar's articles and poems and, taking the local reporter along with him, set out to locate Mr Nambiar. On his way, he picked up two letters, one from the original author and another from the reporter of the magazine who had published the originals. The editor read out the letters pertaining to this issue to the reporter. They said that the materials Nambiar sent were 'lifted' from other authors and that it was the responsibility of the editor to take action against Nambiar in good faith.

The reporter said: 'We'll do it right away. The editor of *Keraleeyan* paper has asked me for a report as soon as we find the man. *Keraleeyan* will publish it tomorrow itself. We must expose Nambiar without any delay. Let us not wait another day. Nambiar's unravelling can appear in our next issue, right? Let these letters remain with me.'

It was four o'clock in the evening. The duo of editor and reporter who went in search of Nambiar's house were exhausted and began to sweat profusely. They stopped in front of a large building at the north end of one of the East Street of Chandrapuram. They saw the house number mentioned in Nambiar's letter painted on the gatehouse. With the relief one feels when a thief is caught, they stood, resting a while. When they were about to cross the threshold of the gatehouse, they noticed the board fixed on a plank mounted on the wall: *Nambiar & Company, Pharmaceutical Distributors*. Both of them read it together. They stood transfixed with surprise and in confusion. They knew the founder of that Company, Dr Nambiar, very well. There was no one more famous or highly regarded than he was. Several of his advertisements for his own ayurvedic products were regularly published in *Sahityaratnakaram*!

Could this gentleman stoop to such a treacherous act?

The reporter, who had recovered from his shock, asked the editor, 'How can this be explained?'

'I never imagined such a reputed person as Nambiar would resort to the mean act of plagiarism; I still can't believe it,' replied the editor.

'Still not sure? Okay, let us find out what he has to say about his petty act! Anyhow, let us go inside.'

'Wonder if he is home?'

'Let's investigate. What a seasoned thief he must be! If he isn't here, we will go to his house and check.' The reporter was all charged up.

The two of them went past the gatehouse. On the verandah of the building stood some youngsters. They asked one of them: 'Is Raman Nambiar in?'

'No, he just left for home.'

'We have to meet Nambiar. Will he be coming back soon?' asked the editor.

'Oh! It must be time for his rounds at the hospital. I forgot about it,' said the reporter soothingly.

'He won't be coming back soon; if you are in a hurry to meet him, you will have to go to his house,' said one of the youngsters.

'Isn't he still in that bungalow near the hospital?' asked the editor.

'No. He now lives in a two-storied building at the western end of North Street. Oh! You must be looking for *Dr* Nambiar! He lives in the same old bungalow. I was talking about our manager, Nambiar. He is the nephew of the doctor. They both use the same name. That is what confused me,' said the youngster and went indoors.

The editor and the reporter stood looking at each other for a long while. In their eyes, the question now was: *Which Nambiar should they go in search of?*

'We made a mistake suspecting the doctor. He won't stoop to such undignified acts. Must be the nephew. Let's go after him.' They walked out.

A nephew who brings disrepute to his uncle! What a shame! Murmuring to himself, the editor followed the reporter.

'We will expose the nephew. Let the uncle also come to know. We must bring in the names of prominent people to add some flourish to the story and jack up our readership. We will flash it as a three-column story. No sleep tonight.' The reporter was excited, waving his arms in the air.

'Hold on! We must show consideration for his social status.' The editor restrained the reporter.

'If *he* is not bothered about it, why should *we* be concerned?'

It did not take them long to reach their destination. As soon as they came to the two-storied building at the end of the street, the reporter exclaimed: 'Here it is! Whether Nambiar is here or not, I won't budge till our purpose is served. Be it midnight or the next morning, I shall wait.' The editor crossed the gatehouse into the courtyard and asked a maidservant: 'Is Raman Nambiar here?'

'I saw him going upstairs a little while ago. Will check,' said the maid and began to climb the stairs. Calling after her, 'Tell him two persons have come to meet him,' they also stepped into the corridor of the house. The maid returned in a minute. 'He is here and wants you to go in.'

The editor and reporter hastened up the stairs, brushing past the maidservant in their hurry. They probably rushed like this because they feared that Nambiar would exit via another staircase or maybe vanish into thin air. It would be silly to let a trapped criminal get away so easily.

When they went into the room upstairs and stood before Nambiar, they were bitterly disappointed. A tall and sturdy man with a pleasant countenance sat in an easy chair. At first impression, he appeared to be a respectable gentleman and not a felon who might engage in theft or treachery. Besides, the room he occupied was tastefully decorated. To judge from its décor, it was obvious that this man had no dearth of money and lived well; to accuse such a man of felony and plagiarism would be a foolish and an unscrupulous act in itself—thought the editor, feeling queasy.

Nambiar did not budge from his seat to receive his guests; yet in his manner there was no tinge of conceit. A pretty little girl of about five was seated on his lap, playing. She had tilted her head to the side. Nambiar greeted his guests with a nod. He pointed to the chairs. Once they were seated, the editor said to him: 'We have to speak to you in confidence. It would be better if you sent the child indoors.' The child, hearing this, clung to her father's neck. Nambiar cajoled her: 'Don't do that. Go outside and play with Lakshmi.' He stood her up tenderly. Glaring at the editor and the reporter, the child pranced out of the room.

Considering the situation, the editor and reporter found the expression on Nambiar's face quite curious. Nothing seemed to fit. Nambiar did not know the people who had come seeking him;

he did not appear to want to know them either. They cringed with embarrassment.

The editor began tentatively: 'I am the editor of *Sahityaratnakaram*; he is our reporter.' There was no change in Nambiar's expression; he remained still and silent. The editor continued: 'We have received the poems and articles you sent us. They are of high quality. Your use of the phrase, "A passion for modernism" fascinated us. However, we find a strong similarity of your poems to those published by another magazine a few years ago. We are here only to understand the reason for this similarity. If we publish them without investigation, our readers will accuse us of stealing the poems of another magazine.'

In reply, Nambiar said without flinching: '"A passion for modernism"? I have never written such a poem. I don't remember it at all.'

They had not expected Nambiar to deny knowledge of it so firmly. The editor was nonplussed. How was one to make so outspoken a man confess his guilt? The editor said: 'That's strange! Having written such beautiful poetry, how can you say you don't remember it at all?'

'Yes. I write a lot; it is possible I forget some of them,' said Nambiar, now lost in thought.

'That may be so. Perhaps if you see the poem, it might refresh your memory,' added the reporter like a mediator.

He pulled out a bunch of papers from his sling bag, picked out the first page of *Parishkarabhramam* and extended it to Nambiar. Nambiar looked at it, turning it over and over carelessly. 'The handwriting on this is mine, all right. But the poem is not my own. I copied it from the book, *Kavyaratnavali*. I never sent it to any publishing house,' said Nambiar nonchalantly.

The visitors looked at each other blankly. Both suppressed the shock they felt. After a firm denial, the way Nambiar wriggled out of it was what surprised them. Nambiar had admitted to having copied the poem; but to say that he had not sent it to any publisher—was that not foolish of the man?

Nambiar had more to say: 'The matter is ... I have a keen interest in poetry. When I come upon a good quality poem, I learn it by rote immediately. If you copy it down in your own hand, it is easier to learn it by heart and to retain it. That is why I copied *Parishkarabhramam*. If I remember correctly, I copied it while in my office. My peons there must have mailed it to you to make me look foolish. My uncle is a man of repute. It is possible that he might want to see me established as a poet. However, I haven't sent it to you. That's for sure.'

Editor: 'In my student days, I too had a habit of copying poetry to learn them by heart; but I didn't have the practise of attesting my name and signing below the poem.'

Nambiar looked down at the sheet in his hand to check the bottom of the page. 'I have not signed at the bottom of the poem here either.'

'No, but you have, on the second page.'

The editor and reporter expected Nambiar to show signs of irritation at this point. What right did they have to barge into his house and accuse him of plagiarism? But they were proved wrong. Nambiar remained stoic. They could not make out if it was his intrinsic character or if he was putting on an act. They even wondered if they had overstepped when they saw the innocence on Nambiar's face.

'Maybe you, Nambiar, didn't sign it; the peon who sent it to us must have written your name and forged your signature,' said the reporter.

Nambiar took the second page from the editor. 'Yes, that is what has happened, apparently. This is not my signature.'

The editor began to lose patience. 'I have received some more of your poems. Here is one that you sent from Unnai Warrier Memorial Library. You are the president of that library, aren't you? Do you think this too has been signed by your peon?'

Nambiar was sceptical. 'That isn't possible. Peons are not allowed in the library.'

The editor handed the sheet of paper to Nambiar. 'This is yours, isn't it?'

'Yes, it is mine.'

'And the signature?'

Nambiar admitted: 'Yes, the signature is also mine. This was written and sent by me. I merely copied *Parishkarabhramam*. But this one is my own creation.'

'Did you also write the address on the envelope in which the poem was sent to us? Is this handwriting yours?'

Nambiar took the envelope from the editor, looked at the address and said, 'This is indeed my own handwriting.'

Editor (feigning nervousness): 'Hold on! My mistake! That envelope is the one that contained *Parishkarabhramam*; sorry!'

The reporter gave a start and sat looking down at the designs of the carpet; while the editor kept turning over page after page of the bunch he held. For a long while, all of them remained silent. The only sound in the room came from the vehicles passing on the street outside and children playing.

When they looked up, they saw Nambiar looking at them intensely. He was cracking his knuckles and shuffling his feet.

The editor broke the silence: 'Where is Unnai Warrier Library situated? Which building?'

Nambiar: 'It doesn't have a building of its own. It is defunct.'

'All right. A certain address has been given on the page in which the third poem was sent. You once stayed in that house, didn't you? Or did some of your relatives live there?'

'No. When that poem was written I was staying in that house.'

The editor looked at the reporter, then turned back to Nambiar: 'We checked as soon as we received the poem. At that time, the house was vacant.'

Once more, silence fell on the room. Nambiar began to squirm in his chair, pressing his hands over his mouth and stroking his face. Then he cleared his throat and asked: 'Are you quite finished?'

Editor: 'The case is closed. Our investigation is over.'

'I do not admit to plagiarizing the poems of others. Let me ask you as a friend: Even if someone does so, is it an offence?'

'What?' interjected the editor and reporter simultaneously.

The editor was aghast. 'Sending pilfered material to a publisher and to collect payment for it; stealing the fruit of another's labour and usurping the fame due to him! Aren't these offences enough? Haven't you still understood that you can't hide such a mean act as this, try as you might—that it will certainly surface someday?'

'But I haven't asked you for money.'

'Even if you don't ask, we are obliged to send you the compensation according to the rules. If we hadn't discovered the fraud you committed, we would certainly have paid you.'

'Where and to whom would you send the money? I have never disclosed my true identity to you. Then how could you send the money?'

'If it wasn't for the money, why did you commit this fraud?'

Nambiar relented. 'I didn't realize that my action was wrong. I still don't think it is. I haven't asked for money. All I wanted was to see my name in print. I wanted my friends to see it. I also wanted to show off to my wife, who is very keen on literature. Apart from this, I had no other interest in doing what I did. I hadn't, in my wildest dreams, imagined that I would accept money from you.'

Again, the editor and the reporter gazed at each other. 'How was I to know that this was your purpose?' asked the editor peevishly. He struggled to sound stern. The man had admitted his mistake and also explained why he had done it. What a simple soul! On the other hand, if he had denied his act of felony and showed outrage and anger, the latter would have had no pang of conscience at all in unleashing his wrath.

'How could I have known your intentions? If we had published your poems, how am I to know that you wouldn't ask for payment then?'

'Now you know that I had no such intention.'

'I know nothing except that you used another's creation and tried to make money out of it. I wanted to teach you a lesson. Let others like you see it and refrain from such pilfering. Is it possible for an editor to read and remember all the poems ever written and published? What protection does a common editor have from the likes of you? Isn't it against the law to let the fraudsters go scot-free once they are caught? I shall go ahead and publish news of your plagiarism without any delay. You can check the paper tomorrow.'

The editor withdrew after delivering this long lecture. Once more, a deafening silence descended on the room. The editor looked at his reporter anxiously ... to see if he approved of his demonstration or if he showed signs of disapproval. But the latter continued to look at the carpet, tapping his chin with his pencil.

'Is your verdict over? Will you not retract your decision?' asked Nambiar plaintively.

'I have made up my mind. It is irrevocable.' However, though his response had come from his mouth, it had not touched his heart. Had he set out alone to track down Nambiar, he would never have spoken so harshly. He thought behaving any other way in the presence of his colleague would diminish his weight in the man's eyes. The reporter must have already envisioned the title, 'Nambiar's Theft' for the long article he planned for the next day's paper. *Oh God*, thought the editor ... *If only the rascal could sink into the ground, what a relief it would be!* The editor squirmed thinking he had no viable justification to restrain the reporter.

Nambiar pleaded plaintively once more: 'Please consider my position. For the sake of a few rupees, you are about to destroy my whole life. Had I tricked you and taken a large sum of money from you, it would be understandable. As things stand, you have incurred no loss of any kind at all. For a small mistake I made, merely to impress my wife, you want to punish me as if I have burgled the state treasury. I have harmed no one. The original authors of those poems received their compensation long ago, along with the fame and stature that go with it. You have lost nothing. Nor have I gained anything. Then aren't you about to inflict this ruthless act on me merely to destroy me? Think of what will follow when this matter appears in the paper tomorrow. My uncle is an important man. All because of me, his image will be tarnished. My own family too will do something drastic about the disgrace they will have to endure …'

The editor's heart melted. He crumpled all the sheets of paper and shoved them into the sling bag. Were the reporter absent from the scene, the papers would have gone to Nambiar. The editor asked the reporter: 'Hey! Do you have anything to say about this?'

The reporter spoke without looking up while doodling with his walking stick on the carpet: 'Nambiar should have thought of the dignity of his family and the stature of his uncle before resorting to these heinous deeds. What is the use of talking about all that now? Anyway, just the two of us can't take a decision on this matter right now; let all the journalists in the publishing house put their heads together and arrive at a decision.'

Editor: 'You are right. We can't pass judgement sitting here. Let them decide.'

The visitors got up to leave. Nambiar, who was convinced that this was the end, stood up disappointed and said: 'Don't you see that I haven't the least need for money? I have no reason to cheat you for the sake of a few rupees. Had I done something like that, I wouldn't object to being punished. My objective was only to make my wife proud of me. I only entreat you gentlemen not to issue forth a punishment that is not in line with the fault I committed.'

The editor-reporter duo walked to the door. Both were distressed and did not want to prolong the scene. They paused at the door and said, without looking back, 'We will let you know of our decision tomorrow morning,' and walked out.

'You mean, I will see it in tomorrow's newspaper?'

Before the editor could reply, they heard someone coming up the stairs towards that room. In a minute, two pretty hands parted the curtains hung over the door to either side. Just as the family deity appears before the devotees who regularly perform stringent penance, especially when they are about to commit a sacrilegious act driven by frustration, Nambiar's wife appeared before the man—who was roiling under the heartless words of the editor—to save him. As soon as Nambiar saw the beautiful young woman, he stood still and looked down silently. The guests too were wonderstruck by the sight of that lady. Seeing strangers emerging from the room, the lady hesitated to enter and, because it was not polite to turn around, stood there, holding on to the parted curtains.

The editor decided that if this lady was Nambiar's wife, he must somehow beat the reporter to it and thwart his plans to publish the story. He could not guess what his colleague was thinking; he now stood with his chest puffed out and eyes popping.

It was neither the lady's beauty nor her dignity that influenced the editor. At first sight, the editor concluded that this was an honourable lady who deserved great respect. Seeing her stance and the way she looked humbly, head tilted and smiling, even a man with a stony heart would not have the courage to hurt her feelings or disgrace her in any way.

'Take the maidservant along with you; I am a little busy. I shall be back by dusk.' Nambiar spoke without looking up. At that, that jewel of a lady bowed, smiled, withdrew from the door and walked down the stairs.

Watching the change of expression on the faces of his guests, Nambiar assumed that the visit of his Lady Luck had saved him from certain indignity.

'If I were an old man, it would have been all right. But I have many more years to live, and I would hate to live under the weight of indignity, with my head bowed. You two are also young. Will you be able to live bearing the burden of infamy ... how would you stand it?' Hope and faith were reflected in Nambiar's voice.

'Anyway, we will inform you tomorrow morning.' Saying so much in a grave tone, the editor and his companion parted the curtains in the room—now sanctified by the touch of that gracious lady—and left it.

Once they reached the bottom of the stairs, the editor turned around and asked, 'What say you? Do you still plan to write that article?' to which the reporter replied with wonder in his words, 'What? Didn't you see that Goddess yourself?'

Sahityaratnakaram lost an excellent scoop. The reporter lost the incentive money that might have been his for exemplary reporting. And Nambiar learnt a lesson. Fortunately, his wife's faith in him remained intact.

That night, when the editor and his companion sat down to dinner, they spoke about the Nambiar episode. Would that simpleton go to the extent of committing suicide that very night, fearing the infamy in store for him? A letter—informing Nambiar that the publishing house had decided not to expose his 'mischief' in view of his family's high status—was dispatched to him through a servant of the Press that night itself, after which, the editor went to bed.

ABHINAVA CHANDU MENON (THELAPURATH NARAYANAN NAMBI)

The Second Marriage of Kunju Namboodiri

'WHAT KUNJU IS doing is quite unkind. I have now become instrumental in causing all the misery that innocent girl is going through. I am unable to bear the thought. Only Thottasseeri can find a solution to this problem. He must seriously apply his mind to it. I know Kunju holds Thottasseeri in high esteem,' said Achan Namboodirippad.

'Of course, I shall do my best,' replied Thottasseeri Namboodiri. 'You know that if I have your permission, I won't bother about Kunju's opinion—as it happened in the matter of his betrothal. When I think of the misery of that poor antharjanam,[1] I am

---

1 Namboodiri woman. Anthar: in doors; Janam: person/existence.

Originally published in Malayalam as 'Kunju Namboodiriyude Randaam Veli' by *Lakshmibhai Pusthakam*, Number 2/June 1916.

inclined to try out even the things that I am not familiar with. What is the state of affairs now?'

'The less said, the better. I have kept it secret. Kunju and his wife haven't met after the auspicious hour of their consummation … I tried to reprimand him. Face to face, Kunju has either nothing to say or only senseless answers to my queries. The matter is very serious.'

'What do you mean, "senseless"? What is it?'

'There are several things …

'How many men-at-arms do the Mullackal family have in their employ—he says a betrothal conducted without considering such aspects is below his stature. This is one of his reasons. Is it always possible to marry only into a renowned noble family? When some youngsters like you make a fuss over consanguineous marriages, how can one complain about arranging a match with an unblemished erudite family, like hers? Then he says the girl isn't pretty enough. Anybody will say his vision must be jaundiced. He has gone and told Ilappalli that he will go ahead and marry a second time. As long as I live, I won't allow it. But at the same time, our family needs an heir …'

Thottasseeri said with a smile: 'In the last-mentioned matter, can Kunju be held guilty?'

Achan Namboodiri raised his voice: 'I understand what you mean. Your insinuation is to *my* second marriage. Mind you, I treat them both equally. I know people blame me for *maintaining* two temple-bound women on the side and formal relations with two more Nair ladies. When there are consorts available through accepted norms of alliance in the permitted quarters of society, why should I deny myself the pleasure? They are ours for the taking.

The Second Marriage of Kunju Namboodiri

Moreover, I am in a position where I have the means to give two bits of cloth[2] to the girls I choose. Apart from all of them, don't we have one or two slaves here as well? Therefore, I continue with my alliances, that is all. All the same, two days after my wives complete their menstrual cycle each month, I do my duty by sleeping with them. Isn't that all there is to the duties of the head of a household? The first proof of that is Kunju himself. Kunju's problem is different. On his birthday, he refused to allow his wife to even drink a drop of water. That pierced my heart. Is this good behaviour? Thottasseeri, please be firm with him.'

'I shall try,' said Thottasseeri and took leave of the Namboodiri for the time being.

Vazhappuram Mana was known all over Kerala for its high status and great wealth; Achan Namboodiri was its karanavar (the head) and sixty-five years old. Of his two sons, Kunju Namboodiri was the elder. He began to visit a Warrier family soon after he completed his religious studies. The father did not display any discomfort at that because he himself had an affair going on, in that very house. This way, the son's alliance matured. It became an accepted union. There were many other houses Kunju would visit as and when it suited him. This way, like many before him, Kunju Namboodiri became a veritable womanizer. He developed an aversion to women of his own community. The ladies of his own illam he derided for their poor attire, poor ornaments, lack of grace, and he scorned them to the extent that he promised all his

---

2 An accepted ritual of giving a length of clothing (called 'Pudava') to a girl to indicate his acceptance of her as his concubine, and that he would provide for her.

lovers that he would never marry one of his own kind, uncultured as they were. That is when he had to give in to his father's wishes and marry a girl from his own community—an antharjanam.

What happened thereafter is what is detailed above.

The alliance from Mullakkilledam was perfect in every way. Sridevi, who was Kunju's young bride, was truly a *Sridevi* to his illam. Her behaviour was exemplary. Because she was married off at a very young age, she lived and behaved like a little girl, utterly innocent of the role of a husband in her life.

During the time of this story, as the antharjanam spent her days in tears and sorrow, the systems and the regimen observed in the kitchen began to suffer. Thottasseeri Thrivikraman Namboodiri, although young of age, had wisdom beyond his years in matters pertaining to knowledge and manners. His ability to turn around people of all types to his way of thinking was truly laudable. The day after Namboodiripad spoke to him, Thrivikraman Namboodiri arrived at the mana.[3] Kunju Namboodiri invited him to tea and escorted him to his pathayapura.[4] Whenever Thottisseeri visited the mana, he would have his tea with Kunju. They began to talk after tea. Beginning with, 'I left early yesterday because it was already late,' Thrivikraman apprised Kunju of his father's concern and what he had told him about Kunju and his wife. Not that Kunju did not counter every line with a reason of his own. It is difficult to detail everything the two said to each other. But I do not have the courage to hide from the reader some of the amusing parts of their conversation.

---

3 The residence of a Namboodiri, also called an illam.
4 Outhouse.

The Second Marriage of Kunju Namboodiri

Thottasseeri: 'Can you say that? Mustn't you listen to your father and do as he bids you to?'

'That is my wish too. Achan has many concubines apart from two formal marriages. I haven't managed to do so much, have I? Parents want their children to become like them, don't they? But with this action of his, father seems to have contracted tuberculosis. I am trying my best to avoid it.'

'It is very sad that you don't give a thought to that girl's plight. Her basic nature is very sweet. There isn't the slightest flaw in her figure. Isn't she the Goddess of Prosperity to the tharavad? Her horoscope is extraordinary! I was there when they studied her chart. In a girl's chart, the ninth house must be strong. The astrologer Korukutty said that he hasn't seen such a good horoscope in recent years. Her seventh house is also sumptuous. The fourth and fifth houses are brilliant!'

Kunju blurted out: 'Let the hundredth house or the two hundredth house be exalted. I always wanted to expose these fraudulent astrologers. If I had done so, what would happen to your fourth house and fifth house?'

Finally, Kunju Namboodiri declared firmly that if the illam must have an heir, he must remarry. Needless to say, it dismayed Sridevi's father and others. That saintly man prayed to all the Gods he propitiated in his daily worship.

Achan Namboodiripad put his foot down and said that he wouldn't give in to Kunju's demand for a second marriage even if the mana fell to ruins. 'In that case, get married without informing father … He will relent later … Things must fall in place …'—such was the advice of Kunju's friends. Therefore, Kunju entrusted the work of his wedding plans again to Thrivikraman Namboodiri.

Kunju Namboodiri detailed his specifications for a bride to Thottasseeri and once the burden of finding a suitable bride fell on his shoulders, the latter set out in search of one and returned after two months. Conveying with his expression that he was successful in his pursuit, Thottasseeri had his dinner and later sat with Kunju, describing his travel late into the night.

Kunju said: 'You are indeed very clever! I know for a fact that Muthukinkadu has sworn that he will never send his daughter anywhere north of Aluva. You have convinced him to do so! As a matter of fact, I have heard that his daughter is the only girl in our community said to be passable as a bride. I had thought that you would but return a Thota-sseeri ('thota' means failed) at the end of it all,' said Kunju, teasing the other about his name.

'The name of my illam doesn't mean what you imply. Haven't you heard of "Thottam"? The tantric ritual performed by the Nairs and the washerman communities to invoke the power of the poltergeists is called "Thottam". That is what I also employed.'

'The place is quite far away. How far do we have to go after getting off the train?'

'It is about twenty-two miles away. Of the two rivers on the way, one is fairly wide. We have to cross them by ferry boat; there's no other way.'

Kunju Namboodiri was firm: 'If you are with me, I have nothing to fear.'

Soon, Kunju Namboodiri and Thottasseeri Namboodiri began their trip after giving a vague explanation to the people in the Mana. Murukinkadu illam was a hundred miles away. What if there wasn't a train to cover the distance? Thottasseeri had ensured that Murukinkadu Namboodiri would arrange for all the people and other aspects needed for the ritual of the betrothal, even before embarking on the journey with Kunju. He had opined that a servant as help was inconvenient. When they got off the train, their journey continued in a bullock cart. Right from the start of the trip, their discussion was about the courtesy of the Murukinkadu illam and the girl's intellect. Nothing else was talked about till then. Kunju Namboodiri's thoughts, which strayed in all directions, returned to settle upon his second marriage. He felt elated to think that he would be the one to put an end to the infamy his father had gained as a man who enjoyed a multiplicity of women. After some time, they reached Olamkali ferry.

There was a large ferry and a small dugout in the jetty. When they saw that the ferry boat was full of lower castes, the Brahmin youths decided to take the dugout to cross the river. Kunju knew that Thottasseeri was an expert sculler. Ignoring the ferryman's query, 'Will the "Thirumeni" duo be able to row across?' Thottasseeri picked up the quant pole and stepped into the small dugout. Kunju followed. After a small stretch of the crossing, the boat began to wobble. Water seeped into the dugout. Namboodiripad began to panic. He thought Thottasseeri had failed this time. He yelled and hooted for help. Ferrymen on the coast began to rush to their help. The ferry boat turned towards them. For as long as he could, Namboodiri tried to keep the boat afloat, but soon it capsized. It sank for a while, but Kunju was in the firm grip of Thrivikraman Namboodiri. By then the ferry boat reached them. They were lifted aboard and taken safely back to the shore.

Thottasseeri escaped unhurt. But Namboodiripad had fainted. All the water that had entered Kunju was flushed out with the usual techniques of the time. What Thottasseeri did was to engage a cart and return to base. Somewhere near a railway station was an illam where he had an alliance. So that is where they went. The people of the house were very courteous and helpful. Right off, they began the treatment that Kunju Namboodiripad needed and sent word to Vazhappuram Mana, following which Achan Namboodiri and others reached there the very next day. When Thottasseeri explained the whole episode, Achan was very upset. Still, he consoled himself, saying *what might have taken the eye merely scratched the face.* Kunju Namboodiripad was better, but his fever raged, and he had not regained consciousness yet.

Kunju Namboodiripad came to his senses at four in the evening one day. When he opened his eyes wide, what he saw was a small face with studs in her ears and a line of holy ash smeared across the forehead. The face was well composed but stained by the tears streaming down her cheeks. Realizing that he was alone with her, Kunju wrapped his arm around that little body and drew her to him and began to talk. As he was still weak and incoherent, all that angelic girl could do was to weep in reply. Soon, Kunju began to recover as his fever left him. His fatigue abated. Matters came to a point when only if this girl nursed him, he would obey all the strictures imposed by the remedy.

Two days later, Thrivikraman Namboodiri came to him and asked with a smile: 'What if we had crossed the river?'

That is when Kunju grasped the fact of the matter. Once he set out for his second marriage, all he could think of was the wedding ceremony. Even when Thottasseeri spoke to him, he was deliberately ensuring that Kunju thought of nothing else. Even as the boat sank, his mind was full of his marriage-to-be. He regained consciousness two days later. When he came to, he assumed that the girl before him was his new bride. There was nothing that diffused his perception of the situation. Being completely emaciated, he could only wallow in the nursing of his beloved and praise every act of hers—nothing else could enter his mind. Because his last thoughts before the boat sank remained with him, when he saw the antharjanam by his bed, he presumed that his (second) wedding had taken place. Previously, every time he saw his first wife, Sridevi, she would turn around as custom demanded, because of which he had not been able to decide if she was beautiful or her figure lithe and attractive. Her nursing was more heartening than he could ever dream of. Eventually, Kunju came to realize where he lay indisposed and who was nursing him when Thottasseeri explained everything. Two weeks later, Kunju Namboodiripad recovered fully, and along with his family, returned to their own mana and lived on happily.

All the good fortune Kunju had hoped would come to him through a second marriage was already his from his first. He accepted now that Sridevi's horoscope was ideally matched with his and regretted that he had treated her with scorn and derision for a long while for no reason at all. From then on, Kunju Namboodiripad lived a happy life committed to his one and only consort.

There is a talk in town that Thottasseeri deliberately overturned the boat.

THACHATTE DEVAKI NETHYARAMMA

An Ideal Wife

The IMPACT OF the assault sent her to the floor. As she hit the floor, her forehead struck the edge of the table and bruised badly. At the start of wedded life, it is impossible to envisage whether or not such incidents would occur later. But so soon! Even a year hadn't passed ... That monster of a man stood staring at her with a smug expression. A ruthless smile played on his lips.

The overseer of their lands had found a way to wring dry some hapless tenant. He reached just in time to ask for the approval of his master. He was certain that he would get permission. Still, ought he not to ask?

When he saw the overseer approaching, the master quickly went to the door. He was worried that the man might have seen his wife lying on the floor. 'Govinda! A diamond in Janaki's trinket is

---

Originally published in Malayalam as 'Oru Yadhartha Bharya' by *Lakshmibhai Pusthakam*, number 10/February, 1919.

somewhere on the floor. She is looking under the table for it. Don't step in here. Go fetch a broom. We must sweep the floor to find it.'

After two minutes, Janakiamma stood up.

'She has found it! No need for a broom,' shouted Raghava Kaimal to his servant.

The freedom she enjoyed before she was married to him, the happiness and joy she dreamt would be hers after she married him … Instead, the frequent insults she had to endure in that house after she entered as a wife—above all, the assault just now—passed through her mind in a flash. She felt anger, disgust, a longing for vengeance and whatever else all at the same time. She thought no woman had ever faced so much indignity in her life.

'You have no right to hit me just because I went to a neighbour's house.'

'Better keep silent. Else you will get some more. Who is to question me?'

'I will pay you back for this,' she said, walking into her bedroom.

With a sarcastic smile, the man watched her walk away.

A well-appointed bedroom, decorated with expensive articles. She fell on a couch and lay there crying for an hour with all kinds of emotions smothering her. Her forehead hurt badly. Suddenly, she jumped up. She picked up an earthenware jug full of water from the table and washed her face. She stood in front of the mirror, gathered her hair and tied it into a knot behind her head. She erased all signs of weeping from her face.

'I will wreak vengeance on this evil man. God has shown me the way,' she laughed.

This is when the servant maid Ammu stepped in. While she

wept, Janakiamma had not noticed the passing of time. She looked at Ammu to ask what she wanted.

'Kochammae[1]! The time is half past five. You said you were going to the chorunu[2] at the Madhom[3] of Mannil. Isn't it scheduled for seven? It is time to get ready for your bath. The house is two hours away.'

'Oh, I completely forgot. Good you came in. Have you prepared my bath?'

'Yes. I placed warm water and soap in the bathhouse.'

Janakiamma was the only daughter of her parents. She had lost her mother when she was just fourteen. Her father doted on her and had brought her up with great affection. Few were the girls who could manage a household as Janaki could. That was an accepted fact. Four years after her mother's death, her father decided to remarry. It occurred to her mind that her father was planning to remarry because her own management of the house was not good enough. It was no use telling her that he, her father, and his bride wanted Janakiamma to continue to stay with them. The day her stepmother arrived, she shifted to her mother's elder sister's residence. The father set apart a portion of his property for Janakiamma.

It was while staying with her aunt that she met Raghava Kaimal. He was related to her aunt's husband and immensely rich. When the wedding was decided and her father was informed, he had not approved of it. He knew Kaimal's nature very well and

---

1 Young Mistress.
2 Grain of rice given to a baby auspiciously—its first solid meal.
3 Brahminical residence.

had said so to his daughter. Father's disapproval only hardened the daughter's resolve to marry that very man. The wedding took place. Within the first month, Janakiamma began to understand Kaimal's attitude. He was very unkind to his servants, because of which no one liked to work for him. When he was in a bad mood, he would treat her like a servant maid.

'Why did you marry me?' Janakiamma asked her husband one day, summoning all her courage.

'Is that what you want to know? You thought you were more exalted in status than all of us. I had a strong desire to pull you down from that perch and trample you underfoot and squash your conceit. There was no other way to do this, except through marriage.'

Both the husband and wife entered the carriage to attend the chorunu. It was their first meeting after the ugly scene that morning. They pretended everything was normal; only the tell-tale bruise on the swollen forehead remained.

'Our horse-carriage needs repair. I forgot to get it done. Remind me tomorrow morning after breakfast. I have to go to Thrissur today, soon after lunch.'

On hearing that he was leaving for Thrissur, Janakiamma's face brightened.

The chorunu went off well. Kaimal and a few others were sitting in the front room playing cards. Meanwhile, Janakiamma and Balakrishna Menon stood on the verandah upstairs, talking self-consciously, trying not to arouse suspicion in others.

Balakrishna Menon was an engineer in Burma on a monthly salary of Rs 500. Janaki and he had been fond of each other since childhood. He had gone to Burma four or five years ago. It was only when he returned home on leave that he learnt that the love of his life had already become someone else's. Balakrishna Menon's reappearance stoked the fires of passion in Janakiamma: *Why should one sacrifice the happiness of one's life for the sake of a heartless man determined to harm one? Cheating on such a man is not going to give her pangs of guilt. Her heart belongs to someone else. So, she must leave with Balakrishna Menon according to the dictate of her heart. People may raise a scandal. So let them. What of it? Was there a better way to take revenge on that animal?* These were the thoughts crossing her mind when Janakiamma lay on the floor after the morning's assault.

She spoke to Balakrishnan: 'I came today only because I could meet you here.'

'Janu! My good fortune that you thought so. What can I do? I now feel that I ought not to have left this country in the first place. I might have waited to discuss our future together before going.'

'No point in talking of things past. Plan what can be done next.'

'Anyway, I am happy to see you are happily married.'

'Happily married? Look at my forehead! Did you hear what I said when some of the guests asked me about the bruise? I said my head struck a table—and they smiled! Guess what really happened.'

'Tell me!'

'That evil man struck me and threw me down. My forehead hit the corner of the table as I fell.'

Balakrishna Menon shivered with rage. If Kaimal had been there just then, it is difficult to say what might have transpired.

'Isn't there a solution for all this?'

'Yes. It is in your hands.'

'In my hands? Janu! Even my life is in your hands. What is it? Tell me!'

An Ideal Wife

Janakiamma dithered for a while. Balakrishnan's anxiety grew.

'I shall go to Burma with you.'

'Janu! You must be joking. You make me happy beyond my wildest dreams.'

'I'm serious. Look at my temple. How much more can a woman tolerate?'

'I am blessed; when should we leave? You must have thought it all out.'

'Tomorrow, he will take the 12:30 p.m. train to Thrissur. We can catch the 2:10 p.m. train to Madras. You must come to our house in your carriage at 1:00 p.m. I shall tell the servants that I am off to visit my father.'

The next morning, the husband and wife had breakfast together. As instructed the previous day, Janaki reminded her husband about the repairs to be done on the horse cart, to which he responded: 'That is my personal matter; I'll take care of it. You're very adept at interfering with other people's affairs.'

Without any change of expression, Janakiamma got up and went inside. Such incidents had become commonplace in that house. After lunch, Kaimal went to Thrissur.

Janakiamma stuffed all the ornaments her father had given her into a leather suitcase, along with some clothes. To the servant maid who wanted to know the reason for the packing, she merely said that she was going to see her father.

As the time for departure drew near, her heart began to hammer in her chest. For a brief moment, she would revel thinking of the happy future awaiting her but the very next moment she would be crestfallen wondering if things would not turn out as planned ...

She kept waiting with these thoughts in her mind. The clock struck one. Her anxiety doubled. Balakrishnan's horse-drawn cart arrived; he stepped out of the carriage. Janakiamma walked to the exit gate.

Both of them got into the carriage. The cart began to travel very fast. As it turned a bend on the road, the horse whinnied and stopped abruptly as if it had been startled by something. Both of them looked out. Spread-eagled near a pile of stones was a man bleeding profusely. Two or three people were standing over him. They recognized Raghava Kaimal, who had been thrown from a cart that had turned turtle. Janakiamma jumped out of the carriage.

Balakrishnan shouted after her: 'Janu! We will miss the train if we are late!'

Janu replied: 'Let it go. My place is next to my husband.'

Unable to grasp what was going on, Balakrishnan Menon froze in his seat.

'Serving my husband is my solemn duty. I must not desert him in this state.'

Balakrishnan gazed silently at the scene with unseeing eyes. Then he regained his composure.

'Never before have I felt the kind of love and respect for you that I do now.'

AMBADI KARTHYAYANIAMMA, BA

Conscience and Avarice

THE DAY WAS ending ... In a major thoroughfare in Calcutta, people bustled about. As it was Christmas Eve, the shopkeepers were closing shop and returning home earlier than usual. By about six o'clock in the evening, all the shops had shut down and the crowd of people had thinned. A youngster who had been watching impatiently till then seemed to wake up with a start and began to look all around. Except for a single shop on the corner of the street, all others had closed. Our youngster, Mohandas, hurried towards that shop. As he approached it, he realized that two or three customers had not left yet. Mohandas stood still for a moment as if unsure whether his intended plan would work. He stood staring at the ground for a while. He looked down at his tattered clothes and dusty feet. He jumped when he heard the sound of the customers leaving. His face lit up suddenly. Shouting, 'Salaam, Sir!' he rushed into the shop. The shopkeeper had begun to close portions of the

---

Published originally in Malayalam as 'Manassakshiyum Mohavum' by *Kairali Pusthakam*, issue 12/Feb–March 1920.

shop in stages. 'You know very well it's Christmas Eve today and that all the shops are closed. The streets are deserted. I ought to charge you double for troubling me at this odd hour,' said the shopkeeper looking intently at Mohan's face. Due to the brilliance of the light in the shop or for whatever reason, Mohan lowered his glance to the floor with obvious discomfort. The shopkeeper's intense look of distrust unnerved him.

'Please state what you need soon; I am in a hurry to leave.'

'It is Xmas. I have come to buy a little something for my friends. I know I ought not to be troubling you for a small matter like this. I need not tell you how important it is to acquire a wealthy bride.'

The shopkeeper, though not convinced by what Mohan said, smiled and said: 'Whatever the fact of the matter, if you are about to win a wealthy bride, I won't stand in your way. I shall look for some gift suitable for your friends.'

When the man bent over to pick up something, Mohan, who had been watching every move of his, flinched. His face, which had paled a while agom suddenly flushed with emotion. Within a span of half a minute, his face resumed its normal state. When the shopkeeper proffered a very beautiful mirror, Mohan's hand was trembling violently. Fortunately, the former did not notice it.

'Oh! A mirror!' Mohan asked in a hushed tone.

'Yes. Wouldn't a mirror be a nice gift for a woman?'

Mohan showed surprise. 'A mirror for a lady? Your lack of thought is alarming. Look into this mirror. What do you see there? Don't the eyes we see in it remind us of all our wicked acts? Isn't this the cursed article that reminds us of all our past sins? A pity. Are you so heartless?'

The shopkeeper did not like Mohan's attitude at all.

'Your talk is meaningless. Are you drunk? If so, let me remind you that I don't have the time to play around with you. Tell me if you need a specific article. Otherwise, please leave!'

'Don't be cross! Show me something else.'

'Maybe this will interest you,' saying so, the man again stooped to pick up something from another box. Mohan put his right hand into his coat pocket and tensed; he took two steps forward with a deep sigh. It is difficult to describe the emotions that played on his face.

Even before the trader straightened up, saying, 'I'm sure you will like this,' Mohan pounced on him with lightning speed. With a guttural groan, the shopkeeper fell to Mohandas's sharp dagger. For a short while, Mohan stood looking around with unseeing eyes. The silence around him was unbearable. Suddenly his eyes fell upon the corpse of the fallen man. He had expected that such a sight would frighten him. But as he stood staring, the impact of his heinous act began to dawn on him. Many theories suggesting that murder has a tongue of its own began to fill his mind and began to frighten him. All of a sudden, there was a commotion in another part of the shop. Mohan trembled in fear. His whole body shrivelled. If he had not held on to the table nearby, he might have certainly fallen over. To check the source of the sound, he looked deep into the inner recesses of the shop.

Ha! Such a simple sound had terrorized Mohan! It was the simultaneous striking of the clocks placed in the shop for sale which had triggered such fear. Look at the power of conscience! The conscience of a criminal drains him of all his valour and strength. On the other hand, an innocent receives the complete support of his conscience.

Once he identified the source of the chimes, Mohan regained his courage. But the ringing of these bells did cause him some distress. He had half a mind to smash them all. As the time was past seven, Mohan decided that everything he planned to do must be executed without further delay. With the bunch of keys he found, he opened all the drawers and began to stuff their contents into a bag. Even when he walked around the shop, he felt that some shadows were following him. His own eyes, reflected in a mirror, frightened him. The complications that would arise from his deed began to trouble him. Might the crime possibly go unnoticed? What would happen to him if someone suspected him? The police would certainly surround him. He would be questioned in the crowded court. The roar of the gathering and the jangling of chains; finally, the hangman's noose. Mohan's whole body broke into a sweat. He hoped that the pounding of his heart would not awaken someone from his sleep. He became aware of the fact that the trauma that he was going through just then would be his for the rest of his life. Even when he felt these pangs every now and then, Mohan did not forget the purpose of his visit. He had to find the keys to the rooms inside the shop. Where could they be? In the pocket of the underclothes of the dead man? Why should he fear anything … what could a corpse do? Mohan approached the body. How impassive and lifeless that face—which had emotions till a short while ago—had suddenly become! Why should Mohan be afraid of it? He groped around and found the bunch of keys he wanted. Outside, it had begun to drizzle. The sound of the falling rain gave Mohan some comfort. He moved to open the door leading upstairs, but then he sensed someone trudging up the stairs very slowly. But summoning all his courage, he pushed the door

Conscience and Avarice

open. A dull light was pouring into the interior through the open door. In that dim light, Mohan could discern the articles placed around. By then the rain had intensified and the pitter-patter of the raindrops had become louder. Through the sound of the rain, Mohan could make out some other noises too, clearly. The sound of footsteps, of sighs, the creaking of a door opening—he felt he could hear such sounds now. More than anything else, what frightened him was the sensation that he was not alone—as baseless as the feeling was. With every step he climbed, he had felt that someone was crouching and that 'someone' was looking over his shoulder. He kept looking back intently. Climbing twenty-four steps seemed like climbing twenty-four hills.

Finally, he reached the top of the stairs and locked the door after him. That gave him some relief. There were many things lying scattered around that room. On one side was a large metal cupboard. Mohan began to look for the key to that almirah in the bunch he had. He found it tiresome to sort through them. While rummaging, his eyes darted to the door every now and then. The rain had abated a little. He could hear singing from a house nearby. Overall these sounds could be heard the tinkling laughter of little children.

Mohan, who had been partially daydreaming and working on the bunch of keys, suddenly stood up with a start. It was as if a very sharp arrow had pierced his heart and passed through it. His hair stood on end. He peered hard at the door. Someone was walking up the stairs. Someone seemed to have reached the door. Somebody was drawing open the latch of the door. The door opened suddenly. Mohan stood blinded by fear. That could be the ghost of the man who had succumbed to his cruel act, or the watchman who had come to punish him as he deemed fit. Mohan could not even guess who it could be. Abruptly, a face could be seen at the door. It smiled at Mohan and turned around. Mohan's terror doubled. His voice was a muffled cry. When he heard this, the man who had looked through the door came back and asked, 'Did you call me?' He walked in through the door with a smile and closed the door after him.

Mohan gazed at the man curiously. Probably because there was a haze over his eyes, Mohan could not see him clearly. He did look familiar, though. He also thought the face resembled his own. But he was convinced that what stood before him was a wicked inhuman ghost. Even the familiarity shown by 'it' to Mohan was unbearable.

'You are looking for the money bag, aren't you?' asked that form with a smile. Mohan said nothing.

'The trader's assistant will return sooner than usual today. If he sees you here, you, Mohandas, know what will happen next, without my telling you.'

Mohan was surprised to hear his name spoken. 'Do you know me?'

'Oh yes, for a long time. I love you. I have also often helped you.'

'What kind of an apparition are you?'

'Whatever form I am, it won't affect the help I intend to render you.'

'Oh, no? Of course, it will. I certainly don't need your help. Thanks to God, my condition is not all that bad. You who are prepared to lead men to sinful acts without distinguishing between the old and the young—if you are not an evil spirit, what else are you?'

Conscience and Avarice

'I know you better than you know yourself.'

'What do you know about me? I have never done anything out of character. If I have at all, have I not been *driven* to it? God knows the state of my mind very well.'

'Whatever you might think are the facts, as far as I am concerned, I never analyse the reason for any action of yours. Sow and you shall reap. But now it is late. Remember, the shop assistant will return soon. Shall I tell you where the money is hidden?'

'Pray, tell me how I must compensate you for that?'

'I need no recompense. Let it be a Christmas gift from me to you.'

'I need no Christmas present from you. Even if I am dying of thirst and should you bring me water, I will have the strength to refuse it.'

'Let me remind you that any sin will be washed away by repentance during the last days of your life.'

'Don't try to make me err by talking about irrelevant things. You yourself know that the popular belief that all sins are forgiven when you repent on the deathbed is a lie. Otherwise, you couldn't have given me this advice. I warn you again as a friend that it isn't safe to go on talking like this.'

'Are you suggesting that I have become your accomplice because of this murder? Will all the goodness in me perish because of this one act?'

'I concede that murder is a sin. But many misdeeds that ordinary people consider harmless are as potent as murder. Perjury, confidence trickery, jealousy at another's prosperity and the consequent slander ... many similar deeds are serious sins. The consequences of all these sins are alike. A man's experience will be in accordance with not just his deeds but also his character. I am no proponent of crime. What I like is your taste for cruelty.'

'Is the affection that you show me based on my character? If that is so, I must tell you that it is misplaced. This despicable crime—born of avarice—that I committed is my last. I have learnt many lessons from this one act of mine. I did this because I lack the strength to bear my poverty. I have gained much wealth and a very useful lesson from this act. This much is certain—I will never sin again.'

'You are going to deposit this money in a bank, aren't you? You have squandered a lot of money like this.'

'Yes. But this time, I'll manage it better without losses.'

'I can assure you that this money too, like before, will run out in no time.'

Huge beads of sweat appeared on Mohan's forehead. All the unholy things he had done and their consequences came back to him. He believed that this ruthless form before him was the reason for all that. Mohan felt anger and sorrow and deep self-hatred, which in turn brought on a strong animosity towards that sadistic spectre.

'So be it. Good and evil dwell equally within me. If such criminal actions can be born of evil, the goodness in me won't go to waste either.'

'Alas! Such lack of thought. For thirty-six years I have been watching you intently. In all those years, never have I seen anything but negativity in your character. Even five years ago, you would have been shocked at the mention of murder. But now? There isn't an evil deed that you will hesitate to do. This is the way it is going to be with you till your dying day. Try to be content with this. Shall I show you the money?'

'Everything you say is true. I now understand the depth of my own savagery.'

At this point, the ringing of a bell was heard from below. Mohan's strange 'friend' suddenly went up to him. 'Quick! The shop assistant has come. Tell him that his boss has a headache and bring him inside. You have your dagger with you. Once that fellow is taken care of, you will have the whole night to yourself. Hurry!'

Mohan looked hard at the apparition. He backed five or six feet away from it. 'Go away. I don't need any help from you. If I can't do good, fine. I turn away from evil hereafter. I don't care if my life ends tonight. Let all my sins end this way.'

By the time Mohan finished talking, the mysterious figure vanished completely. Mohan slowly opened the door and began to climb down the stairs. There was a deathly silence all around. In his mind appeared a vision of the peace that awaited him in the future. When he threw open the front door, he saw the shop assistant. Mohan spoke with a smile:

'Don't just stand there staring. Call the police. I have stabbed your master to death.'

V.A. AMMA

A Sleight of Hand

'Here, Gauri! Your mundu is draped over my chair! You'll never listen to me, will you?' Sukumaran began his tirade as soon as he came home.

'My mistake. When I changed my clothes, I accidentally left it on your chair. I'll be careful in future,' Gauri replied submissively.

Sukumaran had no patience to hear any of it and hurriedly sat down for lunch.

'Again kaalan[1]! It was kaalan yesterday too. Kaalan every day! I've begun to wonder if I can get any other curry at all in this house! Little wonder that I am always unwell. What did you do with that recipe book I bought for you? That's what I want to know.'

Gauri ignored the tirade and asked:

---

1   A common curry made of yoghurt.

Originally published in Malayalam as 'Oru Podikkai' by *Lakshmibhai Pusthakam*, number 4/August 1920.

'What's the matter? Aren't you well? Did something happen to trouble you?'

'Did anything trouble me? With one or the other, has there been a single day when I haven't been bothered? Everyone is hell-bent on harassing me. When will all this end? The cost of coconuts has plummeted. Or haven't you heard?'

'So what? It keeps fluctuating. Since you don't have many trees, your loss will be only a few rupees.'

'Oh! That doesn't matter, does it? Five rupees lost is five rupees lost forever. You must remember that. We don't have money to play around with. About the cost rising again—that is not likely to happen. At least till the time I have sold off all my property, it won't happen. It is a pity that you still haven't understood that *silence is wisdom.*'

After that Gauri said nothing. He began to speak again: 'On my way to the workplace today, the veshti[2] slipped off my shoulder and fell into the slush. It fell off because it was too heavily starched. How many times have I told you that my veshti and mundu must not be starched like planks?'

'That veshti was not starched. It must have fallen off when you walked in a hurry.'

'Are you suggesting that I don't know how to drape a veshti? For the last twenty-nine years …'

'It couldn't be twenty-nine years as your age itself is only twenty-nine—'

'Your calculation is so precise! If only you showed this precision in the matter of money! I already have a lot of things to bother

---

2 A folded cloth draped over the shoulder to symbolize high status.

me—from the moment I step out of the gatehouse without you adding to it. I could've missed the train today. I got into a third-class compartment somehow.'

'That was lucky.'

'Lucky, is it? It is better to miss the train fifty times rather than suffer the clutter of the third-class compartment. When I found a vacant seat and settled down, I heard a girl scream; I had sat on a tray of duck's eggs that she had placed there. The eggs were crushed. The girl began to cry loudly. There was a quarrel; she collected an anna for every egg she lost. Good profit for her. Wherever I turn, I encounter misery. I can do no more. If I put an end to it all, all my troubles will be over.'

'Don't say such foolish things. Yesterday, I saw you playing with that dagger in the house. We must remember that there are many people who suffer much more than us.'

'This is not being foolish. Everybody belittles me. I will tell you the truth: one day I will commit suicide. Nobody has any use for me.'

Gauri (with tears in her eyes): 'Talking like this is not a sign of manliness. In spite of the fact that you find me unsatisfactory and do not trust me, please remember that I am unable to carry on without you.'

'It is very difficult to continue living, suffering constant harassment.'

*

When he saw Gauri, Ramunni vaidyan[3] rushed up to her. The vaidyan was a friend of her parents and someone who treated her

---

3 Country medicine man; a physician trained in traditional medicine.

like his own daughter. He listened intently as she told him all about the change in her husband's behaviour, his senseless actions and his reckless statements.

'I'm worried that he is in some sort of depression,' she ended sadly.

'Have no fear of that. I see no symptoms of depression. This is just neurosis. Don't believe things blindly. Besides, whatever he says is merely to bully you. It is obvious that he lacks the courage to act on what he says. I have the right medicine for this ailment. I'll fetch it.'

In no time, the vaidyan returned with a packet. 'Here, take this. He must take this medicine before he goes to bed tonight. All will be well then.'

That sad woman returned, thanking the vaidyan profusely. When she reached home, Sukumaran lay stretched on the cot.

'I met Ramunni vaidyan and told him about your troubles. This is a medicine he gave me. He has assured me that it will make you completely well. You have to take all of this before going to bed tonight.'

'Medicine cannot help. Nothing will. This illness is incurable. And that doesn't bother me, anyway.'

Like all ignorant and feeble men, he too liked to think that he was afflicted by a disease and needed treatment. Hence, he swallowed the vaidyan's medicine in one go at bedtime.

The next day, when Sukumaran sat down to dinner, someone delivered a letter to him, which said:

Come immediately. Matter is most urgent.

—Ramunni vaidyan

When he read this letter, Sukumaran's face turned crimson. A strange fear seized him.

He said to himself: 'Why would the vaidyan want to see me now?'

The vaidyan was an acquaintance; he was concerned about what the suave vaidyan would make of his behaviour.

'Gauri! Why would the vaidyan want to see me now?'

'I don't know. Why do you look so scared?'

'Of course not. Why would I be scared? Have I done anything amiss that I must fear meeting the vaidyan?'

In a short while, Sukumaran reached the vaidyan's house. A servant escorted him to the vaidyan's room right away. The vaidyan also entered the room.

'Happy to see you. I am sorry to hear that you are not keeping well.'

'Have been like this for a few days now. I am feeling much better today. But sir, I didn't feel too good last night after taking the medicine you sent through my wife. I could not sleep at all.'

'From now on, you will suffer no more. In a week's time, you will have recovered completely. Now I shall tell you about the letter I sent you. There is something I want to tell you. You must promise to keep what I tell you secret.'

'As you wish.'

'Then let me begin. I committed a folly that will torment me forever. But because of that, I did you a favour—a favour that I was not prepared to extend to any living person.'

'That is a great privilege. Why don't you tell me what it is?'

'All right! Your wife came here yesterday. She told me that you often threatened to pick up the dagger to commit suicide. Is that correct?'

'Yes, in a manner of speaking. I—'

Vaidyan said: 'Don't for a minute think that I have called you here to contradict that decision of yours. But to threaten one's wife beforehand with dire consequences is not the sign of a brave person. I consoled her, saying that you lack the courage to commit suicide.'

The last few words spoken riled Sukumaran terribly.

'You are entitled to think what you want. But what surprises me is that you do not have the intelligence to keep it to yourself. One day you will also come to know the facts. That is something I am determined to ensure.'

'That is exactly what I too want to know. Good; your desire is to end your life in whatever manner. My error has turned out to be a blessing to you. You will not live for more than seven days, starting from this day—isn't that enough?'

'What are you saying? That I will not live more than seven days? Dear vaidyare! Please don't joke about this!'

'No joke. Yesterday when I rummaged about in my almirah, I picked up the wrong vial. It contained a potent poison that I had formulated after years of research. I was very sorry to have lost it. I could have minted money on that one concoction. It was the product of years of alchemy. The effect of that potion is quite unique. It brings on a sense of euphoria for seven days—more precisely twenty hours after ingestion. Once that period is over, the patient will experience intense pain in his chest, following which, he will cease moving about till he falls dead. He will feel no discomfort till the last minute before the pain strikes. There is no better product than this for a man who is about to take his own life. I have tried this concoction on some animals and verified the results. What you ingested yesterday was sufficient to put down four or five animals. Why do you look sick, suddenly?'

Sukumaran trembled from head to toe. His face took on a pallor as never before. 'My God! Is all this true, vaidyare? Is there no way to rescue me now?'

'I believe not. Why do you want to be saved? Aren't you the one prepared to end this life?'

'Oh no! Not at all. I am a listless fellow. I ought not to have said such things. I don't want to die. You must save me. When I am dead, it will be proved that you have murdered me.'

'Don't blabber like a madman. Didn't I tell you that it was a mistake on my part? As for the post-mortem (Sukumaran froze) report, they can only prove that the cause of death was heart failure. It is quite possible that I may also be assigned to be part of the autopsy team.'

Sukumaran was in a state of panic. He began to sob and sniffle. 'Please do something to save my life ... If I die, you will be the one responsible for it.'

'Anybody can commit a mistake. For the sake of your wife, I can perhaps try out something. Nobody knows the antidote for this potion but I. The outcome of that will depend on your behaviour in the future. Don't eat too much. Do not touch intoxicants. Above all, you have to sport a pleasant expression at all times. You must lead a life of contentment and peace. Never lose your temper or run on about your disappointments and sorrow—lest the antidote be rendered ineffective. It is my firm belief that all this came to be because you tortured your wife without rhyme or reason. The antidote must be taken on the seventh day.'

'Yes, yes! I too think this is a punishment from God. I swear that if I live, nothing of the sort will happen again. Alas! What a blockhead I have been!'

*

'After taking your medicine, my husband feels much better. I have come to express my gratitude to you. There has been a transformation in him. I am yet to see someone so compassionate and affectionate. He does not even admit that he is ill. Says that he has, never in this life, experienced such joy. At the dining table, he no longer complains about the food he is served but eats with great relish. He only wants simple meals. But because all this change has happened in so short a time, I am worried that it may not last. He whimpers and moans pathetically in his sleep.'

The good-natured vaidyan smiled. 'In a short period, all that will stop. Do not worry about it. I am aware of all that is going on. He has been coming to see me every evening … No, no, I will not tell him that you came here. Don't even think about it.'

*

On the evening of the seventh day, Sukumaran presented himself at the vaidyan's house.

'Vaidyare! Is the antidote ready? Please say yes. I spend the day without thinking about it, but it is different at night. I had many nightmares last night. Like the hoardings of drama troupes, I felt that messages were stuck all over me, which proclaimed: *Last night!*

Tonight is the last night!! Strange that I did not die of fright from that alone.'

Ramunni vaidyan said nothing but walked inside, took out another vial and tapped out some powder from it and gave it to Sukumaran on a small plate.

Sukumaran ate the powder. Replacing the plate, he asked: 'Vaidyare! This medicine looks exactly like the first one you gave me. Are you sure you have not erred again?'

'Now I shall tell you the whole truth. The medicine is the very same that I gave you the first time. I made no mistake either then or now.'

Sukumaran (now stricken): 'No mistake!? Don't make a fool of me. Please have a heart and consider my present state!'

The vaidyan spoke calmly: 'In order to straighten out your mind and to fill your life with peace and happiness, I played a trick on you. Gauri's father is a dear friend of mine. I am someone who will go to any extent to ensure her happiness. When I first heard of your nagging ways and negative outlook, I decided that if a solution to it was not found, Gauri would be in serious trouble. Initially, she told me that you were unwell. I told her that if she did not confide in me completely, I could be of no help to her. On my insistence, she told me everything. I decided to make you understand that when all men—old, young, rich or poor—suffer the little distresses of life, treat them lightly and lead their lives with satisfaction, how joyful life can be ... Life is very short. That life must not be spent oppressing others and oneself. My method has been a little harsh. But given that I did it with a noble intention, please pardon the deed and accept it as a lesson ... This is my humble request.'

'I am curious to know what the medicine was that you administered.'

'It is Ashtachoornam[4].'

The vaidyan feared that Sukumaran would blow up. But on the contrary, the man joyfully grasped his hand.

'I cannot express my gratitude to you. Your medicine worked very well on me. It opened the eyes of a dim-witted person and made a man of me. What a fool I was! It was during the last crucial week that I discovered how enchanting and precious life is and realized how virtuous my wife is. If, God forbid, I cause her the slightest distress in future, may my life truly end that day.

---

4 An Ayurvedic health potion.

E.V. KRISHNA PILLAI

The Superintendent's Bribe

THE STORY OF Police Superintendent Rodriguez is pathetic. There was not a single misconduct on the lists of the Penal Code that he was not capable of. All his friends, parents, relatives and even casual acquaintances like us had advised him to shed some of his bad traits—a huge count. A person with no recognized educational qualification, he had somehow infiltrated the services at a low level, risen in rank merely due to heft of experience in the Force and was now a Superintendent. It is widely known that he had amassed great wealth during his service. However, there was once an important episode in his life. I shall detail it here because it is not widely known.

The modus operandi of the superintendent for raking in money was as follows: when he discovered that a tenant in the vicinity was rich, he would send his stooges over to influence the man's neighbour and extract a petition from him. Then he would summon

---

Originally published in Malayalam as 'Suprantinde Kaikooli' by *Kalakaumudi (Kunnamkulam) Pusthakam*, Number 3/February 1921.

the rich man to a trial, follow it up aggressively, with mediation by his cronies and so on … By the time the auction of the property, the settlement of a compromise deal, etc., were completed, a large sum would fill the petitioner's pocket and the lion's share of it would fall into Rodriguez's cash box. In short, the minute he heard of any case received by any of his subordinate inspectors or that a prosperous man had been incarcerated in some police station, he would order that the trial of such cases be vested with him. Once more would begin the mediation of his cronies as a first step.

Inspector Shanmugham Chettiar was a man with a sense of humour. He was also a good friend of mine who worked under Superintendent Rodriguez. One day, a respectable friend of mine was pulled up by the superintendent and after accosting him and the usual rolling-of-eyes ritual, Rodriguez extracted a tidy sum and filched a couple of imported articles from him. When I heard of this, I asked Chettiar what the matter was. He spread his hands in an expression of helplessness. I next asked his superior officer. They chuckled among themselves and sent me away. I then wrote to the newspapers, complaining about the slander, but my letters were thrown in the trash can. Thus, I couldn't find a solution to my problem. The lion Rodriguez continued his routine of dragging vulnerable lambs into his den, all the while unopposed.

After a month or two passed, a plaint was received in Chettiar's station. I acted as an intermediary and met the inspector and explained all the facts about the case. Although he protested at first, he finally saw my point and supported me. The plaintiff was put in jail. The man was both rich and old. The hawk eyes of the Superintendent fell upon this prey, which meant that his stooges had found out somehow and passed the information on to him.

In no time, the inspector received orders to stop the investigation and send up the papers of the case to the superintendent's office.

In the meanwhile, the inspector met Rodriguez secretly. After much disparaging and twirling of his moustache, he wrote a letter and gave it to the inspector who, in turn, handed it over to me. I decided to use it well to the plaintiff's advantage.

I went over and met the Anglo-Indian superintendent after a long time. Unlike his usual practice when he received me—loud laughter and stroking of my arms—that day he appeared despondent and downcast.

'Why do you look so glum, sir?'

'What can I tell you Menon? These wretched creatures called "parents" are a burden for man on earth. They are exceptionally adept at snatching away another man's wealth by telling all kinds of lies.'

'What happened?'

Rodriguez took out a letter and gave it to me. 'Read it. They have written they need two hundred and fifty rupees immediately. They seem to think that this uniform spawns money. You know how I toil daily. For that Chettiar Inspector, this is a cinch. It is the kind of money he makes in a single day by way of bribes. Where can I go for this kind of cash?'

I read the letter from his father, which said that for a certain matter, two hundred and fifty rupees must be sent over—otherwise, all their property would be auctioned the next week.

'How did he incur such a debt?'

'Says it is because he married off his daughter! Am I the one who should become a pauper for that? I had to borrow from all directions to send that money.'

The Superintendent's Bribe

'I'll tell you something. Playing the saint in life won't solve matters. That Chettiar has got a solid party as plaintiff with him. For the loss of two hundred and fifty, you can extract two thousand five hundred in one go.'

Superintendent (feigning anger): 'I won't snub you because you are a close friend of mine. Take a bribe? Me? Isn't it better to beg on the streets? Even if you die in penury, your children must inherit a good name. That alone is my earning in life. Rodriguez' children must never hang their heads in shame upon hearing their father's name. What do you say?'

'That is correct. Nobody but you bequeathed such a glorious legacy to his children in this Presidency. Some may be corrupt. Some drunkards. Yet others, womanizers. There is only one man in this world who hasn't been besmirched by any of these vices.'

I mentioned these three vices specifically because I knew that he was addicted to all of them. With this, we parted for the day.

Rodriguez's hangers-on began to visit Chettiar's lock-up regularly. As Chettiar had given firm orders that none of them were to be allowed inside, their schemes suffered a mild setback. I caught up with their leader, a head constable. I asked him to work in favour of the jailed victim and try to get him released through the 'good offices' of the superintendent. I struck a deal with him and handed him a packet of cash to be given to Rodriguez. To make sure that all the money reached the superintendent intact, I hid in the stable house near the office to spy on the constable. The head constable, who knew I would be up to something like this, walked right up to the superintendent's table and placed the packet in front of him.

'Who is it from?' asked the superintendent.

'It is from the man taken into custody recently.'

At that very point, I made my appearance.

The superintendent was taken aback. With a loud cry, he shooed off the head constable and asked me to be seated. In the midst of it all, he scribbled something on a piece of paper and flung it to the head constable and left the room.

Rodriguez began to make small talk with me. After a long while, some common friends of ours walked in. A while later, Inspector Chettiar also arrived. As soon as he did, I put up my 'brief'.

'The superintendent sir must listen. Let everyone present also hear this. A man very close to me has been arrested and detained in the police station without any investigation for three or four days. I have come here to submit my complaint about it.'

Chettiar spoke: 'Here comes your "prisoner". (Looking towards the entrance.) Hey, Constable ... Where is the culprit who has been brought here by the order of the boss?'

Rodriguez cringed. I resumed: 'Sir, this packet placed on your desk looks very good. Your name has been inscribed on it beautifully.' I picked up the packet; the superintendent's eyes popped as he looked at it.

'*My* name! *My* name!' he blabbered. By then the elderly prisoner stepped into the verandah and stood still.

The superintendent cried, 'Oh no!' and collapsed, his chair toppling with him. We picked him up and laid him on a sofa. Unable to watch all this, Chettiar left. The agent of the bribe, the head constable jumped forward. The old man yelled. The superintendent sat up on the sofa and shouted: 'False! False!' As the head constable could not hear the 'instructions' of his big boss—because of the yells of the elderly prisoner—he grabbed him by his neck and shoved him hard. 'Rotten old crock! I am not able to hear the boss's orders because of your howling.' With this, that faithful servant of the boss pushed the old man once more. In his attempt to stop the head constable from hurting the old man, the superintendent leapt forward but by then the iron fist of the head constable had already struck the old man who fell to the ground and lay on his back. The superintendent slapped the head constable hard on his face four or five times. He too fell, staggering. To prevent people on the road from watching the farce in progress at the police station, Rodriguez ran to slam the door shut.

What transpired later:

The ruse used to end the corruption of the superintendent was a little far-fetched. His old father was incarcerated in Chettiar's police station and was made to write a letter to his son for that packet of cash to reach the superintendent—it must be clear to readers by now that the inspector and I are the culprits who orchestrated the whole drama. If the old man had known that he was jailed within his son's jurisdiction or if the constables had known the old gentleman was the superintendent's father, our whole scheme would have fallen flat. The end result was that from that day on, Superintendent Rodriguez never acted unjustly. He now lives in Bangalore comfortably, drawing a decent pension. But after being shoved by the head constable in the presence of his son, the old man didn't survive long. On the other hand, with the superintendent's mighty slaps, only three teeth flew out of the head constable's head.

MALABAR K. SUKUMARAN

Cuni's Remedy

Seated on the corner of a tattered reed mat—spread out on the southern end of the eastern verandah of my house, I was daydreaming of meaningless things, flicking off now and then the stubborn flies trying to settle on my nose. My wife came holding a net and sat next to me.

'There's no rice left,' she said.

'There's no money either.'

'How can we cook?'

'Not unless we get a loan.'

'It's always, loan, loan, loan … When are you going to repay all this?'

'Repay? I take loans with no intention of repaying them, as far as possible.'

'Wonderful! When you borrow in times of hardship, shouldn't you pay back when you have the means?'

Originally published in Malayalam as 'Kooniyude Chikitsa'—publisher not known; estimated period prior to 1930—*Kathapallavangal*, 1976.

'My policy is to take loans whenever I can.'

'What on earth for? Is it a good thing to have creditors all over the town?'

'Why not? When I die, won't the whole town mourn? Isn't that a matter of prestige? To earn respect even in death—is that a small thing?'

'Enough. Shame in life and prestige at death! Do you want to have a meal only after you are dead?'

'The rice-rites after death must be for that.'

'Talking silly when we discuss something important has now become a habit with you.'

'Speaking one's mind is the sign of an honest man.'

'Honesty won't sustain life. After I came to live with you, all my silks and jewellery have vanished. Leave alone *my* problems. Can't you think about earning for the sake of our poor children?'

'Thought, in any matter is detrimental. Except to do what comes to mind at all times, planning to do something is rubbish. When you act on instinct, it may bring good or bad results. Whereas, when you plan your actions, the result is always negative.'

'This is another of your quirks.'

'Never. If the bug that bites us and makes us jump out of bed, and remains on the sheets contemplating its next move—instead of disappearing into the folds of the bedspread—what will become of it?'

'I understand none of your neo-philosophy.'

'The example of the bug is an old one. Is the bug a creature that evolved recently?'

'Let the bug evolve or devolve, for all I care. Tell me about what I asked you, "without planning", as you say.'

'About what?'

'About making money.'

'What is so difficult about it? I've found a way!'

'Really? Then we have won.'

'Of course. Why won't we win?'

'What is the way you found?'

'Have you heard about the "Remedy of Cuni"?'

'But for the fact that *Kooni* (the local hunchback) is aggressive, does he also have a method of treatment?'

'The Kooni you talk about is a hunchback. I am talking about the German, Luis Cuni. The remedial treatment is his.'

'Aren't you old enough already? When can you begin making money, having spent so much time learning the method of treatment to become a vaidyan?'

'We won't be treating anyone. We will treat ourselves.'

'Getting treated to make money is news to me.'

'Then let me tell you. Cuni's treatment needs none of the usual concoctions or condiments of a normal meal. No salt, no chillis, no firewood, no fish, no meat—no cooking. No servants, male or female. The result: better than that of eating ash gourd. Benefit? More than that of the celestial bow.'[1]

'But where will the money come from? I don't understand anything you say. *I need no father, no mother, neither wife nor children*—if you chant this the whole day, will money bubble up from nowhere?'

---

[1] Author writes, '*Bhargava Chapam*': the bow of Shiva (from the Puranas) to signify the 'horn of plenty'.

Cuni's Remedy

'If you don't have the patience to hear me out, how will you understand?'

'How can I tolerate your drivel?'

'You can call it drivel only after having heard me out.'

'As far as I've heard, I see no logic in anything you say. If the logic part is yet to come, I shall listen patiently.'

'Then listen! If expenditure is less and income more, isn't that profit?'

'Yes. The converse means loss.'

'Isn't the lifestyle I described profitable to us?'

'If it comes about, maybe, yes.'

'We will make it happen. We have the strength to do it.'

My wife said: 'We don't spend money on non-essential things anyway. How else can we reduce our expenses?'

'That is exactly what I am saying. We will adopt Cuni's method of treatment—a remedy for all our troubles.'

'What ailment do we have to undergo this treatment for? Is there a medicinal remedy for lack of money? Are you senile already?'

'I'm perfectly fine. So is my opinion.'

'What is the treatment?'

'You should be asking that.'

'We must, day by day, or in a *pouna: punnyena* manner ...'

'Can't you please use a language that humans understand?'

My wife had not a whiff of Sanskrit. Therefore, like converting a silver coin to a chip of cheaper copper, I continued: 'Our usual fare is no longer needed. All we need is water and raw peanuts. Vegetables can be had raw. A little bit of powdered sand can also be consumed. It is healthier than sugar, they say. Together, between you and me, the total expense on food won't be more than five rupees. We will become robust. Besides, we can live to a hundred and fifty.'

'Don't mock me! If it were so, wouldn't the whole world follow the diet?'

'The whole world doesn't do it because the whole world is not aware of it. As word spreads, how many dignified men switch to it! I hear that our friend, Chathunni Menon, the lawyer, has also taken to it.'

'Isn't Chathunni Menon's health robust enough already?'

'This remedy has a unique feature. Chathunni Menon is doing it to shed fat and Balakrishna Menon to step up his health. We will be doing it to ramp up the state of our finances.'

'First, let's clear all our debts. Then we will talk about increasing wealth. Do you know how bad I felt the other day when the milkmaid came for her money? When she left, I actually cried.'

'That was your idiocy.'

'Crying because we are reeling in poverty is idiocy, is it?'

'If you don't give the milkmaid her money dues, isn't she the one who should be crying? Why should *you* cry? What loss did *you* incur?'

My wife said tersely: 'Loss of prestige.'

'Loss of wealth is worse than loss of prestige. Therefore, you just listen to what I say. If we resort to Cuni's Remedy, we will be able to save at least Rs 60 every month. That makes Rs 720 every year. Over a hundred years, we can save a lakh of silver coins, including the interest that would accrue from them. Now do you think that my choice of remedy is good?'

Cuni's Remedy

She said: 'I don't see any other way to make money. So, I don't mind trying out this form of *treatment*.'

'One more thing—you will need a little strength of mind. We will have to forego the usual tea and coffee we have daily. When thirsty, drink only cold water, avoid salt and chilly. Rice and curry are banned just as the tuft on the head is in foreign countries.'

'In other words, it would be a life of renunciation.'

'Yes. Like the Vedantins say: "Life is an illusion, yet everything in life is also the tangible fact," although ours will be a life of sanyasins, we won't be sanyasins. Life will be rather odious.'

'All that doesn't matter. Maybe we will find it difficult for a couple of days. Then we will get used to it. My only fear is whether you will be able to stand erect.'

'When I stand like Mister Ramanpillai instructed, although my body takes the shape of a question mark, the fixity of my mind is as stiff as the stem of a sugarcane plant. I fear not about being able to stand erect.'

'In that case, why don't we begin Cuni's remedy today itself?'

'Even for a matter that brings in money, you don't have to be so charged up. You have to understand this method of treatment a little more. We will begin on Monday. First of all, we must inform my mother and sister about our treatment. We must warn them to ensure that our regimen is maintained faultlessly. We must announce this determination of ours to all our relatives and friends. The whole town must celebrate this news. I have another purpose in doing this. It is possible that most of the townsfolk will follow our footsteps and adopt Cuni's remedy. This will bring about the closure of the shop of that audacious, thankless Masala vendor,

Raman, who sent me a registered notice to recover his dues. In all this uproar, let that heartless fellow also learn a lesson. It is said: *When popular demand turns elsewhere, he who thrived on it, will get his retribution.*'

'Why do you want to teach *him* a lesson? You are the one who should be taught that money borrowed must be returned in due course.'

'One must think of returning the money only when it is in surplus with him, like water stagnates in a pool without an outlet.'

'All right. I hope we will get to see a lot of money some day, even by restricting our daily needs.'

I twirled my moustache: 'Upon the voice from my lips, I swear that our money will multiply by the day. We must order a locker soon. I will make you a heap of gold like a haystack. When other people receive titles like Rao Bahadur, Diwan Bahadur,[2] your husband will receive the eponymous title of Kuberan.'[3]

This way, as I propagated our scheme to whosoever crossed my path, my friend, Mr Menon too, came to hear of it. Mr Menon is a committed follower of Cuni's Remedy. He had planned to begin to practise it after the word had spread about the treatment. He published it in papers like *Kerala Kahalam* and a few others. In short, most of the Malayalam-speaking public heard this novel bit of news. People began to view me with awe, as they would a hero.

The first day of the *diet* passed without much difficulty. The second day was harder. On the third day, an inexplicable restlessness gripped me. To a person who would shout at the cook even if the

---

2 Titles of high stature vested during the British Raj.
3 The Hindu God of Wealth.

curry needed a little more salt, living without salt at all seemed as if the curse of providence had fallen upon him. Much as I tried to contain myself, an uncontrollable yearning for rice and curry came over me, not unlike the desire a lover has for his beloved. But I decided to suppress it from the rest of the household to maintain my dignity. Even then, at times when the smell of oil-soaked mustard seeds sputtering in sambar hit my nostrils, I squinted at my wife to check if she had noticed the drool flooding my mouth; but she stood there with no sign of discomfort or misery, with a firmness of mind, like a wooden puppet. Her equanimity surprised me. Nature's laws did not seem to apply to her. I told myself that my wife had surrendered to this frugal way of life, focusing on the ultimate goal of amassing wealth. As for me—my life had become miserable. At mealtimes, my roving gaze fell on not just the snacks but even the salt placed on the wooden tray. I feared that I might have a predilection for thievery too. Another two or three days were spent like a madman unable to focus on anything else but food. I now understood perfectly that it is impossible to give up a behaviour evolved through decades of habit. At the same time, I also thought it is not wrong to act against the laws of nature. But watching my wife's determination, my resolve grew stronger and along with it, my jealousy. She wasn't one to be shaken. My courage dissolved in a minute. My greed for rice became a misery to me. I wonder if my condition of coveting food had transcended the state of that sage of yore—the practitioner of intense penance over fire—who succumbed to the charms of a celestial seductress. When the torment became unbearable, I began to use some tricks. I began to visit my friends making feeble excuses with the hope that they might serve me tea or coffee. Because I had already raved about my chosen treatment, none of them offered either. At one of my friends' houses, I shamelessly said, 'I feel very thirsty.' My friend rushed inside and arranged for something to be served. My face flashed joy. When the smell of coffee brewing hit me, I knew my trick had worked. Coffee with a strong flavour was served. That is when my friend remembered my diet restrictions. He said, 'Oh no! I forgot that you are under treatment. Please bring some cold water; make it a full jar.' Saying this, he drank all the coffee. As I had already told him that I was very thirsty, I had to swallow all the water like it was prescribed medicine.

'Your strength of mind is commendable. I couldn't sustain such a diet as yours, even on pain of death.'

I mumbled with a weak smile, 'Where there is a will, there is a way. It is because we don't try hard enough.' With that I left his house. I felt that I would be in a terrible state if I didn't have at least a mouthful of tea. Finding new reasons, I began to visit even some people who belonged to the lower castes. Maybe because I was not an acquaintance, they didn't bother to entertain me with tea. In some houses, I preached that caste distinction was anathema to me; tried to goad them into offering me something. I could have moved a mountain but not one of them.

One day, as I walked on the path along the railway station, I caught the smell of beef roasting in ghee from a roadside restaurant nearby. I halted like a horse reined in, unable to take a single step forward. Like some prominent people entering a hooch brewer's den, I looked around furtively to make sure I wasn't being watched and slunk into the shack. My heart began to pound. I walked up a short flight of stairs and stood behind a chair placed next to a table in the corner. I called out to the server boy. To my luck,

Cuni's Remedy

there was no one else on that makeshift floor. I ordered stew, cutlets, chops for eight anas each and bread for four anas. I paid the money in advance nonchalantly. In no time the feast appeared before me—steaming stew in a dish and chops in gravy in another. In my impatience to attack the fare, I asked for water to wash my hands. What came later were the cutlets and bread. I scolded the boy harshly for delaying the water. He said someone had gone to fetch the water; saying which, he descended the stairs. I began to pace the floor restlessly like a caged jackal. I heard a sound and looked, now joyful. I was happy to see the boy coming up the stairs with the water jug; but when I saw another man following him, I frowned and looked again—Oh, my God! That man was our friend, Mr M.K. Menon. Menon's presence, which was always welcome, struck me like a flaming arrow this time. I cowered more than a thief caught red-handed. Fortunately, the thought that I was not seated before the spread of the delicacies gave me courage. Seeing my relaxed smile, Menon suspected nothing.

Menon: 'Hey! What are you doing in here?'

'Oh, nothing in particular. I had some casual matter to discuss with the hotel owner.'

That is when the server boy came to me and said, 'I've brought the water. Better eat the dishes before they get cold.' I felt like dunking that boy in the Arabian Sea. What concern was it to that idiot if the food that *I* paid for went cold? I had half a mind to devour that imp of a fellow alive for his undue show of concern. With wrinkled brows and glaring eyes, I signalled to him to scoot. I noticed how Menon had started when he heard the boy's words of 'concern'.

Menon asked me: 'What is this? Have you concluded your fast so soon?'

I replied: 'End the treatment! My, my! Even if I lose my life, would I stop it?'

'Then who is being served all these dishes? The boy was calling you, wasn't he?'

I scratched my head in my discomfort. 'My brother-in-law is coming by the mail train now. He can't contain his hunger. I have ordered all this for him.'

My explanation would strike home, I thought. To my bad luck, Menon had more recent news of my brother-in-law than I did.

'If it is for him, don't bother. I read in the paper that he is breaking journey at Coimbatore today.'

'But his letter to me says otherwise. So, he must come.'

'Please be quiet, sir! The inspector also confirmed it; he received the telegram yesterday. They are to meet in Coimbatore.'

'Oh no! What a pity! All my preparation is wasted.'

Menon grinned. 'Don't say wasted. Aren't I here? Isn't the one who helps in distress the true friend? You sit by me.'

With that, Menon ate the food laid out. 'You must love your brother-in-law very much. You have ordered quite a fare.' He began to eat with great relish all the stuff I had ordered and paid for, right there before my dazed eyes.

Menon spoke between mouthfuls: 'It will lose its taste if it cools. This is very well cooked. I haven't had such tasty food in recent times.'

Menon munched away to my consternation while I sat watching him like the proverbial fox who invited by the stork, was served food in a beaker. How could I make a move? No mean misfortune, having to witness someone else devouring the delicacies I had paid for and ordered for myself; what kind of a tangle have I got myself into? A time has come now when I have to watch helplessly, while others get their way. Menon's good stars, what else? Like Lord Krishna snatching away the bride betrothed to someone else.

Having swiped the whole meal, Menon began to speak: 'Now that you have spent so much, spend a little more and round off your hospitality. Hey bearer! Bring me chops for four anas and a coffee for two anas.'

I mumbled: 'You must be very hungry,' and counted the money.

'Not that I am hungry any more. All the stuff is delicious. A man must eat this kind of food. But for your stringent diet, I would have insisted that you share the meal. The food is so tasty.'

'Oh no! How can a sage be lured by worldly matters?'

'Are you suggesting that you have no desire for tasty meals?'

'I am not interested in these things, in the least. It has become a habit with me. Nowadays, when I smell food, I feel nauseated.'

'May such a state come upon me, by God's grace,' retaliated Menon.

Having polished off what came next from the kitchen, Menon Esquire stood up and let out a loud belch. Thanking me profusely, he walked out with me in tow. Actually, it was Menon who walked out of the restaurant and I who was led out. I let out a deep sigh. Without letting on my acute disappointment, I walked along listening to the prattle of a stingy but grateful Menon.

Although my strength waned, there was no change in my wife's determination. I know by experience that women have a peculiar ability to conceal what goes on in their minds. Even then, I had never figured that, in her despair for money, she would go to this extent. She never once uttered the words rice and curry. I continue to indulge in all kinds of folly to appease my hunger. I began to grow jealous of my wife. That is when I received a letter informing me of the arrival of my uncle to consult Dr Settu. As he had a major ailment, we prepared mutton dumplings and roti for him and waited till eleven o'clock that night. We then went to bed thinking we could get up when he finally arrived. My wife slept in the southern room inside and I in the corridor. All the food prepared for the uncle was stored in the northern room—a room arranged for common use. A desperate greed rose within me. Probably because she saw me sitting up in bed, my wife told me to put out the light and go to sleep. I blew out the lamp and came back to sit on the bed. Thinking of the delicious spread on the table in the northern room, I couldn't sleep. With Indulekha[4] in the next room, can Suri Nambooripad sleep? I slowly left my bed and began to sneak into the northern room, like a thief. That is when it struck me that uncle might still arrive. Anticipating the arrival of the uncle, I decided to hold on for another two hours. An allegory of yore—Lord Indra and the Gods waited thus to wed Damayanti—gave me solace. I was back, reclining on my bed, waiting. Later, when I groped around my wife's door, I found it ajar. That shook me. I couldn't be sure if she hadn't planned to catch me red-handed. How can you trust a woman? Being a part of the male population, who can't lie without prior practice, I decided to wait a little longer to enact my scheme without the knowledge of my wife and tried to nap for a while. I closed my eyes; probably

---

4   Reference to a famous scene in O. Chandu Menon's eponymous novel.

because of the comfort I derived from the thought of the fortune awaiting me in a short while, I fell into deep sleep. I don't know how long I was trapped in that state of sleep. Hearing the clatter of a dish, I started. The clock struck. Because that clock was designed to strike every half hour, I couldn't tell the time from the chime alone. When it struck once again, I surmised the time must be 1:00 p.m. or 1:30 p.m. The right time to act, I thought. I got up like a catfish hurtling out of water. Imagining how embarrassed I would be to face my wife, if caught, my legs quivered. I walked to my wife's door and strained my ears to make sure she was fast asleep. Did she have no thought other than her fixity of purpose, to not think of food at all? Let that be. It was a new experience to steal from my own house, thief-like. When my hunger surpassed my sense of shame and fear, I groped my way into the northern room. I felt around with my foot and spotted the location of the row of dishes. Dying with greed, I sat before the dishes. I tenderly opened the lids, without making any sound. When I dipped into the dishes, I found them all empty. I sat there, stunned like a tree struck by lightning. Thinking I had groped about in the wrong dish, I struck a match and lit a handheld lamp and looked about carefully. I found nothing. I felt sheepish. I was lucky that I didn't faint because of disappointment. Even before me, a blessed cat had swiped the dishes clean. Frustrated and fatigued because of a fruitless exercise, I lay back on my bed and began to chant: *Rice namah; Curry namah* ... till I fell asleep once more that night. I don't know if I continued to chant in my sleep.

The next morning when the day broke, I heard a commotion and people shouting that all the food had been eaten by the cat. I snapped to attention, now fully awake. My wife gave me a queer look. Why should I cringe when I am innocent? I got the impression that my wife suspected me when she saw the expression on my face. When my wife convinced the sceptical that the cat had crawled in through the narrow space between the window bars, I thought she was trying to defend me and felt very remorseful.

Even as my wife began to suspect me, I went into depression. I decided that the next time we arranged a feast, it should be sufficient to outlast the hunger of even four cats. I didn't have the patience to wait for more than two days. The letter from my uncle seemed to set an example for me to use. I was determined to have at least one meal without the knowledge of my wife.

'Tonight your brother and three others are coming for dinner. Keep dinner ready!' This was the message I sent to my wife from the court where I practised. On returning home that evening, I was overjoyed to see a grand feast being prepared. When my wife asked for her brother's letter, I told her indifferently that I had forgotten to bring it from the Court. This time around, as I knew that no guest was due, I decided to gobble up all the food even before the cat got at it. Just like the other day, the people at home waited for a long while and finally went to bed.

'Ever since Sukumaran began his Cuni's Remedy, why has he been receiving notices of guests arriving for dinner repeatedly?' asked my sister to my mother. I froze. I went to bed at ten. Slept a while. When I woke up, I imagined seeing the rice and curry and all the other stuff in the northern room. If I had a hundredth of the courage and determination that my wife had, would I stoop to such a shameful lowly act? What was the use of being a man? I couldn't hold my own against a mere woman! If ever she found out that I was trying to outwit her this way, how on earth could

I face her again? Such emotions and thoughts flooded my brain. I rubbed my eyes and got out of bed silently. Just then I thought I heard the sound of clattering dishes from the northern room. Fearing that the cat had beaten me to it again, I rushed to the room as quietly as I could. I heard the slurping sound of the cat lapping it all up. In order to stop the cat from eating it all, I struck a match. In the light of the flame, what I saw startled me and made me stare incredulously with my mouth agape. What I saw was my *better half*, gobbling up dish after tasty dish, seated on the floor before the array of delicacies.

'You! You thief! Don't you have any remorse?'

'Stop scoffing! You too came here for this, didn't you?'

'If I had known of this, I needn't have taken all this trouble.'

'You go out regularly. Why did you have to sneak up like this?'

'For God's sake, don't finish the rice.'

'Don't worry. There is enough and more.'

'So, you were the cat of that other day, weren't you?'

'Talk softly. Don't wake the sleeping people. What is done is done.'

'The long and short of it is that there is no point in making money by starving ourselves to death, don't you think?'

'I think so too.'

'Good! Like balls of mud for a gun made of wood—you are the ideal wife for me.'

'Oh, shut up!'

This way, our scheme for making money and 'Cuni's Remedy' died a natural death that very minute; but since then, my respect for women has risen by the day.

V.T. BHATTATHIRIPPAD

Illusion or Delusion?

THE EVENING'S DEVOTIONAL boom[1] from the temple had sounded about two hours ago. All the shops along the walkway to the temple were closed. The incessant traffic had dwindled and the town had become tranquil. The stillness that enveloped the town—which had till now been reverberating with the throb of life—was like the silence that envelops the temple grounds after the crescendo of festival drums.

I had my meals at the hotel as usual and walked back to my house in Nadakavu;[2] I reclined in an easy chair and was soon lost in idle thoughts. That is when I remembered that the next day

---

1 A daily ritual of detonation performed in some temples at dawn and dusk, to propitiate the deity.
2 Walk-way; a locality named so.

Originally published in Malayalam as 'Mayayo Manmathibhranthiyo' by *Pasupatham Masika*, 1927/*Rajanirangam (Kathasamaharam)*, Thrissur, Mangalodayam 1928.

was when *Pasupatham* must be published and that the editor had entrusted the task of writing the 'Rajanirangam' column in it to me. I decided to get to work on it and raising the wick of the lamp placed on the table, wrote about four or five sentences. Because I hadn't studied the topic to be covered, my hand froze. I reclined on the chair speechless, rested my feet on the table and stared into the flame of the lamp, listlessly. That is when I heard someone shouting, 'Bhattan, Bhattan!' and pounding on the door. Wondering who it could be at dusk, I got up and opened the door—to find Poonjola Parameswaran Namboodiri. I cannot say that I wasn't startled by his unexpected appearance—cropped hair, clean-shaven face, wearing a shirt and carrying a suitcase.

'Oh, Chelan, is it? What a surprise! Where are you coming from at this odd hour?' I said it all in one breath guiding him to a chair near the table, going back to my earlier perch on the easy chair. Noting the perspiration at the tip of his nose and wilted face, I suspected that something was amiss and tried to make small talk: 'Hope you are all right?'

'Oh, nothing at all; yet it isn't right to say that all is well either. The problem isn't with the body, but the mind. There's no malady without a cure. The sore in my mind can only be treated with the sap of the mango tree. If you must understand that clearly, I must explain to you what I have been through in my life. I am thirsty and would like some water, please!' Saying so, he began to undress and throw his clothes on the floor. Meanwhile, I picked up a couple of soda bottles from my summer's stock, opened one and gave it to him. The man gulped it down greedily. When he was through, he let out a belch of relief, freshness and enthusiasm returning to his face. I too felt a sense of relief.

Moving my chair nearer, placing my elbows on the table and squinting at him, I prepared to listen to his tale of days gone by. The clock struck twelve. He began his story—

It was a hot day. The heat of the smoldering sun subsided and a westerly breeze began to blow across town. The huge banyan tree at the gatehouse, which stood facing the slanting rays of the afternoon sun, shone like the coruscated umbrellas on the elephants during Pooram[3]. Gurunathan, my Vedic tutor, had not come out of the western wing after his siesta. The revered Guru's wife, strongly marked by old age, her wrinkled breasts resting on her chest, lay on a piece of her clothing on the verandah skirting the northern side of the house. My Guru's mother sat with her back against a pillar, chanting prayers, already half asleep. Seizing the chance when the negligent kitchen maid departed, leaving the vessels uncovered, the homeless dog laps up all the strained boiled rice. This is when I reached the eastern courtyard to bid farewell. (I couldn't enter the Akai[4] because I had not bathed and was therefore 'impure'.) The 'Guruputri' stood leaning on the door jamb of the kitchen, lost in thought.

(The author describes her metaphorically here.)

—With lush hair, dark as rain clouds, undone and spread out cleverly with dainty hands the colour of golden stars, a long garland of blossoms hiding pristine breasts resplendent as bowls of gold—

---

3   The premier festival of the state held in Thrissur district.
4   The private chambers for ladies of an aristocratic Namboodiri manor.

Illusion or Delusion?

Caught unawares and seeing my travel clothes, she stood up hastily and after giving me a curious look, rushed inside, calling out to her mother. Since that day, I haven't seen that charming face.

Thathri is only about four or five years younger than me. When I was assigned to the Guru's house after my sacred thread ceremony was over, she was just a toddler with jingling bangles and anklets. Had I not been in the proximity of my Guru's only child—the apple of his eye—with all her childish curiosity, I may not have been able to continue to stay there learning, partly, the Vedas, even for a month. When the setting sun painted the walls with its golden rays, and while I recited the 'Othu' (ritual incantation of the Vedas) *in stanzas, Thathri, who would be prancing around the house, would come to me and, clinging to my hand, ask all sorts of questions and plead, 'Please carry me ...' I can still remember those days like they were yesterday.*

On days when there was no Vedic training, we spent all our time together. All through the day we played in the courtyard and around the homestead. At nightfall, we both would spread mats on the floor of the Akai and tell each other stories of the heavenly cowherds and their consorts, till her mother finished her meals. On one such night, when I lay with my head in my grandmother's lap and absentmindedly and occasionally said hmm in assent to her advice, 'You must recite the Panchaksharam (Namah: Shivayah!); then the God of Death can't touch you,' and then some more, Thathri came running to me and said: 'Kuttetta! Look at the moonlit western verandah! It looks like Father's dresscloth spread over it. Let's go and roll around in it.' She dragged me, without waiting for a reply. It was a full moon night. The moon which had risen over the quadrangle seemed to be smiling at the two of us. I can't recall—without getting goosebumps—all the mischief we indulged in the soothing moonlight, which was like a white mattress laid out.

Time dragged on, unbeknown to us. Thathri began to read under the tutelage of an ezhuthachan (preceptor). She was studying the primary lessons like Ganashtakam, Mukundashtakam,[5] etc. In the evening, on our way to the temple, she told me, 'Kuttetta! Today I learnt Manipravalam[6]. Ezhuthachan said he will teach me Nalakkam (digits) tomorrow. Will you too come with me to study?' She would often shower such words of nectar and soothe my ears. Absorbed in the harmony of her heart, in my desire to continue to soak in that rain of elixir, I would tell her, 'Then let me hear you recite some of the poems you learnt.' In response, she would begin to recite in her melodious voice—now stammering, now pausing for breath—a stanza of her choice which invokes the soothing tones of the flute which yearns to kiss the petals of the blue lotus. At times, when she slipped up, she would say, 'Etta, I haven't learnt this poem properly yet; it is meant for tomorrow's session'—a cute falsehood to hide her dainty flaws. And when I caught her lying, she would retort: 'I was trying to fool you!' With that second white lie, she would encircle my waist with her arms and burst out laughing. This way, the two of us grew up with no sense of the passage of time, loving each other like brother and sister.

I completed my Brahminical rites of initiation and studies simultaneously. Thathri had her ears pierced and began to dress like a young maiden. When the diktats of social norms, like twisted cords, pulled apart our tender hands and the period of innocence of two children growing up together as if born to the same mother ended—it came to a state when even to meet each other freely was deemed improper. But as

---

5 Poems of eight verses eulogizing Lord Ganapati.
6 Poetry in a language which is a mixture of Sanskrit and Malayalam metaphorically described as rubies and corals.

Illusion or Delusion?

we were distanced by our bodies, our minds only drew closer. I say this because by now Thathri had become more and more concerned about my welfare, as if in return for all the love I had showered on her as a little child.

Every day, when I entered the house after ablutions, Thathri would wait for me with a sweet snack consecrated in prayer, along with a jar of coffee. When she heard my voice, she would make her presence known by clinking bangles or jingling anklets. When I chanced to talk to her, she would prolong the conversation by asking for more and more details, so that I might linger. That delighted me too. Often, seeing our endless prattle, her mother would admonish us with, 'What is this! What do you two have so much to talk about?' This happened more frequently as dusk fell.

One day, when all the people in my Guru's house were enjoying their daily siesta, for some reason, I had to go to the western room upstairs. When I went there, I saw Thathri reclining on the parapet backrest, holding the Ramayana and gazing at it sightlessly, lost in thought.

'Is this the way you read the Ramayana?' said I and walked up to her. That was when she noticed me. She hurriedly stood up and asked in feigned anger: 'No card games today? Why have you come up where we ladies rest in the afternoon?'

'Now that I am here, I shall join you in reading the Ramayana,' saying which, I snatched the book from her hands.

'Aiyyo! Don't lose the page! I had made a wish and was riffling for an answer. Please don't turn the page that has been marked.'

'What was the question you wanted an answer for? Tell me!'

'Why should you know? Just give me my book.'

'And if I don't?'

She looked at me meaningfully. 'Two years ago, I would have snatched it back from you.'

'Okay. Then let us both make a wish and riffle the pages to see where it opens. We'll see which of us gets an answer. You think of something. I'll do the riffling.'

'But I have already riffled for what I wanted to know. Let it be the same thought. I only want that.'

In the meantime, I switch to a random page and read out aloud seven lines and seven letters from the page on the right:

'... *pole santhosham poondal*

Kauthukamundaivannu chethasi kaushikanum

Swarnavarnathe poonda Maithili Manohari

Swarnabhooshanangalumaninyu shobhayode

Swarna malayum dharichaadaral mandam manda—

Marnojanethran mumbil sathrapam vineethayay

Vannudan nethrolpalamalayumittal munne

Pinnale varanaarthamalayumitteedinal ...'[7]

'Maithili was as overjoyed as a peahen ...

... the glamorous Kaushikan intrigued—

... Beautiful golden-hued Maithili

... bedecked in gold ornaments and chain

... walked gracefully, approaching in humility,

him of the divine eyes ...

... glanced at him coyly first ... and then,

she garlanded him ...'

[Original lines are in Manipravalam taken from *Adhyatma Ramayanam*].

---

7 Stanza transliterated here.

Illusion or Delusion?

By the time I read as far as this, Thathri lowered her gaze, abashed. 'Don't you recite impertinent lines! I have to go for my daily chanting.' She grabbed the book from me and was off in a second. The unfinished fourth act of the drama of my life ended that day.

Since I left my Guru's house to return home, I studied more, privately, and then joined Parvatipuram High School for further studies. In four years, luckily, I passed the school's final examination. Soon after the results were announced, I began to receive proposals for marriage from the noble families of Thripunithara and Paliyam. As I was against this system created by some donkey of yore, I refused to fall for the inducements of the brokers. In fact, my secret wish then was to marry my Guru's daughter, Thathri. I conveyed this wish through my friends to both my own illam and Guru's, in due course. But Kanimangalathu Achan Namboodiri, a renowned aristocrat, was a candidate who sought Thathri's hand. At that point of time, the man must have been more than sixty years old. From his previous three marriages, he had two or three sons and six or seven daughters—totalling eight or ten children. There was talk of one or two secret alliances, besides. Matters being as they were, either because I was the youngest of the brothers and potential bridegroom-to-be out of turn[8], or because the old man was the eldest in his family which gave him natural precedence over others, he was the one to whom Thathri was married off. With that, all my marriage proposals ended. Unfortunately—or shall I say—fortunately, the old man died of a snake bite on the morning of the stipulated day of the consummation of his marriage to Thathri. This bit of news merely added fuel to the

---

8 In the Namboodiri community, the youngest is the last to marry. A younger sibling cannot marry while his elder sibling remains unwed.

fire of separation burning in my heart. How would that child-bride spend her remaining days? Yet another unblemished flower had been trampled by the typhoon of convention-bound oppression peculiar to my conservative community.

The night train from the west arrived at Shornur Station. In ten to fifteen minutes, the commotion on the platform subsided. The workmen of the station retired to their own corners to rest; some seated and others stretched out on the benches. When I checked the first and second class waiting rooms, they were pitch dark inside. The rooms were filled with the loud sounds of snoring, grinding of teeth, slurping. Thinking that it was impossible to sit waiting among all this ruckus, I peeped into the third-class waiting room. Oh, God! All the benches there were also occupied. Those who remained lay sprawled on the floor jostled against each other like the scattered stone sculptures in a snake-shrine. Dawn was still four hours away. To pass the time till then, I began to slink around on the platform. Some unruly vagabonds wearing stinking turbans moved around, threatening weaklings who dozed alone or in scattered groups on the platform, shouting in Tamil, shooing them away, asserting themselves. Thinking that these fellows won't let me rest here too, I crossed over to the Cochin Line. That platform wasn't too crowded. One or two railway peons were curled up over boxes, fast asleep, having turned down the wicks of their signalling lights. A ditty came to mind, which said, in effect:

'The palace, forever on watch must always remain awake—peaceful slumber pervades the hutments of the poor.'

Food and other stuff discarded by unruly passengers lay scattered on the platform, providing sustenance to the stray dogs who fought over the scraps—this also made the platform an impossible spot for a rest. In the end, throwing caution to the winds, I climbed into the vacant

Illusion or Delusion?

compartment of a stationary rake. Even as I stepped in, a repulsive stench struck my nostrils. I heard a piteous groan from the nearest cubicle. I switched on my pocket lamp to look through the partition, only to see a ghostlike form which seemed to have taken a ticket to Hell and lay there awaiting the 'departure' call. Seeing the terrible state that the orphaned woman (for a woman it was) was in, I was badly shaken. I rushed out to the platform and came back with some candles and a cup of coffee to sit next to that creature. Her breathing was strained and got worse by the minute. When I saw her condition and the situation she was in, my whole body tingled with compassion. Even with sunken eyes and hollow cheeks with protruding yellow teeth, I discerned a past radiance in her countenance. Furthermore, there was something vaguely familiar about her which troubled me. She had wrapped around herself a tattered piece of soiled cloth and had no other baggage to speak of. A battered begging bowl lay beside her, mouth open, crying over the fate of its companion. Her chest heaved and fell into rhythm with her laboured breathing—as if the residual life in that body had failed repeatedly in its attempt to cross over to the afterlife. I sat next to her and shaping the tip of my veshti [9] into a wick, dipped it into the coffee and held it to her parched lips to let the coffee drip into her mouth in drops. When almost a spoonful had gone in, the patient opened her eyes. 'Havoo,' groaned she, groggily. I asked her: 'Do you feel better now?' She stared at me without blinking. Tears brimmed over and began to flow uncontrollably. This expression of hers upset me even more.

'Do you know me, Kutta—' She uttered these words which struck me like an electric bolt—and she went on to speak through sobs: 'Don't forget Ettan's Thathri ... I can now die peacefully. I have been redeemed.' She

---

9 A wraparound cloth.

reached out to me with withered arms which resembled the wilted stalks of hay laid out to dry. I held those arms and kissed her hands lightly.

'Let me go now—' Even before she completed saying it, phlegm blocked her throat and she lost her voice. I trickled some more coffee into her mouth. Before it seeped in, she had stopped breathing.

I started at the sudden whistle of the train. Simultaneously, the burning candle nearby toppled and went out. A horrible darkness settled over us and plucked Thathri away from me. I cried out over and over again: 'Thathri ... Thathri ...' There was no response. Just then I heard a terrible noise from the door and I collapsed.

By the time the narration reached this point, Chelan's body was covered in perspiration. He was pale and for some time, he sat motionless. Even then the clock kept ticking. A large beetle flew in through the window, flew around blindly and fell in a corner with a resounding thud. Helping himself to another soda, the guest resumed his narration:

I regained consciousness. When I looked around, I saw that Thathri's body had shrivelled and become stiff as a log. It was already morning. The cool breeze of the morning filled the compartment. The crows were cawing in all earnestness. Anticipating a loud whistle, the train awaited the auspicious signal to move forward. I made arrangements with the authorities to move the body. On inspecting the bundle next to the body, I found a piece of paper in it. This is it:

[Chelan (Poonjola Parameswaran Namboodiri) began to read out from the paper]

It must be my many sinful acts in previous births, which caused me to take birth in the Namboodiri community. If I had to be born in

Illusion or Delusion?

such a community of heinous conventions, my sins must have been truly terrible. If there is a community in the world which considers the birth of a girl a curse, it is our Namboodiri community. Even so, born into such a family, I had the most festive and joyful childhood. How delightful were those days, when the sorrows of life were totally unknown to me. Above all, the presence of Kuttettan who showered tender love on me and pampered me, was a blessing to me.

—Sharing the same toy,
Playing the same game in the same playpen
With mutual emotions...
One shading the other
Such were we, little children of yore—

We shared everything from toys, the nursery, our emotions—one sheltered the other—such was the way we were, in our childhood, always together.

When I recall that precious period of my life, I get gooseflesh; not just that, I forget all of life's sorrows. As children, we did not notice the days becoming months, months turning into years. When we grew from childhood to early youth, though others noticed the changes, we were totally innocent of them. Even when my parents with their throbbing hearts realized that I was a soon-to-be-prisoner who had to be installed in the corner of some kitchen, we continued to play underneath the mango tree like inseparable friends.

All to what avail? This paradise of fun and frolic did not last long. Social conventions flung me into the dim, inner quarters mercilessly. That was the beginning of the most unhappy chapter of my life.

I attained puberty. I was told that I couldn't talk to Kuttettan as before. My life was confined to the dark and dank interiors of the illam from then on.

Like the verse says, 'The domain of the kitten is confined to the reach of the twitching tail of its mother. Likewise is the life of a Namboodiri girl in the cloister on the western side of an illam.'

There was nothing I could do about it. How could these delicate hands have broken the shackles of convention? Lament is all a girl in my position could do. Although I suffered all this silently, I got relief from the fact that Kuttettan was still in that house. By the force of misfortune, that consolation also disappeared very soon. Kuttettan left us. Along with his departure, a pall of gloom descended over my world. I felt my life was not worth living. I had wished to sail with him in the same boat of life till my dying day. A mere fantasy! I still remember with a thrill, the day when he chanced upon me as I was randomly picking a page to read from the Ramayana, *to get a divine answer to my secret desire.*

Not many days had passed since Kuttettan's departure. Plans for my wedding were underway in the illam. To get rid of 'this useless creature', the people in the illam found a suitable match and finalized the marriage without delay. The law within the community is that the bride has no right of opinion in—nor does she need to know of—such matters, as her own marriage! Like someone said a long time ago:

'Do we consult the snack before we consume it?'

Isn't that our plight?

I thought about Kuttettan. Till tears flowed down my face soaking my breasts, I thought of all those delightful days we spent together, all the time seeing his form in my mind's eye, revelling in it.

Illusion or Delusion?

I do not have the strength to write the following part. What use is it if cattle, driven to the fields to plough, resist? Or if a man taken to the gallows to be hanged—what use is it, if he yells and pleads for his life? I was told that my wedding was over and done with. I became the wife of a total stranger from that day. Neither Kuttettan nor my childhood memories had entry into that world. When my parents let out a long sigh of relief as if a great burden had been taken off their shoulders, my heart burned ceaselessly in profound distress.

A time comes in everyone's life when one is not left with any option but to accept only the most repulsive thing. A drowning man will grab at anything within his reach for his survival, be it even the tail of a snake. He will regret losing even that. The man who became my husband was very old. I have no complaints about it. But I am not sure that I wouldn't have felt derision for him, if thoughts of Kuttettan hadn't pervaded my mind so. Anyway, I set foot in the arena of a new phase of my life. With no other recourse, to whom would I turn to for sustenance instead? Like that tale about the drowning man, I even felt a tinge of sympathy for that old man.

My dear sisters, you might think that my misfortunes ended there. No, the worst was yet to come. On the fourth day of our wedding, my husband died of a snake bite. Could anything worse happen to a girl like me? Even before I could see him properly, he vanished behind the cosmic curtain of life. The boat I was bestowed with to cross the ocean of life—be it rusted and with holes in the hull—crashed and broke apart. I was left to swim alone and thrive among the swelling waves.

Widowhood! This word still causes a tremor in the nerves of my heart. A widowed woman has no right to live like a human being.

Think of the horrible pain of the dying man, whose jar of water, which he takes to his mouth to quench his thirst, is knocked out of his hands! Effervescent youth; desire that climbs like a stubborn creeper has only commenced to bloom; I had merely seen the beginning of the sunrise period when many of my desires could be realized—at that very stage of my life, everything came crashing down! Widowhood, the horrendous fiend, stands before me, with her mouth open. How on earth can fasting as penance or leaves of holy basil have the power to deflect the onslaught of the emotions of youth? Let that be.

I was to live in my husband's house after marriage—his fourth bride. Apart from us, there were even more women to serve him. What a farce called the Eldest Namboodiri and his consorts! All his life's desires had been satiated. I knew his wives, with their frozen hearts, couldn't care less. Whichever way you turn, you are blamed. You can look neither there nor here. Anything you say is offensive. In a manner of speaking, one couldn't even breathe in Akai. People avoid them as inauspicious omens. I have never received a sympathetic word or a concerned look from anybody here. What good will I be to anyone if I live on like this? Day by day the joint family atmosphere of that illam became unbearable to me.

My heart, which is going through the throes of death, often turns to memories of Kuttettan. If I derive joy from thinking of Kuttettan one moment, the next moment, disappointment rends my heart apart. On the whole, I could no longer live in that joint family. The pain in my heart had reached a stage of total recklessness.

Sisters, I haven't much more to say. I admit that I don't know why I ran away from home. I am still undecided about the destination. When the trauma got too much for me, I simply stepped out, driven by some force within me. Even though thoughts of

Illusion or Delusion?

Kuttettan remain foremost in my mind, I have no hope of seeing him again. All I remember is that at that point, I experienced an inexplicable calm I had never felt before.

Oh, what freedom! Happiness born of freedom! Heavenly joy! I drank deeply of that ecstasy. Even the birds and the animals enjoy the incomparable joy of freedom; every human being deserves freedom—except the Namboodiri woman. Why can't we seek that freedom? Look at the women of the other communities. They are free. They have the right to choose their mates.

My very own sisters! The ancient practices, old conventions and societal domination which have smothered you won't give you freedom. Those robust fortresses won't crumble by themselves. Do you yearn for freedom? Do you want to stand in the sunshine and breathe fresh air? Without a doubt, these are the birthrights of every girl. Try you must, to achieve them.

This is my last piece of advice to you.

Parameswaran Namboodiri concluded and went on to say to me: 'This letter in Thathri's own hand, written to her sisters as her last advice—you must publish it in our community newsletter. I am proceeding for my Gangasnanam[10] for the eternal salvation of Thathri's soul.'

With this, he dropped a piece of paper on the table and stood up to leave. By the time I followed him to dissuade him from undertaking that adventure, he had disappeared into the timeless darkness of the night. Brooding over my friend's unexpected visit

---

10 Dip in the Holy Ganges.

and his abrupt disappearance, I stood there in pitch darkness—God knows for how long!

Sometime during my stupor, the resounding boom from the temple heralded the dawn of another day. The rickshaws began to ply; little children in homes in the vicinity began to wail. Suddenly aware that morning had dawned, I headed to the pond for my morning dip.

I still do not know for sure if this was a dream, an illusion, or a delusion.

C. KUNHIRAMA MENON (M.R.K.C.)

The Deposit at Manimanjathu

During a span of six months, I must have read that strip of palm leaf manuscript thousands of times. Turning it over and over again, from side to side, forward and backwards, getting nowhere, I began to bob up and down in a sea of reverie, endlessly.

Manimanjathiduka malallayilnithrithikol adathrinikkabhayayil nipthadhanikshinam—Moorandarukku Moonnu

Read these lines repeatedly from north to south, right to left or every which way, where do you get? Nowhere! *Moorandarukku Moonnu*—what does this mean? What is the relevance of this faintly discernible phrase and the rest of the words in the mysterious verse? Needless to say, I was trapped in a tangle of thorns.

Originally published in Malayalam as 'Manimanjathile Nikshepam' by The Mangalodayam Press, Thrissivaperur (Thrissur). Author's note of first publishing dated 1920/21. Fourth print on Malayalam dated 1930.

C. KUNHIRAMA MENON (M.R.K.C.)

During the Saraswati puja, when I took down bundles of volumes from the loft, among them I found the sheath of a sword. I had heard that of all my grandmother's old tales, the most significant was the history of this scabbard. Members of my family say that this centuries-old article belonged to grandmother's father, Kunju Panicker, a member of Manimanjathu Tharavad, a family of overlords; and that the only memento that remained as testimony to the alliance of my tharavad with the former, was this scabbard. I did not have the courage to destroy such a consequential souvenir, so I placed it along with the books for consecration during the Saraswati puja.

A month passed. Around that time, in a newspaper, I saw a detailed report by the Archaeological Department of the Government of India. The report contained a scathing attack on the recently inducted BA degree holders from India—of which I too was one. In the critique's tirade against the BA degree holders loitering around, seeking government employment, it was stated that no educated youngsters competent to conduct research in archaeology could be found. The statement also propounded in detail that a study of ancient etchings on copper plaques and inscriptions on palm leaves could bring to light numerous details of life in a bygone era, hitherto untapped. I also read, in another newspaper that many nobles and landlords—during the period of provincial battles—had deposited all their wealth in cryptic troves for safekeeping and translocated to other provinces—never to return. This report also mentioned that there was no one now who might seek out and extricate these treasures for the common good.

When I read this, a desire to become an archaeological researcher bloomed in my mind. At the same time, it was not that the primal concern for finding a means of sustenance did not occur to me. I had heard that there was something called a research institute in countries abroad. Enthusiastic youngsters there are paid to conduct research. Our own government or any magnanimous benefactors here have no similar plans for their youth. In the midst of all these thoughts arose the memory of the venerable Kunju Panicker's scabbard. I decided that I would make such a relic—so conveniently at hand—my first object of investigation. With the intention of executing this process before I decided for or against joining the law college, I collected the volumes and the scabbard and began to scrutinize the latter from all angles. I found nothing worthy of attention on it. To check if there was anything lying hidden in the inner recesses of the sheath, which was badly coated with mildew and looked like dried silage, I inserted a thick petiole of a coconut frond into the scabbard and groped around with it. Even with this mild probing, a withered section of the scabbard fell off. Lest I be accused of destroying a valuable relic, what followed was an attempt to split the sheath longitudinally into two halves with the intention of pasting the pieces together later to retain the original shape. That is when I stumbled upon my great discovery! At the farthest nook of the sheath, a palm leaf, all covered in mildew, lay stuck to its wall! The inscription on this piece of palm leaf is what I have quoted at the beginning of this story.

As much as I felt a sense of triumph at having struck upon such a find even as I set out to research relics, I was dismayed when I saw the incomprehensible inscription on the leaf I had discovered. It made no sense at all. Reading the first words of the verse written on a palm leaf found from the inside of the sheath of a sword that once belonged to the Manimanjathu Karanavar, anybody could tell that the message pertained to Manimanjathu Tharavad—it did not call for the wisdom of a researcher like me. But would that do? I understood that if the words in those verses were juxtaposed or untangled and rearranged, they would reveal a comprehensible message—the key to formulating that sentence was the last phrase, 'Moorandarukku Moonnu'.[1] But this did not suffice, yet. My next effort was to decipher the rest of the verse. This is where I failed.

One evening when my mother and I sat down for meals: 'Amme, where do the descendants of the Manimanjathu Panicker live these days?'

'Why ask about the Manimanjathu people now! I heard that that tharavad perished long ago. After grandfather engaged in the provincial battles, the rest of the family has not been heard of. It is said that Muthachan's (grandfather) niece and her brother were killed in battle. Nothing by way of solace has been heard of them.'

'In which province is Manimanjathu Tharavad? How long is it since Muthachan died?'

'I don't have any reliable details about these matters. Their tharavad was situated in Maankkoottam Desam, I have heard. I have no idea where that place is or of the tharavad itself. Many years have passed since Muthachan died.'

'Maankkoottam Desam is more than twenty miles from here. Wonder if there is someone there who might have news of this tharavad!'

'Why all this enquiry about Manimanjathu people all of a sudden, my son? It was known that Muthachan set out from this house to join the forces in battle. I have often heard Muthassi

---

1 Three times two is six—three times.

The Deposit at Manimanjathu

(grandmother) lamenting that the scabbard that you found in the attic is all the wealth that my mother, who was in her mother's womb then, received by way of a bequest from Muthachan.'

The night after this talk with my mother, I lay in bed engrossed in thought. When I came to know that that sheath was the only asset that Kunju Panicker Muthachan had given to Muthassi and that all it contained was the piece of palm leaf that I had found, my curiosity to know what the inscription on the leaf meant knew no bounds. Applying the theory of permutations and combinations to jumble the words on the leaf and attempting to derive a tangible meaning to the verses, I strove to solve the riddle earnestly from that day onwards. As long as this subject occupied my thoughts, sleep eluded me.

If archaeological researchers had such brainstorming to do in the course of their work, I thought I must abandon the plan of becoming a researcher of archaeology and history. In the meantime, I also thought of the *key*: Moorandarukku moonnu. I decided to rearrange the verses thus: Two letters each from three words; the next three letters would be distributed evenly to the other words sequentially. When I applied this technique, what had hitherto seemed an impossible task became, all too easily, a discernible verse with a meaning.

The result was this:

'*Manimanjathu adukkalayil, nithruthikonil adakka bharaniyil nikshiptha dhanam*[2]

---

2 In the corner of the kitchen of Manimanjathu Tharavad, inside the araca cistern, is where the wealth is preserved.

C. KUNHIRAMA MENON (M.R.K.C.)

The only wealth Muthachan had given Muthassi was this scabbard. Unravelling this, I chanced upon the palm leaf with its coded inscription, which when decoded, revealed to me the location of the cistern and the treasure hidden in it. My desire to see the kitchen and the cistern in it reached a fever pitch and I decided to go to Maankkoottam the very next morning.

*

The Manimanjathu clan in Maankkoottam was a revered noble family of warriors. During the invasion of the Mysore Sultan's army, the ruthless vandalism of the forces had devastated this place, and it had since remained abandoned. The homesteads and temples had been demolished. The wells and the ponds of the region revealed the putrid remains of mutilated human bodies. There was no limit to the atrocities committed by the Muslims who had laid siege to this region.

Of late, some Mohammedans had been residing here in scattered groups, cultivating the land. However, these people had no knowledge of the history of the place they had chosen to live in. Such was the state of the place where I arrived at around four o'clock in the evening. Unless I travelled another three or four miles, there was no chance of reaching any Hindu dwelling.

Determined as I was to find Manimanjathu Tharavad, and having set out as a researcher of history, I could not withdraw from my expedition. However much I enquired about the Tharavad from the people I met, I received no clue. Finally, just as I thought of abandoning the mission, I ran into an old man, and upon his advice, decided to go on to some other places to seek more substantial information. Accordingly, through a few more days of investigation, I did gather some details about the Tharavad. The details I collected were these:

There was no longer any Tharavad by the name of Manimanjathu. The Mohammedans who vandalized the house, finding nothing to loot there, took the family members prisoners and set fire to the house, turning it into the blackened ruins it is now; the Manimanjathu family perished during the battle march and a dependent of the family sold the remaining homestead and other properties contiguous to it to a Muslim from Eranadu, whose rightful heirs now had possession it.

This is what I learnt from the locals of Maankkoottam.

As I had collected so much information, I felt it would not be fair to return without seeing the homestead and the spot where the Tharavad once stood. Besides, I would meet the Muslims from Eranadu and try to find out about the dependent of Manimanjathu Tharavad who sold them the property.

It was not difficult to locate the remains of the homestead of Manimanjathu Tharavad. What I saw was an expanse of land with very old mango and jackfruit trees and shrubbery, with a few cows grazing there. In the centre of this expanse of land, I saw what remained of the foundation of a large house with blocks of stones uprooted, lying exposed to the onslaught of weather over the years—and next to it all, a well, covered with creepers and lush weeds.

A young boy—who had accompanied me—and I walked around the house and its compound, checking the ruins. We struggled to climb through the creepers and weeds, on to the platform that was once the floor of the house. Judging from the

Naalukettu[3] design of the house, it was not difficult to locate the kitchen that would have direct access to the well integral to it. We also located the corner specified in the cryptic message. But we could not find 'the cistern', nor could we dig up the floor to look for it to check if the treasure indeed existed.

Within the span of a month, I had met the Eranadu Mohammedan, Assankutty Haji, and taken possession of the Manimanjathu property on a year's lease, having paid a substantial sum as advance. I also located Kumaran Nair in Manjeri, who was the heir to Unikumaran Nair, the former dependent of the family, who had sold the property to the Mohammedan Assankutty Haji.

Kumaran Nair was now a property dealer. When I told him that I was a member of the Thekkeppurathu Nairveedu, the man started visibly. Still, I had no difficulty eliciting answers to all my questions. I gathered that a girl and a boy belonging to the dynasty of the Manimanjathu Tharavad were still alive and the two of them were working as servants in the Ponmaniyottu Mana—I also came to know that during the time of the Sultan's battle march, this Kumaran Nair's uncle had smuggled the lone heir of Manimanjathu family through the Eranadu forest to protect him; later, however, this uncle who was impoverished, sold all the remnant property of Manimanjathu Tharavad and ran through all the wealth attached to it.

I struggled to find the araca cistern by searching all over the Manimanjathu expanse of land I had taken on lease from its present owner. According to the common practice of the region,

---

3 Conventional design of manors that have a quadrangle exposed to the sky in the middle of the house with rooms built around them.

the cistern could only have been buried somewhere on this piece of land. It was a practical dilemma to plough the land clandestinely, to uncover the hidden cistern. Even if I did find something, the government would stake a claim on the find. I was already running out of funds. As it is, I had already spent all the money I had without any reliable knowledge about the Karanavar of my family. However, I decided that having set out to do serious historical investigation, I would not return without finding a closure to my mission.

I built a temporary shed over the wrecked floor area of the naalukettu, ostensibly to begin work on a new house subsequently. I began to live in that shed but had my meals elsewhere.

My servant, Raman, and I would dig up the prescribed corner in the erstwhile kitchen at night looking for the araca cistern. The walls that had collapsed had fallen on the floor and were now all rubble about three feet deep. Through one or two nights, we located the kitchen floor and our hoes and pickaxes began to strike something that could be the buried cistern. The next night I told Raman to go to sleep and began to dig alone.

My efforts paid off.

The cistern was large and deep enough for a man to step into. It was a beautiful object of art. Inside it lay four copper cauldrons filled with currency and gold coins. Another jewellery box contained gold ornaments and precious stones. There was also a volume each of Bhagavat Gita and Ramayanam. Seeing all this, I began to feel faint. I even thought I was having a dream. I thought some demons and ghosts were baring their fangs at me. I also thought snakes with raised hoods were about to strike me.

But these thoughts did not last very long. They were temporary hallucinations.

I did not even have the courage or the confidence to go back to where I had spread a sheet to sleep on and bring back the large portmanteau placed there. The fear that someone would steal all of this wealth—worth four to five lakhs during that time—troubled me. Anyway, I did empty the portmanteau of all my clothes and made a bundle of it. Then I stuffed that hold-all with all the treasure I found and locked it. I then filled up the pits I had dug. To avoid being noticed by prying eyes, I spread dried coconut fronds and other tinder over the covered pits and set fire to it all, leaving behind nothing but ash. I did not sleep that night.

The next morning, I began my journey back home. Riding in bullock carts and on a steam locomotive, I reached home without any hindrance. People who saw me asked, 'Why do you look so pale? Was your journey tedious?' None of this entered my head. I ought to have told them to check my portmanteau. No, not really!

A week passed. After four days of scrubbing and bathing—followed by slumber and ablutions later—I felt the need to speak to someone about my adventure and what ensued. The next day, after lunch, I picked out a gold chain with a pendant from my collection and presented it to my mother as an offering. When Amma saw this valuable chain worth two thousand or more; she became anxious.

'My dear boy! Have you been breaking and boring through walls? Where on earth did you get such a costly ornament to gift to your mother?'

How could I answer her question without revealing all the facts about a month's absence from home? Amma listened to my narrative patiently and intently. I wished to keep all this secret, unknown to the government and the present owner of the Manimanjathu property, the Mohammedan. As a matter of fact, I was indeed the legitimate owner of the assets recovered from Manimanjathu. There was no deception in this.

There is no doubt that this wealth is what Muthachan had planned to hand over to Muthassi. But isn't it true that two of his heirs were still around, as I gathered? Therefore, I said to my mother:

'Amme! Will you please bring those two children Shankaran and Shreedevi here from Ponmaniyottu Mana? Just tell them you merely want to see them for the sake of old times. Why don't you send someone tomorrow itself with money to cover all travel expenses? We are obliged to educate that young man and nurture that girl for life without her having to work for someone by giving them all the money they need.'

'Your thoughts are very commendable. God willing, we can get by in life even without the help of the treasure from Manimanjathu. We must certainly not ignore the plight of these children who today work as servants.'

*

'What now, my dear boy! Shankaran had been admitted to school. What about Shreedevi? She is not amenable to staying on here without doing any work. Because of her aristocracy, she cannot become a servant here either. Not that we need one now. She wishes to go back to that Mana. Are you, Kuttan, going back to Madras when the college reopens?'

C. KUNHIRAMA MENON (M.R.K.C.)

Hearing Amma's questions, I was in a dilemma and couldn't answer her. Shreedevi was no longer a child. She had blossomed into an eighteen-year-old lass. Personally, I would discard my status as a student and become a householder and pursue historical research as a profession. I do not know if our Karanavar would appreciate my plan of renovating the Manimanjathu nalukettu from its dilapidated state, install all required furniture and then take Shreedevi and Amma along with me to start life afresh in that house. Neither did I know if Shreedevi would approve of it. One Shreedevi (Goddess of wealth) *wed* me and made me a rich man. Won't *this* Shreedevi marry me and make a blessed man of me?

I talked to my mother: 'Amme, I cannot continue my studies. I want to see to what avail is the education I have hitherto acquired. I wish to enlist Shreedevi as a helper in all my endeavours. The final say is yours.'

'Say that! I have been suspecting all this for a couple of days now. I did not like the way you have been eyeing and ogling. Shreedevi is pretty and is born to a Tharavad. But if we go ahead with this alliance, people who will not understand the reason for all this, will gossip and raise a scandal.'

'If we set about satisfying the curiosity of the people at large, there is no end to it. I shall convince Shreedevi about it all, in due course.'

*

A year and a half sped by. I am now a prominent landlord and farmer of Maankkoottam. Work on the nalukettu on the Manimanjathu property is progressing well. Amma, Shreedevi and I now live in a small bungalow I constructed on the premises.

The Deposit at Manimanjathu

Shankaran (Shankara Panicker)—Shreedevi's brother—visits often. I have decided to educate him up to the BA degree. I have already prepared a registered will, bequeathing Manimanjathu house and all the landed property attached to it, to Shreedevi and our offspring-to-be, on my demise. On all counts, all this wealth is anyway entitled to them, isn't that so?

> '*Malikamukalileriya mannande*
> *Tholil marappangakkunnathum Bhavan*
> *Randunalu dinanam kodoruthane*
> *Thandiletti nadathunnathum Bhavan*'[4]

Every day, I would listen to Shreedevi recite this hymn to the Almighty in her sweet voice.

In the meanwhile, nobody recognizes my prowess as a researcher of relics. This is the only grouse that bothers me these days.

---

4 'By your will, Lord—He who lives in a palace will be reduced to carrying soiled bundles...In two days a commoner will be borne in a palanquin—Lord, by your will.'

C. KUNHIRAMA MENON (M.R.K.C.)

The Lifespan of Aissakutty Umma

Arakshitham Thishtthathi Daivarakshitham[1]

KUMMINIKUTTY AMMA, WHO had trusted this dictum since childhood, did not actually feel any more secure merely because she wore a talisman, which was 'a protector from all kinds of evil and the decimator of fear of every variant of demon and poltergeist'—as was etched on it by the famous occultist, Chembara Ezhuthachan. Had she foreseen even in her nightmares, that she would have to deliver her baby in a shack in the middle of a desolate field with no help at hand, she would not have stepped out of her Nannambra

---

1 God protects the meek and the downtrodden.

Originally published in Malayalam as 'Aissakutti Ummayude Ayussu' by The Mangalodayam Press, Thrissivaperur (Thrissur) in 1920.

Tharavad and run for cover—even if the greatest of warriors, let alone Tipu Sultan and his army, were to descend on them.

Tipu Sultan and his army had advanced south—sword in one hand and beef in the other like demons of destruction—from Mangalore and had reached Kozhikode. The rulers of Kolathiri, Kottayam, Kurumbranadu, Kadathanadu and others, along with their close relatives, overlords and dependents had relinquished their principalities, boarded catamarans and dhows docked at sea and sought refuge in the land of His Excellency.[2] In all this melee, a ship had arrived at the Beypore harbour to take the kings of Parappanad and their close associates to Thiruvithamkur (Travancore).

In the domain of the Parappanad kings, a prominent overlord was the Lord of Nannambra. During the period of this turmoil, in 1784, the head of Parappanad was His Lordship Veeravarman. His Prime Minister was Nannambra Kuruppu.

Although the Mohammedans in Kozhikode, Eranadu and Ponnani had sworn allegiance to the Zamorin, when Tipu Sultan's atrocities targeting Hinduism began, all these Muslims turned informers and helped the marauding Mysore army.

There were two designs underlying this attack by Tipu Sultan: to make the people of Kerala surrender to the Muslim faith and loot and confiscate all the wealth they possibly could. Other than these two intentions, Tipu had no desire to conquer and rule this region.

The extreme degradation resorted to by Tipu's army included, to cite a few examples:

---

2 The Zamorin of Kozhikode.

Demolition of all sacred icons.
Raping of women.
Defecating in temples.
Burning record books.
Entering homes.
Terrorizing inmates, driving them out.
Murdering religious heads and those with a scientific bent of mind.
Unleashing turmoil in the society through hooliganism ...

By the time the battle march of the Sultan reached such diabolical dimensions to cause so much carnage, his army had doubled in size as it marched from Mangalore to Kozhikode. Traitors and defectors among the Malayalees became the informers of the army and helped the siege in whichever way they could. Under the circumstances, it was of little surprise that people abandoned their homes and moved to other lands in search of refuge. Veeravarman Thamburan[3] ordered that Ramakuruppu and his retinue shift to Nirunkaithakota[4] and reside there till news came of the arrival of the ship at Beypore harbour, whereupon all of them would go to Beypore.

Although the Tharavad of Ramakuruppu had wealth in plenty, the family lacked the blessings of an offspring. The only hope remained in the prospect of Kummini Amma bearing a child. The other two ladies in the house were too old. Two of Ramakuruppu's nephews were swordsmen in the army of Veeravarman Thamburan. Having buried most of the precious articles and entrusting

---

3 His Lordship or King.
4 Nirunkaitha fortress (kota).

The Lifespan of Aissakutty Umma

what could not be 'deposited' thus with some trustworthy Mohammedans, Ramakuruppu and family grabbed what they could of what remained and reached Nirunkaithakota by noon. By then, the Thamburan, his nephews and the inmates of the Kovilakam[5] and other associates had already arrived there.

Nature had bestowed on the Nirunkaithakota a unique feature that no other fort in Kerala possessed—a steep hill from the plateau with a temple both on the top and another down in the valley below. Skirting the hill on three sides coursed a deep river serving as a moat. From the vantage point atop the hill, one could see four to five square miles of the kingdom clearly. Nowhere else in Kerala was there such an impenetrable citadel. This was the fortress where the Parappanattu Thamburan and his entourage had pitched camp.

The decision was to perform the evening prayers at the temples in the evening and thereafter board the boats, traverse the Kadalvand river and coast on to Beypore river.

Kummini Amma was installed in a house adjacent to the fort because women in an advanced stage of pregnancy were not allowed to enter the premises of a temple. By five o'clock, sounds of gunfire came from the north and the south sides. It was obvious that the Sultan's army was approaching to lay siege to Nirunkaithakota. The only thought on the minds of the inmates of the fort was to beat this army and find a way to reach the ship anchored at Beypore. The warriors among the royals and the soldiers were concerned about blocking the advancing army and

---

5 A palace or any other manor where a king or his family resides.

saving the women, children and the elderly within the fortress. The Thamburan and the ladies, Ramakuruppu and his family were persuaded to board the available boats and sail to Beyporepuzha forthwith. Preparations began to execute this plan. It was dusk already. The Mohammedans had surrounded the fort on the other side of the river. The situation had become catastrophic.

Four little dugouts laden with people had reached the middle of the Kadalvandi river. Two remaining boats were still on the coast loading people. Soon, firing began from the opposite banks of the river; the Mohammedan soldiers targeting the people on the boat. Either because of the skill of the oarsmen or by the grace of the Goddess, three of the boats had sailed beyond the range of enemy fire. With the greatest caution, these three boats rowed towards Beypore. The remaining boats in the middle of the river—with all the people on board—sank. A few swam to safety. Others drowned to death.

The Sultan's army attacked Nirunkaithakota because their spies had passed on the information that a ship had docked at Beypore harbour and that the rulers of Parappanad and their families ensconced in the fort were preparing to sail to Beypore to embark on the saviour ship. As the Mohammedans in the attack force did not know where the escape boats were headed, they did not follow them. Their priority lay in capturing the fort and rounding up those in it to loot the wealth they had brought with them to take to the ship.

Unable to cross the deep river, the Mohammedan army stood frustrated and the Parappanad folks remained on the

The Lifespan of Aissakutty Umma

other bank like caged birds. The remaining Nayanmars[6] and the Thamburan's relatives in the fort decided to fight to the death with the Mohammedan army. They planted sentries all around the fort because there was no way of knowing at which point the Mohammedans would choose to cross the river.

Before the stroke of midnight, the Mohammedan army had breached the moat. Many of them were massacred by the Nair defence. Still, because they had not brought along their main artillery in their bid to board a ship to an asylum, they were not prepared to face the fire power of the Mohammedans. The ruckus caused by the invading army as they entered the fortress was beyond description. Through the war cries, the yelling and the sound of the guns, there was nobody there who was in his right senses. The Nairs and the Thamburan folk engaged in hand-to-hand combat with the Mohammedans and attained the coveted salvation of the valiant in combat. The weak among them just fell to their deaths. All the remaining inmates of the fort were imprisoned and dispatched to Kozhikode. They vandalized and looted the temples, the treasure chests and all the homes in the vicinity, chanting raucous victory cries as they did it all, before they returned to Kozhikode. Nirunkaithakota was smothered in blood. All that remained was a pile of a thousand corpses. Of the people who were present in the fortress, Veeravarman Valiya Thamburan,[7] Nannambra Kuruppu, the royal ladies and a few dependents

---

6 Nairs of Kerala, known for their valour, were usually recruited by kings for warfare.
7 Valia Thamburan is the title used for a king.

survived; all others succumbed to the onslaught of the Sultan's army. Those who boarded the ship finally mourned the death of so many of their own people. With sinking hearts, they sailed to safety in Thiruvithamkoor.

We began the story of the battle by narrating how a pregnant Kumminikutty Amma was made to stay in a house adjacent to the fortress—Kummini Amma, who was informed that she would be escorted to the boats after the evening puja concluded, panicked when she heard gunshots. She understood a calamity was about to happen. Even after a long wait, she saw no one coming to take her along. On the opposite bank of the river, she saw fearsome men armed to the teeth, standing in formation. She also witnessed a boat in the river capsizing, the corpses of the people who fell off the boat floating around and even the death throes of some others. She was in a state of horror-stricken frenzy, maddened with fear. There was no way of knowing who had died and what was going on inside the fortress. She decided to leave the house before dark and walk north. After she walked about two furlongs, she came upon a vast paddy field. The place was desolate, and she could find no one there.

As the verse goes:
Due to the atrocities of the Army of Tipu Sultan
Not merely the faith and karma of a land was lost,
Wealth and paddy crops, health and conventions lost to them, all the citizens left home and land, sought refuge in forests and the high ranges, and remained hidden there.

As described, the people of Parappanad, who could not go to Nirunkaithakota, heard of the approach of the Sultan's army and escaped into the jungles and the eastern mountains, abandoning home and fields to save their lives. Nothing living was left in the land where the fortress had been demolished. Engrossed in troubled thoughts, Kummini Amma walked a mile with no sense of direction. Darkness had descended and grew deeper by the minute. She could not see any more. She felt drained and an extreme weakness set in. She suspected if it could be the beginning of delivery pains ...

At a short distance away, on a raised plot of land stood a shack that appeared to be a lookout shelter for farmers. She walked towards it. Fortunately, it was indeed a shack erected by farmers to protect their crop. She climbed onto it. She spread a length of cloth she had on the floor and lay on it. In the span of two hours, she delivered a baby and lost consciousness. By morning, Kummini expired, leaving behind a flailing, female newborn.

During that very night, the Mohammedans had patrolled this field to chase people fleeing for their lives. But by good fortune or not, nobody spotted the baby and its dead mother lying in the lookout shelter.

It was ten o'clock of the next morning. Neither in Nirunkaithakota nor on its premises could a single soul be seen. Even the birds and the animals had fled from the place when the gunshots rang out. Inside the lookout shelter, a baby lay thrashing about its limbs and crying in agony. Who could possibly hear its cry in such a desolate place?

Chemban Alikutty of Parappanangadi had come to know by morning something had transpired inside Nirunkaithakota.

Ee duniyavinde aathu, enthellam ikkumathappa padachon undakunnathu! Ee haramboranna Makkal halakkakkunnu!

(What all calamities the Almighty creates in this world! And these worthless fellows here cause such devastation!)—babbled Alikutty and set out for Nirunkaithakota. Those were the days when there was no such thing as a 'Noos paper'. That is why Alikutty decided to personally go over to the fort and investigate for himself.

By about ten, Alikutty, who was in the middle of the field, heard the faint cry of an infant. Though he said to himself, *Ithenthuru Ikkumathhu aanu*! (What a dilemma this is!), he decided to walk over to the lookout shelter and check. It was when he entered the shack that he understood the gameplay of his *Padachon*, the divine creator.

There lay on the ground a lady covered in gold ornaments and bathed in blood. Next to her lay a crying infant, five to six hours old, still alive merely because it was destined to live. Alikutty, who was not by nature a cruel man, stood there stunned for a while, contemplating God's designs for man. Then he looked all around. On one side, far in the distance, he could see that the temple of Nirunkaithakota had been set on fire and razed. Far away in the fields, he could see decapitated bodies lying scattered. He stood transfixed, not knowing what to do. Coming to his senses, he climbed a tree on the raised piece of land and plucked a tender coconut. Using a knife that he always carried with him, he pierced the coconut and trickled some of its water into the infant's mouth. The baby stopped crying and soon fell asleep.

Alikutty felt that it was his duty to save this infant. He gathered all the gold ornaments on its mother's person. He dug a grave for Kumminikutty on the plot and buried her there; he picked up the child and returned to his home in Parappanangadi.

The Lifespan of Aissakutty Umma

With the satisfaction that in doing so, he had converted a refugee Kafir[8] to the Muslim faith, he handed over the child to his wife, Amina Umma. They named the child Aissakutty.

Over ten to twelve years passed. Tipu Sultan was dead and gone. The Malayalee districts fell to the control of the British East India Company. The people who had left the land during the turmoil began to return by and by. Parappanad Veeravarman Valiya Thamburan and Ramakuruppu had returned almost four years ago. Whenever they spoke of Nerunkaithakotta, their eyes brimmed over. The Thamburan grieved over the demise of his valiant nephews, while Ramakuruppu blamed himself for not being able to save his daughter, Kummini, who was to carry forward his dynasty. Ramakuruppu did not have any reason to believe—even in his dreams—that Kummini Amma had survived the battle and was hale and hearty.

Chemban Alikutty lived in penury with many commitments. By the time Aissakutty turned ten, his wife passed away. Alikutty was in no condition to live without Aissakutty. He had sold most of Kummini Amma's ornaments to meet their expenses. All that remained was the golden amulet consecrated by Chembara Ezhuthachan for protection from evil forces. This was worn by Aissakutty since childhood to keep the demons away. Aissakutty was capable now of doing a bit of the chores of the house but was not old enough to be working for a living. Alikutty too had grown old.

Finally, Alikutty decided to sell the gold talisman worn by Aissakutty. He was not at all happy about selling this precious

---

8 A non-Muslim, implied here.

ornament. But he thought he would merely pawn this gold for the time being and later, when matters improved, he would retrieve the piece. He took the amulet from Aissakutty and stepped out of his house. He headed to the Beypore Kovilakam of the Parappanad kings.

Once he reached Beypore Kovilakam, he had no difficulty in meeting the Prime Minister of the Thamburan, Ramakuruppu. Alikutty convinced him that he had always been an obedient subject of Parappanad Swaroopam (reign), that he had never done anything seditious during the days of the battle, and that he had, in all honesty, returned the precious objects and other forms of wealth entrusted to him by the people who had fled during the battle and had come back when peace prevailed. He also told the Prime Minister that he was in some financial difficulties just then and had the responsibility of supporting a motherless child; therefore, he said he wanted some monetary help for which he would pledge a gold talisman that belonged to his foster daughter. He handed over the gold plaque to Ramakuruppu.

Ramakuruppu froze when he examined the tiny plaque. Remaining silent for a long time, he glared angrily at Alikutty. Without saying a word to Alikutty, he ordered a Nair in attendance not to release him and then went over to the Thamburan's quarters.

Not just because Kummini Amma's name was etched on the plaque, but as Ramakuruppu himself had arranged for the making of it along with the inscription by Ezhuthachan, he recognized it and assumed that Alikutty had murdered his daughter, Kummini, and taken possession of the talisman. He had gone over hurriedly to the Thamburan to tell him what he suspected.

The Lifespan of Aissakutty Umma

There is no need to drag out this story any longer. When Alikutty was subjected to intense questioning, Ramakuruppu understood the fact of the matter. His anger towards Alikutty evaporated, and in its place grew a deep sense of gratitude. But he also felt a little regret that the girl who would carry forward his dynasty had grown up in a Muslim household till the age of ten.

In no time, the head priest of the Thamburan was sent for and Aissakutty was brought to the palace, and a purification ritual performed; Kuruppu's tharavad was attached to the clan of Chelavil cherna Nayanmars; [9] Alikutty was endowed a lifetime pension.

To this day, the descendants of Aissakutty reside in the district of Eranad.

---

9 Nair families who are declared rightful dependents of the Royal Family, entitled to lifetime sustenance from the King.

NOTES ON THE AUTHORS

Ambadi Karthyayani Amma (1885–1990) was born to father Kochu Govinda Menon and mother Ambadi Naniyamma on 12 December 1885 at Thripunithura.

Ambadi Karthyayani Amma was a great journalist of the colonial period; she published many articles on different subjects such as educational reforms, women in India, and children's literature.

After her school education, she was sent to Maharaja's College for intermediate studies at a time when girls were rarely admitted to college. After her intermediate studies, she went on to Queen Mary's College in erstwhile Madras for higher studies. She was appointed as Head Mistress of the Government Girls' School at Eranakulam and later promoted to Inspector of Schools. She retired from service in 1951. Karthyayani Amma has also served as Vice President of Sahitya Akademi, Senate member and member of the Advisory Committee, All India Radio. She also co-operated with the work of forming a sub-committee for Children's Literature. *Panchathanthram, Padinjare Kathakal,*

NOTES ON THE AUTHORS

Tharanga Viharam, Nadodikathakal–Punarakhyanam Karshika Jeevitham Bharathathil, Mahanaya Viplavakari are some of her important works.

B. Kalyani Amma (1884–1959) was a writer, editor, teacher and social reformer from Kerala. Kalyani Amma's most notable works are *Vyazhavattasmaranakal* (*Memories of a Cycle of Twelve Years*) and *Ormayilninnum* (*Reminiscences*). She was one of the editors of two of the earliest magazines published for women in Kerala, *Sharada* and *Malayalamasika*. Kalyani Amma was the wife of Swadeshabhimani K. Ramakrishna Pillai, a political writer, journalist and editor.

She was born in Kuzhivilaakathu House, Kuthiravattom, Thiruvananthapuram.

Kalyani Amma was one of the well-known early contributors to women's magazines from Kerala. She wrote on various subjects like women's health, education, home management, and so on. Her autobiography, *Ormaiyil Ninnum*, is one of the few existing personal documentations on how untouchability and the caste system worked in that period in Kerala from the point of view of a Nair.

C.P. Achutha Menon (1862–1937) was born to Kuruppathu Kunyan Menon and Changaramponnathu Parvathy Amma on 27 April 1862. Alongside his school studies, he enrolled for Sanskrit classes at Kozhikode. He graduated from Madras in Philosophy in the year 1885. He was placed first in Sanskrit at the University. While working as a lecturer in Pachayappa's College in Madras, he was appointed tutor to the heirs to the Kochi Kovilakam in 1886.

For a short period, he worked as the editor of *Vidyavinodini*.

He laid a sound foundation for the field of literary criticism through several articles he wrote, while he was the editor of *Vidyavinodini* during 1889–95. The nuances of literary criticism and his profound knowledge of it are evidenced in the short notes he wrote on the subject. He was an admirer of Western critics like Mathew Arnold. In his reviews of books on literature, he did not shy away from expressing candidly his contempt for lacklustre creations and mundane writing in literary studies.

C.S. Gopala Panicker (1872–1930) was a Malayalam-language short story writer from Kerala along with Vengayil Kunhiraman Nayanar, Oduvil Kunhikrishna Menon, Moorkoth Kumaran, Chengalath Cheriya Kunhirama Menon (M. R. K. C.) Ambadi Narayana Poduval, and was regarded as a pioneer of the short story in Malayalam literature.

He was born in Chittur taluk in Kerala, studied at Peruvemba School near Chittur and passed his matriculation from Palghat Victoria High School. He completed his FA from Calicut Zamorin's Guruvayurappan College in Cochin and Bachelor of Science from Madras Presidency College.

He married his uncle's daughter Chittur Valiyathachattu Meenakshiamma. His daughters, Devaki Nethyaramma, the wife of Cochin sub-judge Thampuran, and Dakshayani Kettilamma, the wife of a Thampuran from the Kadathanadu royal family, together translated Taraknath Gangopadhyay's Bengali novel *Swarnalata* into Malayalam.

Panicker, who specialized in natural science, was the chief science reporter of *Vidyavinodini*.

All pioneers of Malayalam short story writers like him were inspired by the emergence of the short story as an important genre in Western literature, particularly the writings of Nathaniel Hawthorne, Edgar Allan Poe, etc. Panicker, along with E.V. Krishna Pillai and K. Sukumaran, is also said to have been a link between the old and new generations of story writers. According to Ulloor S. Parameswara Iyer, 'Oru Muthalanayattu' published in *Rasikaranjini* is an important short story in Malayalam literature.

Chengalath Cheriya Kunhirama Menon (1882–1939), also known by his pen name M.R.K.C., was a Malayalam-language author and journalist. He was associated with prominent newspapers and periodicals such as *Kerala Pathrika* and *Mangalodayam*. Some of his famous books include *Velluva Kammaran Allenkil Sardar Sheikh Ayaz Khan* and *MRKC Yude Cherukathakal*.

Menon was born in Valarpatanam in Cannanore district. Chengalath Kunhirama Menon, who founded one of the earliest Malayalam newspapers, *Kerala Pathrika* in 1885, was his maternal uncle.

In 1904, he became a head clerk for the land reforms work of the local ruler of Punnathur.

M.R.K.C. based his stories on history rather than on contemporary society. Though the background is history, the characters and events were mostly imaginary, and the author was not concerned about the historical accuracy of the narrative.

NOTES ON THE AUTHORS

E.V. Krishna Pillai (1894–1938) was an Indian writer of Malayalam literature and a member of Sree Moolam Popular Assembly of Travancore. He was a multi-talented personality and excelled as an advocate, Member of Legislative Assembly, editor and writer. During his short life, he wrote comedies, dramas, short stories and an autobiography. He was also a columnist and a caricaturist. He was an eminent satirist and a genius in comedy.

E.V. Krishna Pillai was born at Kunnathur Taluk of Quilon.

After completing his schooling at Kunnathur, Krishna Pillai went on to graduate in Arts and Law and started his career as a government servant. He married Maheswari Amma, the youngest daughter of writer C.V. Raman Pillai. The couple had five sons and two daughters. Chandraji (Ramachandran Nair) was the eldest, the second son was Adoor Bhasi (Bhaskaran Nair), and the third was Padmanabhan Nair (Padman), a journalist and the writer of the cartoon *Kunchu Kurup*. His other children were Omana Amma, Rajalakshmi Amma, Sankaran Nair (who died at the young age of 18 due to heart disease) and Krishnan Nair.

He edited publications such as *Malayali* and *Malayala Manorama*.

K. Ramakrishna Pillai (1878–1916) was an Indian nationalist writer, journalist, editor, and political activist. He edited *Swadeshabhimani*, the newspaper that became a potent weapon against the rule of the British and the erstwhile princely state of Travancore (Kerala, India) and a tool for social transformation. *Vrithanthapathra pravarthanam* (1912) and *Karl Marx* (1912) are among his most noted works in Malayalam. The latter is the first-ever biography of Karl Marx in any Indian language.

K. Sukumaran (1876–1956) was a short story writer, humourist, poet, essayist and playwright from Malabar, India. He was one of the pioneers of the short story in Malayalam. He is sometimes referred to as Malabar K. Sukumaran to distinguish him from other writers with similar names.

K. Sukumaran was born on 20 May 1876 to Kambil Thattailathu Govindan and Idamalathu Neely. His uncle Diwan Bahadur E.K. Krishnan was a sub-judge in Calicut. He graduated in Zoology from Madras Presidency College in 1894. Then he started working as a civil court clerk. He passed the civil judiciary test in 1915.

Sukumaran started his writing career by writing slokas (verses), inspired by the Venmani slokas. His initial poems were published in *Bharathi*, a magazine run by some prominent writers such as M.R.K.C. Later, he turned his attention to prose.

According to literary critic K.M. Tharakan, the short story as a literary genre evolved and attained perfection with the arrival of K. Sukumaran and E.V. Krishna Pillai. In *Kerala Sahitya Charitram* (*History of Literature in Kerala*), Ulloor S. Parameswara Iyer mentions seven writers as the pioneers of the short story in Malayalam: Vengayil Kunhiraman Nayanar, Oduvil Kunhikrishna Menon, Ambadi Narayana Poduval, Chengalath Cheriya Kunhirama Menon (M.R.K.C.), Sanjayan (M. Ramunni Nair), E.V. Krishna Pillai and K. Sukumaran. Sukumar Azhikode said, '[T]he unrestrained use of wit and humour gave the stories of K. Sukumaran remarkable entertainment value.'

M. Saraswati Bhai wrote 'Witless Women', a story now considered to be the first-ever story written in Malayalam by a woman.

NOTES ON THE AUTHORS

Moorkoth Kumaran (1874–1941) was a social reformer, a teacher and a writer in Malayalam. He also published some of the earliest short stories and novels in Malayalam.

Moorkoth Kumaran was born on 23 May 1874 into the Moorkoth family of North Malabar. After completing his training at Teachers' College, Saidapet, Kumaran became a teacher at St Joseph's European Boy's High School in Calicut in 1897. He worked at St. Aloysius College and at Telicherry St Joseph's School.

Writer Moorkoth Kunhappa has noted that Kumaran's short stories follow the principle of *'singleness of effect'*, which was lacking in most of the early short stories in Malayalam.

Kumaran also wrote the biographies of O. Chandu Menon and Vengayil Kunhiraman Nayanar and biographical essays on Kandathil Varghese Mappillai, Kerala Varma Valiya Koil Thampuran, A.R. Raja Raja Varma and Kumaran Asan.

Vellithuruthi Thazhathu Karutha Patteri Raman Bhattathirippad (1896–1982), also known as V.T. Bhattathirippad, was an Indian social reformer, dramatist and an Indian independence activist. He was best known for his contributions to the reformation of the casteism and conservatism that existed in the Namboothiri community. He wrote a number of books that include a play, *Adukkalayail Ninnu Arangathekku* and his autobiography, *Kanneerum Kinavum* (*Tears and Dreams* in English).

Bhattathirippad participated in the Allahabad session of the Indian National Congress due to which he was expelled from his community.

Bhattathirippad sought the emancipation of Namboothiri women and encouraged widow marriages, which was a taboo during those times. Along with M.R. Bhattathirippad, popularly known as MRB, he campaigned for widow remarriage by putting it in practice in his own household; he gave his sister-in-law, a widow, in marriage to MRB, which was the first widow remarriage among Namboothiris in Kerala.

Vengayil Kunhiraman Nayanar (1860–1914) was a Malayali essayist and short story writer, and a prominent landlord of Malabar. Nayanar was born in an aristocratic Nair family known as 'Vengayil' in Chirackal Thaluk, northern part of Malabar district in British India.

In 1904, he became a member of the Malabar District Board, and in 1917, he was elected to the Madras Legislative Assembly.

Nayanar came to the literary world through *Keralapathrika Vidyavinodini*, *Keralachandrika* and the English Journal *Malabar Spectator*. He was a critic of social injustice and a close friend of Dr Hermann Gundert and William Logan—both of whom contributed greatly to the history, language, and culture of Kerala.

For the following authors, little or no information at all about their personal life or their publications was available:

- Abhinava Chandu Menon (Thelapurath Narayanan Nambi)
- Chembathil Chinnammu Ammal
- Kalyanikutty
- Lakshmikutty Varasyar
- Thachatte Devaki Nethyaramma
- V.A. Amma

ABOUT THE TRANSLATOR

Venugopal Menon

VENUGOPAL MENON retired from Larsen & Toubro Limited where he worked in sales, marketing and finally, training—wherein his writing and workshopping skills were widely appreciated. He turned his attention to literary pursuits in a preliminary manner, beginning with proofreading for Paragon Prepress Journal, Delhi.

He stepped into the field of translation when Thunchath Ezuthachan Malayalam University launched its translation programme in 2015. Beginning with S.K. Pottekkat's *Oru Theruvinte Katha* (The Saga of a Street), he translated a compilation of short stories by the same author, titled *The Story of a Time Piece*, which was published by Niyogi Books in 2019. He then translated an exclusive interview by M.N. Karassery, renowned scholar and social commentator of Kerala, with ninety-six-year-old Venkatram Kalyanam, one of the last surviving eyewitnesses to the assassination of Mahatma Gandhi—the book is titled *Gandhi Alive* (2023).

ABOUT THE TRANSLATOR

His forthcoming translations include works by Shihabuddin Poithumkadavu, one of the most popular contemporary writers of short stories in Malayalam.

Venugopal lives in Kerala and publishes occasionally in the national media while other translation works keep him busy.

ABOUT THE SERIES EDITOR

Mini Krishnan

MINI KRISHNAN worked with Macmillan India Limited (1980–2000) and Oxford University Press (2000–18), editing textbooks for the Indian school market, and literary translations. She has co-authored textbooks for the Translation Education industry: *Word Worlds*; *Words, Texts & Meanings; Wordscapes*; and *Short Fiction from South India* (all published by Oxford University Press) and edited two volumes of translated fiction for the Aleph Book Company: *Tell Me a Long, Long Story* (sourced from fourteen languages) and *The Greatest Tamil Stories*. She is the series editor of *Living in Harmony*, a programme of peace education textbooks for schools (Oxford University Press).

She is currently Managing Editor of the Tamil Nadu Textbook and Educational Services Corporation, working with twenty English-language publishers to take Tamil to the world through translations of poetry, fiction and non-fiction, and on the editorial board of the Murty Classical Library of India, Harvard University Press.

She writes for *The Hindu* and *The Indian Express* and selects short stories in translation for the *Frontline* magazine.

HarperCollins *Publishers* India

At HarperCollins India, we believe in telling the best stories and finding the widest readership for our books in every format possible. We started publishing in 1992; a great deal has changed since then, but what has remained constant is the passion with which our authors write their books, the love with which readers receive them, and the sheer joy and excitement that we as publishers feel in being a part of the publishing process.

Over the years, we've had the pleasure of publishing some of the finest writing from the subcontinent and around the world, including several award-winning titles and some of the biggest bestsellers in India's publishing history. But nothing has meant more to us than the fact that millions of people have read the books we published, and that somewhere, a book of ours might have made a difference.

As we look to the future, we go back to that one word— a word which has been a driving force for us all these years.

Read.